# THE SUITORS

*The*

# SUITORS

## Cécile David-Weill

TRANSLATED FROM THE FRENCH
BY LINDA COVERDALE

OTHER PRESS
NEW YORK

Copyright © Éditions Grasset & Fasquelle, 2009
Originally published as *Les Prétendants* by
Éditions Grasset & Fasquelle, 2009

Translation copyright © 2012 Linda Coverdale

Production Editor: Yvonne E. Cárdenas
Text Designer: Jennifer Daddio/Bookmark Design and Media, Inc.
This book was set in 12 pt. Filosofia
by Alpha Design & Composition of Pittsfield, NH.

10  9  8  7  6  5  4  3

Library of Congress Cataloging-in-Publication Data

David-Weill, Cécile, date
[Prétendants. English]
The suitors / by Cecile David-Weill ; translated by Linda Coverdale.
p. cm.
ISBN 978-1-59051-573-0 (trade pbk. : acid-free paper) —
ISBN 978-1-59051-574-7 (ebook)   1. Sisters—France—Fiction.
2. Rich people—France—Fiction.   3. Upper class families—France—Fiction.
I. Coverdale, Linda.   II. Title.
PQ2672.A162174P7413 2012
843'.914—dc23
2012014605

PIERRE, LAURE, AND ALICE

# CONTENTS

*One: Prologue*

*1*

Spring 2007                                              3

*Nanny*                                                  38

*The house*                                              51

*Two: Weekend of July 14*

*55*

Friday, 7:00 a.m.                                        61

*The Rules of the Game*, film by Jean Renoir (1939)      66

Friday, 12:30 p.m.                                       84

Friday, 3:00 p.m.                                        91

Friday, 6:30 p.m.             .                          95

Friday, 8:00 p.m. 108

Dinner, Friday, July 14 122

Saturday, 9:00 a.m. 150

Luncheon, Saturday, July 15 156

Saturday, 6:30 p.m. 166

*The beach in winter* 167

Dinner, Saturday, July 15 178

Sunday 191

Luncheon, Sunday, July 16 193

## *Three: Weekend of July 21*

*195*

Friday, 6:00 p.m. 204

Dinner, Friday, July 21 232

Friday, 11:00 p.m. 242

Saturday, 9:30 a.m. 254

Saturday, 1:30 p.m. 267

Luncheon, Saturday, July 22 270

*The shortcut* 278

Saturday, 7:00 p.m. 285

Dinner, Saturday, July 22 288

Sunday, 9:30 a.m. 299

Luncheon, Sunday, July 23 304

# Four: Weekend of July 28

## 309

Friday, 6:00 p.m.     315

*Trop bien élevé*, 2007, by Jean-Denis Bredin     319

Dinner, Friday, July 28     336

Saturday, 8:00 a.m.     351

Luncheon, Saturday, July 29     366

Dinner, Saturday, July 29     378

*The road to Eden-Roc*     395

Sunday, 1:00 p.m.     398

*Thank-you letter*     403

# Five: Appendices

## 407

The Characters     409

Staff Menu Notebook     413

Kitchen Cabinet Inventory     415

Recipe Inventory     418

Recipes     420

*One*

# PROLOGUE

*Spring 2007*

It was a Sunday like any other. My son, Felix, was with his father. My sister and I always arranged to have dinner at least once a month with our parents, and now that May was almost over, the weather was becoming pleasant, so our conversation that night would inevitably focus on our plans for the summer. I must have been really bored given that I was looking forward to an evening I had already been through year after year, like clockwork! I felt a twinge of melancholy; my life was decidedly uneventful. I had Felix's well-being and my patients' anxieties to keep me busy, but no passions of my own. I felt empty. In the end, though, I convinced myself that there was nothing wrong with taking pleasure in a family ritual I knew completely by heart.

I could see it all in detail: Marie and I would meet in the courtyard at five to nine to compliment each other on our outfits before braving the indifference of our mother, who never seemed to notice our efforts to meet with her sartorial approval. Sunday dinners were a contest of couture: we had to appear both stylish and relaxed, in a gently tailored suit, for example, or some chic sportswear. It was a game at which my sister was an acknowledged champion.

We would troop to the kitchen to fetch the light supper the cook had left for us on his day off, and then the table conversation would naturally turn to the approaching summer.

"Always the same guests!" my father would complain with a sigh.

My mother, her chestnut hair in a chignon, elegantly thin in a smart housecoat (that old-fashioned garment halfway between a robe and an evening gown), would protest that she was doing her very best. Wasn't she working hard enough as it was to bring fresh faces to the usual cast of characters? It was much more difficult than it looked to come up, year after year, with people who were well mannered, interesting, clever conversationalists, but not freeloaders. Then my mother would pause, pretending to surrender.

"After all, you're right. Still, I don't know . . . My latest attempts . . . Remember Joy, Moïra, Samuel . . . The graft didn't . . . didn't take. They seemed charming, and then . . . disaster."

Marie and I would simply look at each other to make sure we weren't imagining things. Since no one else ever seemed to notice whenever our mother fumbled, disconcertingly, for words, any comments my sister and I might have made would have sounded mean, bringing a sour note to the pleasure of discussing our summer house.

Because for us, L'Agapanthe was a haven of happiness.

Sheltered from time, it was a world of its own, one of luxury and lighthearted enjoyment. We spoke of it with pride, the way other people talk about the family eccentric or some colorful character they feel privileged to know. L'Agapanthe was not the ordinary summerhouse of rose-colored childhood, conjuring nostalgia and memories out of bread and jam, French toast, and skinned knees. No. During the summer months, just like an ocean liner, the house required birds of passage and a large staff. In short, it was what is properly referred to as a "*bonne maison.*"

This shameless, snobbish understatement referred to the handful of houses around the world on that same grand scale, combining luxury, perfect taste, and a refined way of life. In the same way they would have said *"grandes familles"* or *"grands hôtels,"* the servants in such houses referred to them as *"grandes maisons,"* and without describing them or defining what they had in common, these experts could have rattled off a list on Corsica, in Mexico, in Tuscany, or on Corfu, an inventory far more private than the host of palatial European hotels touted everywhere in travel guides and magazines.

These houses always had:

Dumbwaiters
Walk-in cold rooms
Bell boards for the upstairs rooms
Vans for grocery shopping
Cupboards for breakfast trays
A kitchen (for the cooks)
A pantry (for the butlers)
A laundry room with linen closets
A room with a copper sink for arranging flowers and
    storing vases
Cellars

Storerooms

And extensive servants' quarters

From these houses were banished all dishwashers, microwave ovens, televisions in lounges, TV dinners, easygoing informality, and any form of casual attire.

One of the chief criteria of a "good house" was the beauty of the place, from which the patina of time must have effaced all triviality, a requirement that disqualified even the grandest of modern houses. Not even historical monuments were allowed into the fold, those stately homes whose owners, rarely wealthy, often found themselves the guardians of traditions it was their duty to uphold, even at the cost of bankruptcy. For unlike a chatelain, the master of a "good house" devoted his culture, his fortune, and his *savoir vivre* to the pleasure he offered his guests. His objective? To make them forget all material cares and thus freely enjoy the beauty of his house, his works of art, his bountiful table, and sprightly conversation in good company.

Plainly put, in a "good house," chambermaids unpacked and repacked—with a great flurry of tissue paper—the suitcases of guests, who found their rooms provided with pretty sheets, mineral water, fruit, flowers, and a safe, as well as matches, pencils, and writing paper all embossed with the name of the house. But most important, the guests were not obliged to do anything—not to play sports, or go sightseeing, even though all that and more was available and easily arranged, should anyone wish it. The only compulsory ritual was mealtime, like prayers at a lay convent where one's thoughts were otherwise free to roam at will.

And L'Agapanthe clearly fit this long and curious definition of a "good house," so handsomely did this magical place succeed in halting the passage of time, which hung suspended in a bygone age of breathtaking yet unpretentious luxury.

During our family discussions at the dinner table about potential houseguests for the summer, if Marie or I ever dared agree with our father's gentle criticism, our mother, like the sensitive soul she really was, would immediately go on the attack, pointing out that at L'Agapanthe, she had to be more like the manager of a luxury hotel than merely the mistress of the house.

Once again, Marie and I would be relieved to find that when it came to running her house, she spoke with her usual commanding confidence. Then we'd flatter her shamelessly, to satisfy her thirst for recognition and bring us at last to our favorite headache: Casting the Guests.

Increasingly dispirited by the lackluster impression left by our last few summers, my father would finally sound sincere when he asked us to suggest ideas for new table companions.

For if my mother was reluctant to go looking for new faces, it was probably to avoid admitting to herself that she had no idea how to go about it. She would have had to accept that even she had aged, and that it was increasingly difficult for her to "do her shopping" within her generation. Not that her peers were keeling over left and right, no, but the increasing ravages of old age were turning more and more of them into embittered cranks, self-righteous prigs, snobs obsessed with honors and distinctions, or blowhards puffed up with self-importance. Yet turning to the younger generation for fresh blood, she feared, would leave her as vulnerable and intimidated as a new kid in a schoolyard.

"But Flokie," my father would ask impatiently, "how do others manage?"

"Others?"

"Yes, the people we know."

This is where Marie and I would intervene, reminding our parents that they traveled so much that they no longer had the opportunity to make new acquaintances at dinner parties in town. We'd explain to them that most of their friends simply picked up their phones to invite whomever they felt like seeing: a writer in vogue, a powerful government official, an up-and-coming scientist, or a greedy financier—celebrities whose dazzling, sexy, and prestigious presence would reflect brilliantly on their hosts.

My parents would gape with astonishment to learn that people in their circle were now behaving like television personalities preparing the guest lists for their talk shows, a tactic that would never have occurred to them.

For they had no idea, either, how many people would have given anything to receive an invitation to L'Agapanthe, and if Marie and I had told them the names of people who we knew for a fact were dying to come, they would still have only half believed us. Since they themselves went no farther than identifying and avoiding the more obvious social climbers, they seldom noticed the discreet nudges and subtle maneuvers of aspirants who craved such an invitation, and as they personally had never yearned to belong to any "in crowd," of course they couldn't imagine why others would feel that way about them.

My parents had been brought up with the idea that they represented the pinnacle of chic. The tranquil arrogance of their modesty was proof of that. They were completely unaware, however, that their acquaintances saw them in such a light. Did other people even exist sufficiently in my parents' eyes for them to notice this? Blissfully ignorant of the insecurity that drives human beings to study their reflections in the eyes of others, my parents simply weren't observant enough to imagine that anyone might fantasize about them.

Too honest and intelligent to let themselves succumb to narcissism, my parents had decided to pay no attention to the illusion of success or the thrill of having one's picture in the papers. And so, far from being the caricatures of art and business moguls that they had become in the press, my parents thought of themselves as timid people, courteous and ill suited to the excessive familiarity in vogue with fashionable folk.

And this was part of their charm. It was not celebrities they invited but people chosen for their conversation, their beauty, their culture, or because they were jolly, kind, inspired sympathy, or were simply owed a return invitation. Sometimes my parents just wanted to offer a week of luxury to a friend in the doldrums or a cousin in dire financial straits. Their principles, however, could affect their decisions: they would refuse to invite a minister then in office or anyone basking in the glory of a career at its zenith, while they made it a point of honor to have those same people over when they faced dark times.

In any case, to the great surprise of the rare newcomers invited to L'Agapanthe, my parents' hospitality was genuine. Puzzled by such unselfishness, some guests wondered why they had been invited at all, but in the end, lulled by the old-fashioned and candid sense of propriety that clearly reigned in the house, they relaxed and realized that they had been chosen simply for themselves.

Well, that was the romantic version of the facts. But L'Agapanthe really did have a strange effect on a surprising number of people, changing some, while revealing the true nature of others. Impressed by the house, the quieter guests worried that they might not appear sufficiently elegant or cultured, and some would begin to talk loudly or laugh at every turn to boost their self-confidence, whereas a frivolous creature might suddenly start pontificating on politics and the economy, hoping to be taken for an intellectual. Unfortunate shortcomings came occasionally to light: I once caught a populist politician bullying the servants, and one of France's grandest dukes stuffing his pockets with the Havana cigars set out for guests.

So it's not surprising, really, that my parents were cautious with their invitations.

"Why don't you invite Claude Lévi-Strauss or Martin Scorsese? That could be interesting," Marie would quip.

She knew as well as I did that we were really there to amuse our parents, not to give them ideas, since neither of them was ready to relinquish any of their prerogatives as hosts. Quite the opposite: they needed us to witness their powers of decision so as to reinforce their own sense of authority. Not that we minded, for these sessions strengthened our family bonds in the name of certain values, which, because of our constant fear of seeming pompous or pretentious, we simply called "our kind of beauty."

Although unspoken, the selective criteria for these values were many and precise. Good manners topped the list. The formality of life in L'Agapanthe required a comfortable command of conventions, which naturally closed the door to anyone unfamiliar with such standards. Houseguests were well advised to be accustomed to servants and possess a sure mastery of table manners and household protocol—the proper usage of finger bowls and salad plates, and the correct distribution of tips—even though this knowledge of etiquette served our guests chiefly by allowing them to flout the rules with the necessary knowledgeable flair.

To tell the truth, we were particularly amused by outdated yet still picturesque fashion precepts such as the Brits' *No yellow shoes after six*, or the strict injunction *No velvet after Easter*, which only my mother still respected. We likened the Americans' outrage at the wearing of light-colored pants after Labor Day to the British restriction of port drinking to months with an *r* (like the French and oysters, only from September to April), and the wearing of blazers to months without an *r* (May to August). In other words, a man in a blazer drinking port would be a lost cause.

All else paled, however, before our devotion to the most basic politeness, which demanded tactful and attentive behavior toward others. We would never have put up with a guest rudely interrupting someone, or entering a room before an elderly person, or—if he were a man—remaining seated when a woman joined our company.

Although we relied on such conventions in judging the quality of people's upbringing and character, we really judged our guests only according to their practice of *understatement*. This discipline, at which Marie and I excelled thanks to extensive training and observation, implied a certain modesty of tone and attitude. For example, we were reprimanded as children whenever we called the château where we spent our weekends anything other than a *house*, or the two-hundred-foot yacht on which we occasionally cruised anything fancier than a *boat*. We noticed that our grandmother ordered her sable coats shaved to make them look like mink and that our parents seated their guests on patio furniture without announcing that it had been designed by Sol LeWitt, and served them dinner on plates they never mentioned had been created by Picasso.

At the end of our Sunday evening, Marie and I would make one last effort: "What about Moumouche de Ganay? Gary Shoenberg? Or Perla de Cambray?"

"Now *that's* a good idea," our parents would murmur. "We really should think about that."

But we already knew they would ignore our advice completely, because they'd never intended to take it in the first place. As usual, they would do as they pleased. And we would have to wait until we arrived at L'Agapanthe to find out whom they had cast as their guests for this summer and to discover that, in spite of all their precautions and the vaunted qualities of their visitors, the assembly would include, as everywhere else, its share of hypocrites, boors, and spongers.

That Sunday, however, nothing happened as expected, although my father did open the proceedings by complaining. Visibly depressed, my mother then bluntly declared that perhaps they were getting too old for the demands of such hospitality, so my father felt obliged to crack a joke.

"Do you know what the English say about the calamities of old age? *Consider the alternative!*"

Marie and I looked at each other: this was the first time our parents had ever revealed their vulnerable side. The first time they'd ever seemed to simply give up in front of us, in front of those whose role was supposedly to push them into their graves and take their places. We both hoped they hadn't really thought about what they'd just said and wouldn't take the shocking implications to heart.

For some time, now, we had been careful not to draw attention to the fact that we had grown up. Our friends, our lovers, our patients, our bosses had now become cabinet ministers, ambassadors, film directors, writers, CEOs of giant companies. In other words, we were sought-after young women, and they were getting old. We had done our best to let them stay in the spotlight, and Marie, who worked as an interpreter for the President of the Republic, was even careful not to let them know that she was privy to the results of national elections before the official announcement.

There was something odd, though, something disquieting about our parents' behavior. It was as if there were a kind of faint haze between us. To my surprise, I found myself offering to provide them with new guests, home-delivered like a box of chocolates.

"Why don't you just invite the usual suspects, and we'll bring along the new ones? That way you won't have to deal with any of it."

My father agreed.

"That's a good idea," he said solemnly. And as I sat stunned by the enormity of what he had just said, he continued: "A very good idea indeed. Particularly since we're feeling less enthusiastic this year . . . because . . . you see, girls, we've decided to put L'Agapanthe up for sale."

"*What?*" my sister and I exclaimed.

"Are you in some kind of financial trouble?" Marie blurted out, crossing in an instant a line we had always respected, the quid pro quo we honored in exchange for our parents' tacit assurance of financial support.

"No."

"Well, then, why?" I demanded, almost shouting.

"Come now, girls. It's the only responsible thing to do, because no matter what you say, I don't think either of you can afford to spend the millions necessary to maintain the place."

That was a low blow, because he knew the state of our finances better than anyone else. Aside from my salary as a psychotherapist and Marie's paycheck as an interpreter, our income came from him.

The verdict had been delivered. Contesting his decision was useless. Was my father hiding money problems from us? Or, thinking rationally but unfeelingly, did he consider it absurd to have us bear such a burden when he would no longer be there to foot the bill? Having been taught never to contradict a man, or even openly question the validity of his decisions, we said nothing further.

We needed time to learn more about the family's finances, assess the situation, and plan a counterattack.

Before getting into her car to drive home that evening, Marie turned to me, exhausted.

"We'll talk soon," she said sadly.

The first person I called the next day, however, was Frédéric, the uncle I would have loved to have. Ever since I was a child, he's been telling me, "You, you've got that *sparkle* in your eye!"—although he also used to say he found me very serious for my age, probably his way of letting me know he thought I looked bullied and unhappy. He was on my side and made no bones about showing his preference for me by making me laugh and giving me the affection I craved.

"I don't understand a thing you're saying." He sighed into the phone. "You're talking too fast and I'm too hungry to think. Meet me at one o'clock at the Relais Plaza. You know their *escalopes de veau viennoise* are—"

"To die for, yes, I know. Thank you, Frédéric. I'll see you later."

Arriving a trifle early, I sat at his usual table across from the bar. He walked in looking dapper: oatmeal-colored suit, lilac handkerchief in his breast pocket, cashmere sweater draped across his shoulders, because he is always cold, even in midsummer. He's an old man, now. More soigné than affected, he might seem sad and frail, but he's a mischievous little devil.

"Monsieur Hottin!" cried Serge, the maître d', rushing to greet him.

"Bonjour, Monsieur," added the cloakroom lady, brightening into a smile.

It's undeniable: Frédéric is fantastically popular.

First of all, he's a celebrity. In fact, he and his late side-kick, Brady, are to the world of variety theater what Ben and Jerry are to American ice cream: a gold standard. He is also very generous, particularly with the staff, whom he tips royally even though he isn't rich (although he does live comfortably off copyrights since Brady's death). And breaking every rule in the book with the naughty insouciance of an old man who's nobody's fool, he treats duchesses and chambermaids exactly alike, refusing to take anyone seriously, especially himself. He has even become something of a cult figure among trendy young authors, TV stars, culture vultures of all kinds, and nostalgic souls yearning for a Paris of caba-rets and flash parties. They endlessly repeat his best lines and make a fuss over him in clubs where reality TV stars have taken over from the band of buddies he once formed with Françoise Sagan, the painter Bernard Buf-fet and his wife the actress Annabel, a society columnist named Chazot, and a few actors and comedians.

"Darling, bring me a bullshot with lots of ice, will you?" he asked the waiter. "So tell me. What's all this about L'Agapanthe?"

I summed up the situation; Frédéric understood perfectly. He was one of the habitués at L'Agapanthe, a "pillar" of the house, my parents would have said, since they classified their guests according to their level of familiarity and seniority at the villa, and even treated them accordingly, like frequent flyers whose memberships vary in prestige and worth, depending on the regularity of their journeys.

Frédéric was at the apex of this hierarchy, as was Gay Wallingford, his nearest and dearest friend for over thirty years, and the family had more or less adopted this picturesque couple. Then came the regulars of the house. The term might seem dismissive, yet it referred to the *happy few* who were invited each year and had their designated rooms. Their role? To guarantee the basic ballast of visitors required to stabilize the villa on its cruise through the summer, and to mentor novice guests, whose very novelty was meant to spice up our season.

Then came the luncheon crowd known as the "cafeteria club": neighbors who were writers, museum curators, artists, golfers, more often than not single or down on their luck, who came for lunch every day, attracted by the quality of the food and the company. Last came those run-of-the-mill arrivals who rolled in for lunch from Monaco, inland, or Saint-Tropez, and who—not being handpicked like our overnight guests—brought an eccentric midday fauna of rich Texan dames pumped full

of Botox, drug-fiend photographers and gallery owners, demimondaines, artists in floppy hats, and self-
made men tanned to within an inch of their lives, whose
sole redeeming feature was their ability to animate the
conversation.

"Could our parents possibly have money problems?"
I asked Frédéric.

After looking thoughtful for a moment, he replied,
out of the blue, "Tell me about your love life."

"Ex*cuse* me?"

"No, I mean it, I'm interested," he said in an insinu-
ating tone I found irresistible.

"Well, it's a catastrophe."

"Oh, come now. When was your divorce?"

"Three years ago."

"And then nothing, nobody?"

"No. Or, not exactly. You really want to know? I scare
men away. It's unbelievable. There isn't one who'll dare
pin me down on a sofa or hop into bed with me for the
night. Before they even kiss me they're already wondering if they'd be willing to leave their wives or marry me.
That she's-the-daughter-of thing, albeit a social plus, is
toxic. I am too chic, too independent, and probably too
smart, because I'll spare you what happens when I confess that I'm a shrink. In fact, I've come to the conclusion

that the world is awash in men who aren't meant for me. Actually, not meant for us, because ditto for Marie."

"No!"

"Well, sort of. She does have more lovers than I do, seeing as she's got more choices, what with all those security and secret service guys she works with."

"Who?"

"You know, the ones with earpieces who are in charge of security whenever world leaders have those summits— she hangs around with them all day. They haven't a clue who she is and wouldn't give a damn if they did, because they're *tough guys*, right? But as for finding a lover with whom she might actually like to live, Marie's in the same spot I am: nowhere. And for the same reasons. Even though she does her absolute best not to scare them away. Listen, on the phone she'll tell them that she's in Limoges for a radiologists' convention when in fact she's in Davos or Rio—with the president!"

"This is ridiculous. You're both young, beautiful, rich . . ."

Serge brought the order to the table.

". . . Ah! My *escalope viennoise*. Do you know it's the best in Paris? Look at these little condiments they give you on the side, what a lovely presentation!"

"Lovely," I repeated, gently sarcastic.

"Sorry, you were saying?"

"I was telling you that the closer men get to us socially, the farther away from us they stay. What can I tell you! That's just the way it is. What about you? Still crazy about François?"

"Right, go on, make fun of me . . ." He blushed, as he did whenever I mentioned his heartthrobs. The current candidate was an understudy whose career he was trying to launch.

Despite having been married three times and having lived with at least as many boyfriends, including a well-known transsexual, Frédéric was the least liberated of men: reserved, old-fashioned, and he simply hated talking about sex. I changed the subject.

"And what about Gay? How is she?"

Gay is Frédéric's great friend. It was she who introduced Frédéric to my parents and smuggled him into the family like a fox spirited into a henhouse. Indeed, who would ever have imagined that one day this night bird, this court jester, the intimate of lowlifes and drag queens, would even meet my parents, let alone get them to like him! Gay and Frédéric each have an apartment in the same building and are inseparable. Calling her several times a day and taking her everywhere, he brings fantasy and gaiety to her life, while she pampers him like a mother, trying to protect him from himself with a few moral lectures she trots out for form's sake, and which he promptly forgets, rushing off to the casino at Enghien or the racetracks at Longchamps. In short, this charming and discreet couple keep their personal worries and ailments to themselves, sharing with each other only the best of their moods and lives. And they have a ball party hopping through the hottest spots, where they slip in among the young and beautiful to watch the show, on which they comment conspiratorially to their hearts' content.

Gay was fine, said Frédéric, but he seemed more interested in the dessert cart, which he was examining with great care, requesting a description of every cake before finally announcing, "No, I don't really have much of a sweet tooth. But perhaps you could bring us a small plate of petits fours?"

"So, Frédéric, what's your big idea?" I asked impatiently.

"My idea?"

"Yes, your idea about L'Agapanthe going on the market and how we could prevent that."

"Listen. Your father's a true gem, but he's always had trouble reading other people and the effect he has on them. Is this because he's so modest? So preoccupied with his own concerns? So self-involved? I don't know. In any case, he probably couldn't begin to imagine how attached you are to the house, just as he doesn't have any idea how much you girls love him."

"And?"

"And so you have to show him how you feel, because you know how useless it would be to argue with him in the hope that he'll change his mind."

"Fine, but how do we do that?"

Frédéric's idea was outrageous: he suggested that Marie and I look for a sugar daddy willing to foot the bills for L'Agapanthe and the lifestyle it deserved!

"And your next step would be to pitch the deal to your father."

"Deal? What deal?"

"Well, 'Either you leave us the house, or we'll each marry a Mr. Moneybags who will buy it for us.' I'll bet you anything your father will be furious and humiliated that you'd been driven to behave like common gold diggers. So: he'll be furious—but convinced that you mean business. And he'll keep the house for you."

"And if that doesn't work?"

"Then you'll just have to marry those Mr. Moneybags. So be careful to pick nice ones."

I was laughing hysterically. "This is some sort of joke," I said at last and then nervously ate up the petits fours, one after the other.

"Simply organize some tryouts. Invite a few candidates to L'Agapanthe this summer for an audition. Say, one per weekend. Just like those people I knew who used to do this in August. During the week, it was the family, period. They only had guests on the weekend. They always planned separate weekends for golfing, poker, and the crème de la crème. Why don't you do the same with a CEO, a film star, an heir to a fortune . . . ?"

"But I don't know any."

"Oh, please. As if that were a problem."

Frédéric was right. There was no need to know a person to invite him or her to L'Agapanthe. All I needed was to know someone who knew that person.

"Think of Laszlo and the Démazures," he added, referring to Laszlo Schwartz, who'd been introduced to my parents by a couple who were now regular guests at L'Agapanthe.

Henri Démazure was an insipid international lawyer, Polyséna Démazure a dull Italian who mangled every language she spoke, and they bored the pants off my poor father. Yet they came to L'Agapanthe every summer because they had introduced my parents to Laszlo Schwartz, a gallery icon whom my mother admired and whose paintings, acquired by museums throughout the world, were worth a fortune. The Démazures, however, were total pills, and now my mother was stuck with them.

"Well, thanks a bunch, but I'd rather not! They came to dinner and never left!"

The problem was that my mother had had to invite the Démazures to L'Agapanthe in order to ask the artist to come: it was a question of manners, as elementary as not seating engaged couples and newlyweds separately at a dinner party. The Démazures accepted eagerly, but without bringing along Laszlo Schwartz, who was busy in Japan with a show. My mother persevered and renewed her invitation the following year, when Laszlo did come along with the Démazures. The third year, relieved of her obligations toward this couple, whose vapid personalities were now only too obvious, my mother tried to think of a way to keep inviting Schwartz but without the Démazures. This was risky, because she didn't want to offend either them or Laszlo, who might decide to stop coming. But when Henri Démazure lost his job that year, it became impossible for my mother to drop him after such a blow. And so the Démazures notched up another summer. Then, when it was finally acceptable to get rid of them, they called my mother to whine about their straitened circumstances, beating around the bush before finally saying what a joy it would be for them to return to L'Agapanthe. Embarrassed, my mother let them have their way. This had been going on for years now, and I'd eventually realized that unless they committed some unforgivable faux pas, the Démazures could count on their heavenly holiday for the next twenty summers.

"No, no," Frédéric said with a laugh, "it doesn't have to be *that* complicated. You can even invite your candidates sight unseen, without knowing them. I'm sure they would come."

Frédéric was right. Knowing people can mean so many things. It's like books: there are plenty of gradations between the books one has read and those one hasn't. There are the books one has heard of, those with a plot or style we already know by heart, those we can tell by their cover, those whose jacket copy we've read. Those we want to read and those we never will. One can also read a book and forget it—in fact, that's my specialty—or just skim through it. It's the same with people.

Can I say that I know the guests I've seen summer after summer at L'Agapanthe for all these years? Their political opinions and literary tastes are familiar to me, of course, and I know whether they're funny or wearisome companions, chatty, timid, or reserved. I have an informal relationship with them. And yet I hardly know them. What are their characters like? Are they happy? What kind of childhood did they have? What do they think of one another? I haven't the foggiest. At L'Agapanthe, the courtesy de rigueur in a "good house" encourages us all to keep up the finest of fronts, thus preventing anyone from speaking from the heart, just as our luxurious life in the villa shields us from those petty details of day-to-day existence that inevitably reveal our deepest natures in their failings and virtues alike: thoughtlessness, fussiness, generosity, stinginess, devotion, silliness, or lazy self-indulgence.

Sometimes this paradoxical intimacy plays tricks on me. Unable to say much of importance about any of these often prestigious people with whom I've been superficially acquainted since forever, I rarely mention that I know them from L'Agapanthe. If I happen to run into one of them anywhere else, my real friends are then surprised when I say hello.

"You know So-and-so?"

"Yes, a little."

And the next second, So-and-so calls out gaily, "Laure, dear heart! How's your backhand? And how are your loonies? Don't cure them too much, or you'll do yourself out of a job. Don't you think I've slimmed down?"

So right away I look like the modest little hypocrite who pretends she can barely stand up on skis, until, having dazzled her companions on the slopes, she confesses that she's the all-around champion of France. And my friends, wrongly assuming that my discretion stems from my loathing of name-dropping or my professional habit of keeping secrets, remind me that not saying anything can be just as annoying as boasting.

Eyeing Frédéric, who was leaving an astronomical tip on the table, I remarked fondly, "I gather that you'll be perched in a box seat at L'Agapanthe, eager to critique any dramatic developments."

"Precisely."

"What do you mean, a rich husband?"

Marie had actually gasped in disbelief when I suggested Frédéric's solution on the phone the next day.

"Why not?" I countered.

Wasn't that the oldest game in the book? Women from Paris to Moscow and on to New York went husband hunting! All right: the idea would never have occurred to me before my conversation with Frédéric, because I'd always considered this sport something reserved for women who were flat broke, which I wasn't. So joining the hunt, I'd felt, would be immoral, a ploy as unthinkable as my applying to get my health expenses reimbursed from the Sécurité sociale.

"Why not? Because we already are."

"Are what?"

"Rich, dummy!"

Marie was right. We were rich. At least on paper. We were shareholders in companies that didn't pay dividends, but we were still good catches.

"And so what?"

"But . . . how would we get started?" Marie insisted.

Ironically, unlike true gold diggers, we were used to being courted ourselves by people dazzled by money, and we could smell them a mile away.

Romantic idealists, my sister and I were interested only in love and friendship. Money turned out to be a most inconvenient advantage, attracting fortune hunters while often driving everyone else away. Few decent men even dared approach us if they weren't well-off, and if they were, they couldn't quite stomach the fact that we frankly didn't need them to get by. It was the same thing with friendship. How could we invite people on holiday or to a restaurant if they couldn't return the favor? It was equally complicated for us to give our friends gifts without unintentionally making them feel obligated to us.

"No arrogance, no ostentation": the mantra of our childhood. As if we'd needed that! Because we were so miserably conscious of our wealth that we had always tried obsessively to hide it from our friends.

Sometimes that was easy. We never mentioned our trips on private jets or those endless afternoons in the changing rooms of couture houses with our mother, the couturier, and his head seamstress. And we hardly risked bumping into our little pals chez Givenchy, Saint-Laurent, Ungaro, or on the tarmac at Le Bourget, Teterboro, or Biggin Hill.

Our predicament turned dicey when we had to convert our nanny into an English granny, or the driver picking us up at school into a family friend. It became frankly hair-raising when we had to keep coming up with the appropriate traffic jams to explain being late for school on Monday morning after a round-trip to New York on the Concorde.

Our house betrayed us. Rare were the friends Marie and I dared invite home. We'd tell them that our town house was just an ordinary apartment building sheltering many families. Already puzzled by the maze of service stairs we climbed to reach our floor (thus avoiding our imposing front door, which would have given the game away), our guests invariably wondered why there was no kitchen and no bedroom for our parents. So we'd casually refer to our "duplex" to reassure them, as well as to account for the dumbwaiter that delivered our meals, which were revolting, actually, because our chef, no doubt considering himself too distinguished to feed mere children, handed this chore off to a kitchen boy.

Later, during those tough internships when our father decided to introduce us to the real world, Marie and I continued honing our skills in the art of dissimulation. At one point I was a lowly employee in the accounting department of a construction and public works firm where I wasn't allowed to leave the building without permission from my boss, a truly odious bully. I used to slip quietly away, however, to the office of the CEO (a living god accessible only to department heads), who just happened to be a friend of my parents and welcomed me with piping hot coffee and a game of chess. One day my creepy little boss discovered the scam. Drenched in sweat and worry, he buttonholed me in a hall to apologize while begging me to put in a good word for him. His obsequious flip-flopping disgusted me, but I was chiefly relieved that my colleagues, who had taken me under their wing (and for whom I surreptitiously punched in every other day), did not suspect a thing. Otherwise, they might have felt like fools, and in a way, they would have been right, since I had never really been one of them and thus had never needed their protection, which my visits with the CEO would have made cruelly clear.

I'd been a coward, behaving like someone safely ensconced in a cushy position. In my defense, though, I should say that at that time, the wealthy were all considered assholes. And it didn't help that most people I met flaunted their "political consciousness" mainly by posing as enemies of the rich, a situation that would reverse itself ten years later, when heirs and heiresses would be welcomed to parade around in magazines like movie stars. Deep down, though, nothing had changed, because money, having neither reputation nor personality of its own, is a constant magnet for fantasies and projections, and will always channel its share of bitterness and dreams.

"As for knowing how to hunt down a rich husband," I finally admitted to Marie, "you're right, we're probably not up to this. And I'm only attracted to weirdos. I like trying to fix problem men, I can't help it."

"Yes, so I've noticed," said my sister slyly, alluding to my two years of nightmare wedlock to a man I'd found irresistible and who'd proved mad as a hatter. "But why couldn't you fix up a *rich* weirdo?"

Good point. I laughed. "Shall we give it a try?"

"You bet!"

"But how do we find these Prince Charmings?"

"Oh, *please!*"

Marie and I are very close. I'm thirty years old, she's thirty-two. We live a few blocks from each other. At the local café we're known as "the sisters," even if we go there separately, I with my son and Marie with her lovers. Our close relationship hasn't always been obvious because we are quite different, almost opposites. My sister looks Swedish, while I could be Brazilian. She has our father's blond coloring and the svelte silhouette of our mother, a brunette like me, and I got my solid, down-to-earth looks from our father. Marie is always impeccably turned out, whereas I seem to be at loose ends, my curly hair and curvy figure creating an impression of undisciplined excess, the way words can sometimes outrun thoughts.

When we were children, though, we had even more reason to feel different from each other. Taking her lead from our nanny, Miss Ross, our mother had declared that Marie was the pretty one and I the smart one, insisting all the while that she simply doted on both daughters, a charming affirmation we learned to periodically reinterpret as time went by. In fact, our mother never quite knew what to do with us or, what's more, what to make of us. Beginning with our conception. What if pregnancy spoiled her figure? True, she was a beauty. A tall, whippet-thin brunette with superb cheekbones, she had glowing skin, an aristocratic nose, slightly almond-shaped black eyes, and she carried herself like a dancer, as truly beautiful women so often do. Her anxiety over losing her figure soon gave way to that of losing her marriage, and she resigned herself to pregnancy only under pressure from a husband so resolute that he threatened her with divorce. She was determined, however, never to become one of those "loving and frumpy mothers who devote themselves to their children and give up trying to look attractive," as she put it. So she hired an English-woman in her sixties to take charge of our upbringing, an undertaking with which our mother was most careful not to interfere.

# Nanny

*I'm ten years old. No one suspects a thing. Not even Marie, who is incapable, luckily, of imagining Nanny's duplicity. So I keep quiet. Just as I keep to myself all the terrible ways she mistreats me. Because I don't want to spoil Marie's fragile happiness by revealing how our governess tortures me as soon as we're alone together. That madwoman actually beats me, using any pretext to take her resentment out on me with vicious blows. And I am in such fear of these violent episodes, which leave me staggering in terror, that I live mesmerized by her moods, like an appliance plugged into a wall socket, picking up on the fluctuations of her emotional current and preparing myself for the next crisis.*

*Her anger comes on like wind billowing a sail: I can see the rage course through her, taking over, and I await in despair the moment when Nanny will take me away with her,*

out of sight, to vent her fury by attacking me like an evil giant.
A formidable opponent, she has endless tricks up her sleeve.

She has decided, for example, that I am absentminded
and has made it her mission to root out this flaw that seriously threatens my chances in life, when in reality I have
found in daydreaming a way to escape from the nightmare
she forces me to live. The upshot is that Nanny spends her
time testing me in front of my sister and parents by sending
me to fetch a certain paper in the library, or a phone number
in her address book, or some object on the night table in her
room, when the object is actually in her closet.

Off I go, my eyes already blurry with tears. Beginning my
search, I lose time looking without seeing, hunting without
thinking about what I want to find in the room. Like Gretel, I
am lost, as surely as in a forest at nighttime, but Gretel didn't
know how lucky she was to have Hansel by her side when
she met the witch who ate children. I am alone when Nanny
walks in, supposedly to help me in the task she has set me.
"You're useless, you stupid girl," she screams, "clumsy and
pathetic! You'd better hop to it, you hear me? Or I'm going to
lose my temper!"

She often pulls my hair or slaps me, when she's not throwing dictionaries, chairs, or even small tables at me. Sometimes she just crosses her arms and hisses through her teeth,
"Go on, look, show me how you do it. Oh, you're a fine sight,

*with your runny nose and that hair in your eyes, you poor thing, I feel sorry for you." And before I find anything, always before I can succeed, she points a long finger at the object I seek: "And that? What's that?" I bow my head in submission and defeat, but she piles on humiliation, stoking her fury: "What is that? Are you going to answer me or not!"*

*Then I tell her what she wants to hear, but I already know that her excitement has crested and must subside. And in fact, sated with violence, she quickly emerges from her trance to tell me coldly, "Go wash your face, it's an ugly mess." Then she turns on her heel to rejoin my parents, my sister, and the eventual guests before whom she immediately plays the model employee who has just had to deal with the teary tantrum of a poor neurotic child. And when I reappear, she pats me on the head, pretending to forgive me: "Oh! She's still all upset . . ."*

*An apparently well-meaning exclamation I correctly interpret as an extra insult intended to let me know that my face is swollen from crying, so I now look a fright.*

*"There's no reason to make such a fuss, after all!" she concludes, letting me know that the incident is closed, that I'd better not tell my mother about it, because Nanny is the boss, able to disguise her cruelty as affection and turn my tears of suffering into the whimpering of a little girl prone to overdramatize. I could have killed her.*

*After such episodes, Nanny avoids my eyes for a few hours,* no doubt unnerved by the hatred she can read there, as well as my understanding of her pitiful attempt to dominate her charges by buying the good graces of Marie—who looks up to her—while trying to destroy me, even though I could unmask her.

She hasn't even enough goodness in her character to realize that I would never do that, wouldn't ever deprive Marie of the illusion of having a kind governess who dotes on the delightful little girl in her care. For that would spoil the tiny bit of joy my sister finds in her relationship with the woman we've nicknamed Louis XI because she shares that sour, stern profile found in our history books. I can tell that Marie quite often pretends to be happier than she feels. Why let her know about the vile injustice I endure? Complaining about it would make me seem jealous, as if I envied Marie instead of taking comfort in her naïveté for accepting at face value the simulated love of a substitute mother. For I have already understood that despite appearances, our governess doesn't love Marie any more than she does me.

In reality, my sister isn't better off than I am. When she worries about receiving bad grades in school, for example, Nanny tells her it isn't serious instead of encouraging or helping her. Scholastic achievement, she says, is useless because the world is full of intellectuals with fine diplomas who amount to nothing in life. A speech offering the triple

*advantage of telling my sister that since she's not an intellec-*
*tual, she's probably an idiot; informing me that my successes*
*in school and supposed intelligence will get me nowhere; and*
*playing the two of us off against each other, as usual.*

*Deep down, our governess is a fool. Wishing to dominate*
*us, but incapable of fulfilling her ambition, she must both clip*
*our wings and divide us, for fear that we might denounce her*
*if we finally find strength in our true beauty and intelligence,*
*and pool our forces to put together the puzzle pieces that will*
*reveal her weakness.*

Nanny always wore a white smock and was dreadfully
ugly, with skin tanned by the sun in Egypt, where she
had spent much of her life. She had a slender hooked nose,
lips as thin as a scar, red-rimmed, washed-out blue eyes,
and breasts that rested heavily on her stomach. Marie's
beauty so bewitched Nanny that she really seemed never
to tire of it. She would take Marie in her arms, touching
her as if somehow to strengthen her claim on the child,
and she photographed her everywhere, all the time.

Did my mother, who lived in constant fear of our governess giving notice, find this attachment convenient?
Or did she allow herself to be swayed by our nanny's

preferences? In any case, following her lead, our mother crowned my sister the star of the family. Our closets contain entire albums devoted to Marie at all ages: an infant as perfect as an Ivory Snow baby, a giggly little Goldilocks, a mischievous young lady miraculously untouched by the indignities of puberty. And hundreds of snapshots of the ravishing and lissome blonde she became are tacked to the walls of my mother's private rooms, framed on the chintz-skirted tables of her boudoir, or displayed on silver easels on the mantelpiece.

My mother could thus claim to have gone perfectly gaga over Marie, at least in the etymological sense of the word, as she literally spoiled her silly with the toys that cluttered our playroom: pretend grocery stands, playhouses shaped like castles (where we tried to hide from the governess), rocking horses with real horsehair manes (to which I was allergic), and pedal cars that seated four. In short, these expensive and exquisite playthings were accessories intended for the nanny's own satisfaction, objects she could then parade before her colleagues to show off *urbi et orbi* the extravagance of her employer's taste, lifestyle, and love for her children. Above all, this avalanche of toys allowed Miss Ross to savor the sight of Marie on a horse, in a car, or playing lady of the house, enjoying everything our nanny had never had as a child. Because she was really playing dolls with Marie, dressing her, arranging her hair, constantly asking my mother to buy my sister new clothes with matching barrettes and bows.

Of course, my mother didn't buy clothes and toys only for Marie. I had some, too. But when she gave Marie a miniature kitchen with a working oven and real china, I received an exercise mat as well as a children's encyclopedia intended to make up for the difference in the cost of our presents. Her unfairness to me was not that obvious, for my mother simply thought she was granting wishes we had supposedly expressed to our nanny and was thus taking into account our respective characters, which Miss Ross was actually inventing to gratify her own desires.

The same thing happened with our clothes. When it came to Marie, the governess would insist that we were growing so quickly that our mother needed to replenish our wardrobe. In my case, however, she thought it best to have my mother save a little money. So I often wound up wearing my sister's old clothes, so tight they turned me into a sausage. In other words, I looked like the shabby plump one, trotted out as a foil for Marie's charm when we were summoned to politely greet the guests. Even if we were already in our pajamas, we had to get dressed all over again, complete with matching hair ribbons, to perform to perfection our role of model little girls who knew how to bob a curtsy: Bonjour, Madame, how do you do . . .

With feigned modesty, our governess would caress Marie's hair before pinching my cheek, in a brusque gesture of apparent affection and reinvigorating comfort for my desperate fate as a homely little ingrate. It was as if she were trying to say, Don't worry, your mother loves you anyway, even if you're not as pretty as Marie. While she was wearing a fake smile to fool my mother and her guests, however, she was really pinching me, and it hurt. She was punishing me, I realized sadly, punishing me for being less lovely than my sister and thus spoiling the pretty picture she wanted to present to these society people, and I steeled myself not to cry in front of "the grown-ups."

I was too young, unfortunately, to confide in Marie about how I suffered from our mother's neglect, or even to reveal the nanny's treachery toward me, since her cruelty was so insidious that Marie would never have believed me and might secretly have thought me mean and twisted. This must have been what led me to psychoanalysis: the desire for enough knowledge and authority to persuade mothers not only to take a real interest in their children, but also to be intelligently aware of their own behavior, for mothers may well be irreplaceable— and with the wisdom of my experience (bolstered by that of Alice Miller, D. W. Winnicott, and Melanie Klein), I was certainly in a position to know!—but they may also do more harm than fathers, if they are all-powerful like the unhinged matron in charge of my upbringing.

As for my father, he paid hardly any attention to us at all. Like many men, he had handed over to his wife the bothersome chores of daily life, including the raising of their children. And so, vacillating between gratitude and guilt, he felt our mother was acquitting herself splendidly of this task through the aid of a governess, and he never gave a thought to protecting us. In any case, he considered our mother's lack of interest far healthier than the obsessive attention mothers these days lavish on their children.

As a result, I did not know my father. Rather, I knew only what my mother said of him: "Hush, your father is sleeping" or "He's working." He was the figure at the end of the upstairs hall. A blond giant with bushy eyebrows, who made silly faces and smiled kindly when addressing his children. Although hardly a stranger to us, he was inaccessible, a sphinx enshrined in work that was never, ever to be disturbed. He was the Man of the House. And we were brought up in the cult of his well-being, thus burnishing the halo of prestige with which our mother had endowed him. Isolated by all this deference and devotion, however, my father was like a walk-on dignitary in an operetta: he never had a say in anything. My mother was merely giving him the illusion that he was the center of her life, for no matter how often she claimed that "between her husband and her children, she had chosen her husband," I just could not believe in her self-styled role as a loving wife. Because in my eyes, she was as incapable of caring about her husband as she was about her children.

Given the adults in our lives, L'Agapanthe was a fixed point in an unreliable world. Our life there was comfortable and unchanging, in spite of the onerous rules and prohibitions Marie and I had to observe, which left us with a faint but constant melancholy ennui. We knew that this misery sprang from a noble motive, which our parents called education. Ours was Jansenist in inspiration, except that far from inculcating in us a characteristically aristocratic and religious contempt for money, our austere upbringing made us familiar with luxury while forbidding us to enjoy it. As a result, impressed by the sumptuous décor of the house, guests at L'Agapanthe imagined us living pampered lives they would never have conjured up for us had we been observed in a house in Brittany or on a farm in Limousin, and they never suspected that not only were we excluded from the privileges reserved for adults, we were also deprived of their pleasures, such as swimming, which we could enjoy only while they were napping, and with strict instructions to abandon the beach under some pretext as soon as any grown-ups showed up, so that we would not be a bother to them.

We learned, therefore, to be self-effacing. A lesson in tactfulness for which I am grateful to my parents, although it condemned my sister and me to watch others take bold advantage of the opportunities of life, whereas in our chosen professions, we sit on the sidelines, interpreting their language or unconscious minds. With that same reserve, we have both conformed to the images assigned to us since childhood, Marie as the pretty girl who picked a career in which her beauty works wonders, even though she could have gone into academia, astrophysics, or banking, and I as the smart girl who decided on a profession in which I can use my mind without being put on display.

Still, L'Agapanthe did bond us together, my sister and I, as soon as Nanny began going on her own vacations instead of accompanying us there. Marie and I "rubbed off on" each other. I pushed Marie to break free of the idea that she was simply some dumb blonde, and I succeeded so well that she quickly rose to the top of her profession and set up her own agency. She no longer works as an interpreter for anyone but the President of the Republic, whom she accompanies on all his travels. And Marie in turn has helped me to find my own beauty, even though my work has always been more important to me than my appearance. I was so used to being not much to look at that I had to make a real effort to stop feeling invisible. Thanks to Marie's guidance and assistance, though, the glances I get from men these days tell me that I'm nicely visible indeed.

And L'Agapanthe has become part of our identity. By demonstrating the subtle framework of our codes and contradictions, this house, all by itself, could illustrate our education, how we became who we are, as well as the refinement and culture of our parents. We had come to realize, of course, that L'Agapanthe was being changed by time, even deformed, in a way, through repairs and renovations, and we knew that the life we led there, already anachronistic, would soon become almost an aberration. But the house was still standing, and up and running for a few months every year. And I was glad that my young son was able to join me every August after spending a month with his father. That way, he could understand the upbringing I had received there and inherit this culture naturally, without any formal instruction. Because L'Agapanthe was also, like any other family house, a wonderful instrument of transmission linking the past to the future.

So it was hardly surprising that Marie and I were trying to save it from being sold. And I was thrilled by the idea of experiencing there for the first time an adventure with my sister, one in which we would more fully discover ourselves and each other.

# The house

L'Agapanthe has nothing flashy about it. No balustrade or row of columns overlooking the sea. It is a Mediterranean villa, built around a loggia like a monastery around its cloister, the complete opposite of a house with a view. As if the sea had decided to behave like an experienced courtesan and simply suggest its presence, with bright touches shimmering through the shade of lush plants and undergrowth, instead of flaunting itself under the windows of L'Agapanthe like a trollop, as it does before the other villas along the Riviera.

Instead, the garden, with its graphic lines and dramatic effects visible from every part of the house, is an invitation to reverie. The lawn unrolls its green carpet beneath a canopy of umbrella pines whose long silhouettes, like slanting strokes of charcoal, are softened by the silvery grays of their rugged bark. A triangle of sea frames itself in the opening of *a hedge at the end of the lawn, like a vanishing point on the horizon.*

*Here nature is tamed by constant care. The grass preserves the trace of our steps like fingerprints on silk velvet. Pine branches and trunks, like paintings, must be supported with cables to keep them from drooping or falling over one another. Thus domesticated, the garden takes on the artificial airs of a stage set, where one might glimpse a dirty old man trotting after some luscious creature, or a married couple making a scene.*

*And yet the garden, by creating harmony between indoors and outdoors, links the house to the sea. And that gradual movement from architecture to nature can be seen in the careful arrangement of the landscape. The olive trees, which make an almost urban impression on the front terrace, where they are set within flagstones like plane trees in a schoolyard, seem wilder a little downhill, among the clumps of lavender dotting the strip of open space halfway down the stone steps to the pine grove. There the cypresses and pink laurels must be content with their decorative role at the bottom of the steps, where hedges, in turn, complete the transformation from vegetation to the mineral world, framing the lawn down to the gorse-studded slopes among the rocks at the beach.*

*L'Agapanthe is a theater à l'italienne, where the lawn is the stage, the rooms are the box seats, and the terrace forms the orchestra pit, with identical flights of steps on both sides.*

*One particularity of this house is its perfect symmetry. From the guest lavatories to the shower rooms, everything was conceived in duplicate, and often assigned separately to men and women. Which is certainly not the case for the two sets of steps on the terrace, so why do people always use the ones on the right?*

*Perhaps the inhabitants of every house establish tacit traffic patterns that may defy all logic and even the challenges of home improvements? At L'Agapanthe, the steps on the right draw us as if marked by invisible and imperious tracks, and we still instinctively avoid the other steps even though the new swimming pool is on that side of the house.*

*Two*

# WEEKEND OF
# JULY 14

# *Weekend of July 14*

### THE FAMILY

Marie Ettinguer               Laure Ettinguer

Flokie Ettinguer              Edmond Ettinguer


### THE PILLARS

Gay Wallingford               Frédéric Hottin


### THE LITTLE BAND

Odon Viel                     Henri Démazure

Polyséna Démazure             Laszlo Schwartz


### THE NEWCOMERS

Jean-Michel Destret           Laetitia Braissant

Bernard Braissant

# SECRETARY'S NAME BOARD

| | |
|---|---|
| M. and Mme. Edmond Ettinguer | Master Bedroom |
| Mme. Laure Ettinguer<br>(*Arrival Air France Thursday 8:00 p.m.*) | Flora's Room |
| Mlle. Marie Ettinguer<br>(*Arrival EasyJet Friday 5:00 p.m.*) | Ada's Room |
| Lady Gay Wallingford | Peony Room |
| M. Frédéric Hottin | Chinese Room |
| M. Odon Viel<br>(*Juan les Pins Station Friday 6:00 p.m.*) | Turquoise Room |
| Count and Countess Henri Démazure | Annex: Coral Room |
| M. Laszlo Schwartz | Lilac Room |
| M. Jean-Michel Destret<br>(*Arrival Air France Friday 5:30 p.m.*) | Yellow Room |
| M. and Mme. Bernard Braissant<br>(*Arrival EasyJet Friday 5:00 p.m.*) | Sasha's Room |

In alphabetical order for the pantry and telephone
    switchboard.
In order of arrival, with departure dates, for chauffeurs and
    chambermaids.
In chronological order with the number in attendance at
    each meal for the kitchen.

My sister and I had no need to discuss how we would each prepare for the weekend of July 14. Relying on her charm, Marie managed to confirm that our father's finances were still flourishing, while I scouted around to draw up a list of suitors to whom an invitation to L'Agapanthe would seem both welcome and perfectly natural.

Jean-Michel Destret had the advantage of being a friend of Laetitia and Bernard Braissant, who knew my sister. Destret was rich, but just how rich? Not as much as all that, probably, in spite of his astronomical salary, golden parachute, and holdings in the investment group he managed. A reliable estimate was difficult to come by with celebrity CEOs like him, over whom the newspapers went wild. At last: a French entrepreneur! As for the

Braissants, they were delighted at the idea of bringing him along for a weekend at the house, thus introducing this new star in the financial heavens to such prestigious members of the Establishment.

The Braissants were by no means my cup of tea. They belonged to that category of phony leftists whom Marie ran into while on the job, important "cultural figures" who'd found their place in the sun by exposing the official cultural elite for their lack of social consciousness through their endless petitions and loudly righteous indignation. Their role models? Scott and Zelda Fitzgerald for beauty and glamour; Sartre and Beauvoir for charisma, moral authority, and the art of pulling strings. Tirelessly trumpeting their political righteousness, they appropriated the allure and importance of any problem they championed, be it the tragedy in Darfur, the Rwandan genocide, or the plight of illegal aliens. And they expected to be treated with the gravity and respect such weighty issues deserved. Anyone reluctant to show them enough deference they dismissed as callous, brainless or, even worse, bourgeois, in which last category they naturally filed me away as a rich "daddy's girl."

Marie, doubtless benefiting from her association with powerful people (and the Braissants' healthy self-regard), escaped that fate. The couple treated her with a mixture of condescension and benevolence. They had selected her to be their "rich heiress," the way anti-Semites invariably befriend a "good Jew." Except that instead of proving they weren't racists, they sought to show that while making an exception for my sister, they despised money. It was the least that could be expected from the editor in chief of a satirical magazine and the communications director for a politician, and from left-wing intellectuals in general. In short, the Braissants were freeloaders. I found them as unbearable as they were pretentious. Still, as Marie reminded me, they were serving us up Jean-Michel Destret on a silver platter.

*Friday, 7:00 a.m.*

"Can you possibly explain to me why this young man is bringing his car and chauffeur down from Paris when he's flying into the airport at Nice this afternoon?"

Even at seven in the morning, my mother was determined not to be impressed by the prestige of her daughters' guests, since a success achieved by anyone other than herself, my father, and their friends irritated her purely on principle.

"What do you mean?" I asked.

"Just imagine, his secretary called yesterday to ask if we could accommodate his driver. Couldn't he rent a car like everyone else? It's unbelievable! And so ill-bred."

"I have to admit it's rather strange, and certainly cheeky, but would you be able to put him up?"

"Yes, luckily enough, in one of those two small rooms over the garage."

Having arrived late the previous evening, I was eager to take a tour of the house, making it my own again the way I did at the beginning of every summer. I felt that I bloomed at L'Agapanthe like those Japanese paper flowers that unfold their petals in water.

I went down to the beach. Carved out of the living rock and jutting like a promontory into the water, it nestled at the midpoint of a bay wide open to the horizon and that seemed to hold the sea within its arms. At this early hour, the water was as smooth as a slick of oil. I looked to the left, at a house that was constantly changing hands and where I'd once seen a James Bond movie being filmed. This time, the flag flying near the water's edge was Russian. Probably a "Russkaya" mafioso. Mother must be tickled pink, I thought treacherously, forcing myself to stand at the edge of the boardwalk even though I felt dizzy. At the bottom of the ladder, I dipped a foot into the water but found it too pale and cold in the early-morning sun for swimming.

I breathed in a scent of curry from the plants growing among the rocks, and the smell of kelp, lying stagnant in the grotto fitted out as a shower, and the intoxicating musty odor of the little cave that had been made into a bar. Then I strolled along the seaside path to the other beach on the property, a triangle of flat rock at water level reserved for the household staff. An entertaining irony of fate thus made our servants neighbors with one of the world's richest men, a Saudi prince who had bought several houses on the bay to the right of ours. Posted every thirty yards, the armed guards of his security force all stared at me intently as I walked along his beach, and I nervously quickened my pace. Wishing I'd thought to bring the cigarettes I allowed myself from time to time, I climbed back up to the house, arriving out of breath.

"So, all's well, you've done your little victory lap? Ask for your tray and come sit with us," Frédéric said firmly.

In the pantry, the butlers were already busy in aprons and shirtsleeves preparing the apricot and raspberry juices for breakfast, the pyramids of dainty cucumber sandwiches for teatime, and grating the lime zest indispensable for the evening's cosmopolitans.

"Madame Laure!"

"Marcel! How are you? And your hip, it's getting better? The children are well?"

Marcel was a sturdy, good-natured fellow from Mont-de-Marsan. He was married, had arthritis, and two daughters, one of whom was beginning a promising career in banking. And that was all I could say about him, because like the other members of our staff, he belonged to a shadow army about which we knew almost nothing.

Numerous and omnipresent, they worked so discreetly, silently, and invisibly that it remained a mystery to us how they managed to complete their tasks. Through what miracle were our rooms made up? And how did the living room, which we abandoned late at night, become spotless again by seven in the morning? Not to mention the towels left at the beach or around the pool that turned up, freshly laundered and neatly folded, in baskets by the pool or in the grotto down by the water.

The staff shifted constantly between work and discretion, at times preferring to quietly withdraw rather than attract notice. And their choreography—with the imperceptible refinement of our grandmothers' hems, sewn with lead weights to muffle the rustling of their skirts—produced an effect close to perfection. Like a pleasure dome freed from all material contingency, the house inspired reverie, and even happiness. It was only upon leaving this womblike world that we could realize or remember that no one lived like this anymore. No one lived like us.

# The Rules of the Game

## FILM BY JEAN RENOIR (1939)

CHRISTINE de la CHESNAYE, lady of the house:
*Jean isn't here?*

CELESTIN, kitchen boy:
*Ah, no, Madame la Marquise! He has gone to Orléans in the
van, for the fish.*

CHRISTINE de la CHESNAYE:
*Do explain to him about Madame de la Bruyère's diet. She
eats everything, but no salt.*

MADAME de la BRUYERE, guest:
*No, on the contrary, lots of salt, but it must be sea salt, added
only after the cooking. Oh, it's quite simple, a child would
understand. After the cooking!*

CHRISTINE de la CHESNAYE:

*Do you have any sea salt?*

• • •

(At the servants' table)

LISETTE, personal maid to the marquise:

*Some asparagus?*

GAMEKEEPER:

*No, thanks, I never eat canned. I only like fresh, because of the vitamins.*

• • •

CELESTIN:

*Chef, did you remember the sea salt for old lady la Bruyère?*

JEAN, the chef:

*Madame la Bruyère will eat like everyone else. I will put up with diets, but not with fads.*

• • •

JEAN:

*La Chesnaye may be a Jew, but the other day he summoned me for a dressing-down over a potato salad. As you know, or rather, as you do not know, for a potato salad to be worthy of the table, the white wine must be poured over the potatoes while they are still boiling hot, which Célestin had not done because he doesn't like to burn his fingers. Well! The boss, he picked up on that right away. You may say what you like, but that—that is a man of the world.*

"Roberto isn't here?" I asked.

"No," replied one of the butlers in the pantry. "He's out shopping."

"Of course, silly me . . ."

Roberto, the head butler, was responsible for buying our bread, newspapers, flowers to make up bouquets, the fruits and cheeses he arranged on serving platters, on dishes for the guests' rooms, and in baskets for centerpieces. He was also in charge of slicing the larger fruits served at breakfast and shelling the fresh almonds set out on the little tables in the loggia during cocktails.

"What would Madame like for breakfast?" asked Marcel, opening a large cupboard.

Some twenty trays laden with coffeepots, milk pitchers, and jam jars of brightly colored Vallauris china were lined up inside, next to a small notebook hanging from a hook. Warped and blistered by moisture, this recorded the customary preferences of our guests. Beneath Lady Wallingford's name was written "Lemon tea + plain yogurt + fruit + *Herald Tribune*," whereas the requirements of Laszlo Schwartz demanded an entire paragraph: "Scrambled eggs, bacon, sausages, croissant, toast, jam (no orange marmalade), café au lait, *Herald Tribune*, *Nice Matin*, *Le Figaro*, *Le Monde*."

"Tea with milk?" replied Marcel, astonished by my request, "but usually you have—"

"Black coffee, yes, I know. I apologize for changing my mind like this, Marcel, which doesn't make things easy. It's a good thing not everyone is like me!"

I went back to the loggia, a sort of covered patio extended by an awning above the terrace, which looked out over the lawn and the sea. Furnished as a living room, the loggia was connected to all the reception rooms in the house, thus serving as a forum to the "city of L'Agapanthe," a center for intrigues and conversation. I sat down beside Gay and Frédéric in one of the wicker armchairs from the 1940s, across from the huge green linen sofa where my mother held court from the moment breakfast began. Comments on the day's news were enriched by the appearance of each freshly awakened guest, and everyone got quickly up to speed. What had the finance minister said yesterday evening? How many dead from that earthquake? How had this or that guest slept? Who wanted to go for a swim or into town?

"Which of your clients have already arrived?" was the first thing I asked my mother.

I should explain that my parents, always happy to "go slumming," liked to call their guests clients, often comparing L'Agapanthe to a family boardinghouse and themselves to its "bosses."

"Well, aside from Gay and Frédéric right here, there are the Démazures, Henri and Polyséna . . . and also Schwartz, who arrived two days ago."

"Bingo!" I thought, wishing Marie had been there to exchange knowing smiles with me, because my mother had just betrayed once again her attraction to Laszlo Schwartz by using only his last name, unusual behavior for one so addicted to etiquette. In fact my mother was scrupulous about using absolutely everyone's first and last names, saying for example, "Henri Démazure just telephoned." If writing or making an introduction, she would add the person's title, if necessary: "Let me introduce you to the Baroness de Cadaval" or "Lord Fraser." Unless she were speaking of a merchant or other businessperson, in which case she graced the last name with a "Monsieur" or "Madame" that was all the more condescending for its appearance of respect. This led to remarks like, "Monsieur Lefèvre, you won't forget that estimate for my living room curtains, will you?"

So, although my mother was careful to appear casual and unconcerned whenever she mentioned Laszlo Schwartz, modulating her tone with a care she imagined went unnoticed, we couldn't help detecting her interest. True, Laszlo was attractive. Tall, elegant, with an imposing silver mane, and intimidating in the manner of those who make it clear that they follow only their own rules, he could even appear haughty. He did to my mother, in any case, who was timid and insecure by nature, in spite of all her elegance and irreverent airs, and who would have found him overpowering if he hadn't been introduced to her by the Démazures, whose friend—inexplicably—he was.

Enthralled by his talent, fame, and freewheeling conversation, she was still amazed that he paid attention to her. For Laszlo, who had always been curious about the rich, had swiftly succumbed to her hospitality and had also begun to flirt with her. Openly, but without any real impropriety, for the pleasures of the chase, of gently teasing a sophisticated woman—and for the more refined rewards of experimenting with a dalliance from another age, which he had never had the time or means to explore.

"And Odon Viel, he's not coming this year?" I asked her.

For we were still missing our astrophysicist, the Nobel Prize winner of the family, whose major failing was to believe us all capable of fathoming the nuances of quantum mechanics and molecular and atomic physics. Viel would complete my mother's group of intimate friends—along with Gay, Schwartz, and the Démazures—whom she proudly called her little band, and whom Marie, my father, and I referred to as her pets. They were cultured people, intellectuals and, with the exception of Gay, sometimes crashing bores, according to my father, who much preferred eccentrics like Georgina de Marien or Charles Ramsbotham, whom my mother dismissed as "oddballs" or "duds."

"As it happens," she told me, "he's arriving at Juan-les-Pins on the six o'clock train."

"Someone," intoned Gay lugubriously, "should perhaps explain to dear Odon that it's now cheaper to travel by plane than by train. Because I truly doubt that his ticket was a better buy than the thirty euros for a Paris–Nice on EasyJet, even with his beloved senior-citizen card and those discounts he so adores."

Her theatrically sinister delivery tickled Frédéric and me so much we couldn't help laughing. To hear Gay talking about the price of public transportation was simply bizarre, because she was a great lady. An elderly one, now, but still lovely: she was tall, thin, and had *such* class! Like Ava Gardner in a Hollywood film, she always seemed ready to grab the spotlight, even first thing in the morning in her champagne-colored satin dressing gown and matching mules with Popsicle, her Maltese bichon, on her lap.

She wasn't the type to sit around mulling over her memories, so no one ever asked her about her life. Except me, and the one time I did ask her I learned she'd had her share of tragedies. She had started out in life as an adventuress, at least so I imagined, by reinventing herself with a new name, Gay. That career had ended in the camps, however, a part of her life she never mentioned. After that, she'd collected husbands, the last of which, Lord Wallingford, had brought her into society and left her a widow.

Frédéric and I were still laughing when my mother—who has always been peeved by our complicity—asked me loudly about Marie.

"And your sister, when does she get here?"

"At five. On EasyJet, actually. With the Braissants."

When she pretended to be momentarily confused, I added, "You know, Laetitia and Bernard Braissant, friends of hers . . ."

"What is it they do again?"

"They work in the media, communications."

"Oh, yes, television, or something along those lines," she replied with a shrug of disgust.

"Well, let's say public relations for her and journalism for him."

"How awful! When I think that your father and I had managed until now to avoid having any journalists in this house . . ."

Her comment was all the more unfair since our parents hadn't raised the slightest objection when Marie and I had gone over our guest list with them. And Marie had been particularly careful to reassure them about the exclusively political nature of the Braissants' professional interests, because she knew how much they distrusted journalists. Besides, Marie and I thought largely as our parents did, since we considered journalists incapable of loyalty to anyone once they smelled a possible scoop, and they were often disinclined to respect the boundary between what was fair game or not—that famous "off the record" they flung all over the place to create a climate of confidence they would betray the first chance they got, overwhelmed by the desire to release an exclusive report or write the breaking story.

Our parents had often told us: If you're a public figure, it's impossible to be friends with a journalist. How can you ask a friend to put feelings before professional interest? Besides, such discretion represents a sacrifice so exorbitant that you'll wind up paying for it ten times over. The proof? Allow a journalist "friend" to write an article about you: afraid of being accused of concocting a puff piece, the writer will come down harder on you than anyone else. And it's always possible that the critique, based on intimate knowledge of your life, will wind up being too painfully intimate by far.

My mother, however, had picked the wrong target, because if any one of our guests was open to her accusation, it was surely Jean-Michel Destret. Marie and I really did think it hopelessly vulgar to chase after notoriety the way he seemed to do, waltzing delightedly across television sets and through photo sessions on his way to the ghastly stardom of the VIP: a catchall category comprising the likes of sarcastic old novelists, decrepit social butterflies giddy with gratitude for a photo in the advertising section, and empty-headed pundits pontificating at full blast in televised debates. So if either Marie or I took an interest in this Destret, his deplorable taste for publicity would require prompt correction, because the Duchess of Windsor's "You can never be too thin or too rich" paled in importance, in our eyes, before the wisdom of "You can never stay too far away from the press."

Fortunately, my father chose to make his appearance at that moment, nipping my mother's growing ill humor in the bud.

"Good morning, everyone!" he cried cheerily, then gave me a kiss.

Raising an eyebrow in my direction, he asked how I was doing, to which I replied with a demure flutter of eyelashes and a smile. He must have sensed that I'd be well advised to cede center stage to my mother, leaving her to reign uncontested over her husband and guests, so I sat back, and a child once again, let the grown-ups do the talking.

My father couldn't keep quiet for long about his passion for art. For a good part of the night, three Renaissance paintings had kept him awake, lost in the contemplation of color slides sent to him by Sotheby's, which he quickly showed us with greedy zeal.

There was a Cranach the Elder (1472–1553) titled *Young Woman Holding Grapes and Apples*; a Titian (1485/90–1576), *Mary Magdalene Repentant*; and *Descent into Limbo* by Andrea Mantegna (1430–1506).

His enthusiasm was touching.

"So, you're tempted by all three?" Gay asked him.

"Oh, no! I'd love that, but it's impossible. Besides, I'm not really captivated by the Mantegna. It's superb, but the subject is quite austere. And it's simply too expensive."

"But it's tiny! 38.8 by 42.3 centimeters, that's eensy-weensy!" cackled Frédéric, holding the Ecktachrome up to the light. "Me, I'd go for the Cranach, and what do you know, it's a steal at only one and a half million!"

"Yes, but the Cranach's 81.5 by 55 centimeters: it's smaller than the Titian estimated at four to six million dollars, which measures 119 by 98.5 centimeters. And that comes to, per square centimeter . . ."

"You sound like a couple of accountants!" exclaimed my mother. "It's shocking!"

My mother was not really shocked at all by these trivial comments and was herself often quite blunt when speaking of artworks, which were all the less sacred in her eyes because we lived among them. My father was the collector and scholar of the family, a man who studied art history for several hours a day, but my mother wanted to remind us that she had a good eye, too. And it was true that through her familiarity with the works coveted or purchased by my father, and by visiting assiduously all the museums in the world and observing dealers in art and antiques at their trades, my mother had acquired such expertise that she rarely erred in her evaluation of a canvas. As on the day when she had appalled a well-known dealer in New York who was showing us a Caravaggio.

"Actually, it should be cut in two! Because the infant Jesus lighting up the picture is sublime, as is the angel in the bloodred robe whirling above him. But the entire right side is a botch . . ."

And she was right, because carbon 14 dating revealed that the right side of the painting was speckled with pentimenti and overpainting.

"I'm with Frédéric, I'm leaning toward the Cranach," announced my father. "Especially since it's the gentlest, most civilized version of a subject he used several times. In general the young woman holds a severed head, whether it's Judith with the head of Holofernes, or Salome with John the Baptist's, or Jael with Sisera's."

Henri and Polyséna Démazure, wearing varied shades of blue, now made their entrance into the loggia to such spectacular effect that everyone suddenly realized we were all dressed in blue, except for Gay, who was in yellow.

"What happened?" Frédéric asked her in mock dismay. "You didn't receive the bulletin informing us that blue was the color of the day?"

After a courteous little laugh, Polyséna hurried to revive the conversation about art, eager to take advantage of this chance to mention the beautiful book she was working on, in which photographs of current celebrities—actors, politicians, singers, sports icons, and TV stars—were paired with their doubles from the past, immortalized in famous portraits dating from the quattrocento. James Gandolfini, lead actor in *The Sopranos*, revealed a striking resemblance to the Doge Giovanni Mocenigo, as painted by Gentile Bellini, while Sonia Rikyel seemed to have inspired Otto Dix's portrait of the dancer Anita Berber.

"I suppose Cate Blanchett corresponds all by herself to a number of Holbein portraits," observed Gay.

"And Nicole Kidman might find herself as a beauty with rippling red hair by Dante Gabriel Rossetti," added my mother.

I saw my father's face cloud faintly with annoyance. Cate Blanchett and Nicole Kidman meant little to him in comparison to the grandmasters of painting, about whom, on the contrary, he could hold forth forever, but he preferred to keep quiet rather than offend Polyséna.

"Well, Laure," said Frédéric brightly. "It's high time to get a move on! You promised to drive me into town, remember?"

Like many fun people who disdain to conform to modern life, Frédéric had no idea how to drive. Surprised for a moment, then grateful for the diversion, I was about to reply when my mother beat me to it.

"Don't be silly!" she told Frédéric. "Roland, the chauffeur, will take you. And if it's to buy your *Paris-Turf*, I don't see why you can't ask Roberto to get it for you."

"Flokie, darling," said Frédéric, rising to kiss her hand, "you're a sweetheart, tried and true, but I absolutely need Laure for my little jaunt because I'm going hunting for a present for her *birthday*, which—as you know—is only a few days away."

Mollified by this logical explanation for Frédéric's desire for my company, my mother let us go.

"Just give me time to call my son," I told him.

"Fine, come get me in my room when you're done—I know it might take some time . . ."

And he was right. I missed my son so much when he was with his father that I could bear the separation only by breaking it up with phone dates, replacing "See you next month" with "Till tomorrow" or "Talk to you later." And he missed me. He was only seven, and he needed me. But his moods varied, and that day, busy getting ready for some fishing with his father, he barely said hello. I felt hurt, but relieved as well, because that meant he was happy.

"So, what's the form?" said Frédéric after we'd settled in with our coffee on the terrace of the Hôtel du Cap.

He always came on like a punter checking bloodlines when asking about the pedigree of one of my lovers or a guest at L'Agapanthe.

"Jean-Michel Destret? But haven't you seen his picture? It's in all the newspapers."

"You mean the one who looks like the class nerd with his hair parted on the side?"

"Exactly."

"Hoo boy! Are we in for some fun. Who's he for, you or Marie?"

"Whoever gets the first hit—we're going to play it by ear."

"Like flipping a coin?"

"That's great, laugh at me! You know what I mean . . . and by the way, this is the first time you haven't told me that a guy isn't good enough for me."

"I'm on my best behavior, just for you! I'm keeping my beady eye on the sugar daddy prize."

"Hey, real sugar daddies are old, so if you don't mind, I'd rather call this a blind date."

"Blind date? I'm good with that! See how nice I'm being?"

I have always confided in Frédéric about my love life and always been able to count on him whenever I wanted to go AWOL or hit the hottest underground club of the moment.

"I think that's a stupid idea," he usually told me, "but I'll totally support you in whatever stupid idea goes through your head."

And he meant it, like the year when I had a crush on French movie star Daniel Auteuil. I went on and on about him to Frédéric (who knew him a little), asking what he was like and if there was a chance that he might like me. I always got the same answer.

"You're pissing me off with your Daniel Auteuil!"

Until my birthday. I was blowing out my candles when he handed me the phone with a mischievous look. "Call for you."

"Who is it?"

"Some guy named Auteuil, I think," he told me, casual as you please, when he'd been pestering the actor relentlessly to please call me up and invite me out for coffee.

My mother had a strange look on her face when we got back from Juan-les-Pins shortly after noon.

"Flokie, what's wrong?" said Frédéric.

"It's Roberto. He fell. I'm afraid he's broken his hip. Roland and Pauline just left with him in the ambulance."

"Oh, shit, the poor man! Is there anything you want me to do?" I asked her.

"Yes. If you could find me a new head butler, that would be a big help, because with our guests already here and now your friends arriving . . ."

"I'll take care of it," I promised quickly, refusing to respond to her insinuation, although I figured that at this rate, my guests—a definite thorn in her side—would soon be held responsible for tripping up Roberto.

"And what about Roberto? Would you like—"

"I'll handle that," she answered brusquely.

On that point, I had complete confidence in her. She was fantastic in difficult situations. I knew that she would reassure Roberto, pay all his expenses, and have him cared for by the best specialists, even if it meant moving him to another hospital.

I considered my options. Our staff had already been requisitioned for the summer at L'Agapanthe. Streaming in from my parents' other residences, these chambermaids, cooks, and butlers, who had worked for my parents for ten or twenty years, seemed happy to come back to fulfill their assigned tasks. In fact, some retirees even returned to service for the occasion, to plump up their savings and renew old ties.

With a long weekend coming up, my only course was to find an open employment agency. I had no illusions: finding another treasure like Roberto would be a miracle. He'd been with my parents for twenty-eight years, a paragon of kindness, professionalism, and refinement. And it would not be easy to find a head butler who would share our approach to domestic service.

As we saw it, the expertise of our staff depended on years of apprenticeship and experience. The servants were expected to perform their duties appropriately and without any instruction from us. It would never even have occurred to us to advise our employees regarding their work, and why would we have done so, since we knew ourselves to be incapable of ironing a fluted sleeve or whipping up a soufflé Mornay? The new butler would have to be up to the job, because our long acquaintance with impeccable service made us excellent judges in the field.

He would also have to understand our devotion to protocol. We were never on familiar terms with our staff, because displaying any growing affection or general sympathy for them would have smacked of demagoguery. That was our way of showing them respect and appreciation for their skill. Sticklers for form, we addressed our cook as "Chef." And we would never have disturbed the servants during their meals or leisure hours by entering their living or dining rooms, or have meddled in their personal affairs of the heart, family, workplace, or pocketbook. In short, we left them to their own devices. We kept a distance we considered ideal for a long-term relationship. Familiarity breeds contempt, as the saying goes. So we all stayed where we belonged: we, by behaving like employers, by giving orders respectfully, unemotionally, without any attempt to manipulate our employees; they, by sheltering behind a tradition requiring them to address us in the third person—"Would Madame like . . . ?" Behind that facade, they were free to think whatever they wanted, and even not to like us.

Our staff enjoyed, if not our affection, our esteem. And so they deserved consideration and pleasant working conditions. L'Agapanthe was a "good house" for them as well. The laundry, kitchen, and pantry were air-conditioned. The servants received excellent wages, had everything they needed for their jobs: professional-quality appliances, the latest model steam ovens, workstations worthy of the very finest restaurants, plenty of *sous-chefs*, even a raft of "scullions" to do the washing up. They had a private beach at their disposal, dining areas both inside the house and on a patio outside, simple but tasty food, a television lounge, comfortable bedrooms with their own bathrooms, and cars available for going out in the evening. And judging from the noise and laughter from their dining room at mealtime, the atmosphere "belowstairs" was good.

But our family ideal of service was possible only in a house like L'Agapanthe, where we could all live together. Because the social gulf between us was not as wide as the chasm between city centers and their suburbs, fashionable neighborhoods and slums, elegant town houses and tenements—although the town houses were becoming increasingly middle class, doing away with the social distinctions formalized by the parlor floor and the maids' rooms up under the eaves.

Nevertheless, the invisible barrier between us was impossible to cross. The servants, so close to us and seemingly as varied and picturesque as our houseguests, formed a mysterious tribe whose proximity aroused my curiosity. I sometimes wondered how they lived and thought, like a student in a girls' boarding school dreaming about the boys' school next door. When

I was younger, I'd even ventured out on a few nocturnal expeditions into the unknown realm behind the forbidden doors, but I felt distinctly like a trespasser when I studied the staff menu notebook, the cupboard inventories, or the recipe boards hanging on the kitchen walls, or when I tried to eavesdrop from convenient rooms on their conversations during mealtime.

They, of course, knew a lot more about us. The butlers witnessed our conversations and how we behaved at the table. The chambermaids could tell a great deal from the quality of our garments, the way we packed our suitcases, or the state in which we left our rooms. And they evaluated us according to how demanding and polite we were, the generosity of our tips, and our general behavior. But they also judged us by the benchmark of too-daring a décolleté, an arrogant attitude, a tendency to drink too much or to spout unreasonable opinions. And I felt that they were rather conservative, preferring couples to single people, moderates to reformers, people who kept busy to those who lounged around. They had a moral viewpoint on people and things. And I would have been willing to bet that they preferred employment with a traditional family like ours rather than with a Russian mafioso or a movie star.

Denounced at one time under the banner of class struggle, this rigid social barrier between servants and employers now evoked a certain nostalgia for the past. Having died out elsewhere, it was no longer really under attack, especially since nothing more equitable or persuasive had replaced it. Such an organization was now an anachronism, a weird and wonderful curiosity. And that's what made it precious.

One had only to look at the servants of our nouveaux-riches neighbors. Because although we still accepted invitations inland, from around Monte Carlo or Saint-Tropez, we no longer had much to do with the houses on the bay, which now belonged to Greeks, Arabs, or Russians whose security concerns required an army of bodyguards with walkie-talkies and machine guns. Aping the aristocracy, some of our neighbors in their Palladian villas kitted their servants out in white gloves, gaudy uniforms, and even full livery, delighting in the spectacle of entire brigades of costumed minions marching at attention into a dining room, subjecting a captive audience to their ostentatious choreography. Other neighbors, envisioning their staff as an advertisement of their own fortunes and cultural savviness, hired young and beautiful people whose irreproachable "look" complemented the designer furniture and clean, pure lines of their employers' glass-and-concrete houses.

Whether they aspired to splendor or to the *very* latest fashions, our neighbors had one thing in common: all were all jumped-up vulgarians in our eyes. Their desire to broadcast their status and lifestyle betrayed way too much social insecurity. They might be rich, hip, swooned over by the press, pursued by paparazzi, and courted by the owners of art galleries and clubs, but they hadn't a clue how to run what we considered an inherently gracious household. And they didn't impress us with their noisy hired help, who brayed their announcements or demanded immediate replies to their questions, not to mention those flunkies who looked us over like maître d's in trendy restaurants, just long enough to decide if we were worthy of the lousy service they might deign to bestow on us.

Such parvenus, however, had every right to show off to their guests instead of demanding proper household service. And we would have bowed before the onslaught of history, feeling simply out-of-date, like dinosaurs, if these people hadn't *all* mistreated their staff. They did so for various reasons, but chief among them was their contempt for underlings who were in essence interchangeable yet burdened with the task of enhancing their employers' standing. Lashing out, the nouveaux riches could savor the full exercise of their power only by oppressing their hirelings, whose beauty, inexperience, and sheer numbers they found wearisome in the end. Demanding of them anything and everything, our neighbors played their roles as lords of the manor by being condescending, capricious, and abusive.

The funniest part was that we inspired exactly the same disapproval in these upstarts. Our conception of luxury was too subtle for them to grasp: they recognized neither its standards nor its stereotypes. And they despaired over our refinement, which they saw as an appalling lack of comfort and luxury. Where were the massive flowerbeds, the statues, the fountains they considered the sine qua non for any self-respecting garden? What about our cars, our boats, our helicopters? And where was our staff? Had we no security personnel? No control rooms with plasma screens and intercoms, no loudspeakers on the grounds? What was behind this inadequate, ridiculous, pathetic setup? Were we broke, or just cheap? And so we seemed as vulgar to them as they seemed to us.

*Friday, 3:00 p.m.*

Someone named Gérard, bristling with references, was assuring me over the phone that he had always dreamed of working "in a bourgeois house" when the sound of a diesel engine out on the front drive informed me that a taxi had arrived. Just what I needed! I hired our new butler then and there, arranged for him to get here in time for dinner, and went downstairs.

"Talk about a warm welcome!" remarked my sister. "Did we miss Roland at the airport, or did you simply forget about us?"

"Sorry, we forgot about you, because it's total chaos here. Poor Roberto has just broken his hip, and Roland went to the hospital with him. Which means he must have forgotten to alert the caretaker about your arrival, so no one came to pick you up."

"Poor Roberto! A broken hip, that's not good, is it. . . . I'm sure you remember Bernard and Laetitia Braissant?"

Although Bernard looked rumpled and sweaty, he seemed pleasant enough, but I took an instant dislike to Laetitia in spite of her glowing complexion and masses of dark hair. There was something vaguely superior about her attitude. She was wearing a tank top with a long peasant skirt in the Provençal style, and I would have sworn that the affected simplicity, the fake "local color" of this outfit had been intended simply to give a lesson in authenticity to us rich people, whom she was visiting only reluctantly.

"Where are you putting us?" asked Marie, looking exquisite in beige and white pants and a bush jacket.

"You're in Ada's Room; Bernard and Laetitia are in Sasha's Room," I told her, consulting the room assignments posted in the secretary's office just off the entrance hall.

"And I suppose you're in Flora's Room, and Jean-Michel Destret has the Yellow Room?"

Marie had supposed correctly, and I smiled in reply, because this distribution of bedrooms observed an unspoken hierarchy we both recognized. By giving us the two smallest and least attractive rooms in the house, my mother was reminding us that we were merely her daughters, not honored guests, and that our friends would receive nothing more from her than a carefully calculated graciousness.

Had we been in a hotel, my parents' room would have qualified as the presidential suite. A vast room with four windows and a fireplace, it had a linen closet, a dressing room paneled in cedar, and a spacious bathroom worthy of Hollywood. Half boudoir, half ballroom, this bathroom was where the family often got together to chat, far from our staff and guests. With its pearly pink light, the veined yellow marble sinks, the bronze faucets shaped like dolphins, and the 1930s furniture laminated in beveled mirror with valances of raw silk, the room seemed to await a visit from Lauren Bacall or Katharine Hepburn in satin slippers, trailing the fragrance of tuberose and rice powder.

Next in grandeur came the Peony and Lilac rooms, which had perfect proportions and a fantastic view of the lawn and the sea. Less sumptuous, the Turquoise Room looked out over a small terrace that seemed to relegate the sea to the background. Although they were huge and enjoyed an oblique view of the water, the Yellow and Chinese rooms were one notch below the Turquoise, since they overlooked the staff's outside dining area, a nuisance that in a hotel would have justified a distinct reduction in their rates. Finally, dead last, came a trio of rooms at the entrance to the hall leading to the servants' quarters, rooms that no amount of remodeling could change into bona fide guest rooms and now named after Flora, Ada, and Sasha, frequent guests in the house in my grandparents' time.

L'Agapanthe had originally had so many more staff rooms than guest rooms that my parents had built what we called the annex, over by the entrance to the property.

The annex so lacked the charm of the main house that guests lodged there sometimes felt slighted, but others were flattered, because my parents gave those rooms only to previous visitors whom they were inviting back for another stay.

Colette, a lovely young woman from Normandy with a Louise Brooks bob, was already in Sasha's Room when Marie and I escorted the Braissants upstairs. Laetitia stiffened with indignation when the smiling chambermaid asked her, "Would Madame like me to unpack her suitcase?"

"No, thank you, I'll manage by myself," she replied, with the studied manner of someone who, scandalized, refuses to participate in a degrading ritual from another era.

The dismayed Colette was about to withdraw when Marie returned her smile and asked, "Colette, would you be good enough to unpack mine?"

*Friday, 6:30 p.m.*

I heard the sound of crunching gravel again. Was it Odon Viel arriving, or Jean-Michel Destret and his chauffeur? (It turned out to be Jean-Michel.) While Marie and I were heading for the front door, I remembered a sidewalk game we used to play when we were younger: you had to pick, from the first ten men who came toward you, the one who would be your husband for life. I always panicked; should I be cautious or optimistic? Take the first one who wasn't either elderly or repulsive, or wait for a good-looking boy, at the risk of missing the boat and getting stuck with the tenth passerby, who might well be a ghastly old man?

Sex was a topic often and broad-mindedly discussed in our presence by my parents and their friends, who for the sake of appearances would pretend to lower their voices around our innocent ears. They treated sex with the humor and relaxed detachment expected of cultured people, because a light, bantering tone was to them an essential ingredient in any civilized conversation. Artful and amusing, amorous dalliance was thus a required subject, just like literature or the opera. Compared to my friends' parents, who never broached the subject and certainly not in front of children, my own parents sometimes even struck me as obsessed. Marie and I were privy, as it turned out, to a real education. Whether down-to-earth or laced with literature, those conversations instilled in us the vocabulary and aesthetic nuances of a libertine freedom of thought that never stooped to a vulgar familiarity, ranging from the naughty, spicy, smutty, and just slightly perverse language of a Choderlos de Laclos, to sensual and voluptuous concupiscence, or brazen Rabelaisian ribaldry—and from the grandiose debauchery of a Sade to the crudest, ugliest, most unsettling pornography and all the raunchy, sordid, lubricious, salacious, libidinous depravity drawn along in its wake. Thus educated in indecency by proxy, as we had been in wine and painting, we ended by appreciating this cultural inheritance passed down by parents who were most unusual, to be sure, but who had the merit of being emancipated and nonconformist.

Which by no means meant that in our family sex was allowed, authorized, or approved of. The sexual education my sister and I received from our mother was summed up in a few principles: we were to begin our lives as women only after a visit to the doctor, and only if (she always said *if*, not *when*) we were in love—the sine qua non, she said, for making love, thus making the gift of oneself out of what otherwise would be simply an easy lay.

In that department, though, Marie and I have always been different. Marie is romantic and dreams of meeting her soul mate, but that doesn't stop her from collecting lovers. She has never found it compromising to sleep with whomever she pleases. It gives her pleasure, especially when she comes across a hardy and enthusiastic partner with self-assured moves but no real emotional involvement. In short, nothing to write home about. Sometimes she even has to think twice about her scruples when she turns down men who seem to attach great importance to sex. But she's too sought after to yield to her admirers just to be considerate, so to rein herself in she has come up with some inhibitions and apprehensions: unseemly, occasionally embarrassing noises made by interlocking bodies, and self-consciousness about her nakedness, or about the folds and bulges created during the choreography of love's embrace. And these barriers keep her from giving in to just anyone, without preventing her from letting herself go whenever she feels like it. Particularly with her pals in the security details for summit meetings, guys for whom my sister, who's crazy about officers and uniforms, feels a guilty fondness.

I'm the opposite of Marie. Men never leave me indifferent. Arousing desire or disgust, their skin, their bodies wield a power over me that proves sometimes inconvenient. I'm incapable, for example, of dancing cheek to cheek with a man who doesn't appeal to me. And I make sure I never touch or brush against a man, even by accident—in the back of a car, say—for fear of shuddering with desire if he attracts me or with aversion if he doesn't. In my life, sex has always intruded in an unexpected and uncontrollable way. Falling in love is an invitation to chaos and commotion: I feel immediately on fire, overwhelmed by a painful desire for the man who fills my thoughts. Sleepless, I lie moaning, writhing with longing, capable of climaxing or becoming prostrate with frustration at the memory of a word, a gesture. So it goes without saying that I set great store by physical love. Without any "technique," I abandon myself to my partner and lose all sense of time. For me, sex is like an elixir that cures me of everything, of both worry and pain. It's like a prodigious journey that sweeps me up from head to toe, a journey on which I cannot embark unless I love the man to distraction, even if only for a few hours.

Like the narrator's aunts in *Remembrance of Things Past*, who thank Swann so obliquely for the case of Asti wine, I tried to be tactful by not looking Jean-Michel Destret straight in the face, so that he wouldn't feel too ill at ease upon arriving at a strange house. I did sneak a peek at him while he was getting out of his car and noticed that he'd sat next to his driver instead of in the backseat.

Marcel, who was in charge of the luggage, welcomed the chauffeur and led him off to his room, while Marie and I escorted Jean-Michel into the loggia, where the other guests were chatting over their tea.

"Jean-Michel Destret, delighted," he said to my mother, bending crisply to kiss her hand before adding, "Allow me to thank you for your invitation, Madame Ettinguer. I'm very happy to be here."

Marie and I looked at each other, stunned by the disastrous impression he had just made. Managing to cram so many gaffes into one greeting was in fact a kind of triumph. Beginning with "Delighted,"[1] *totally* provincial, at least when trotted out for an introduction—an absurd rule, perhaps, but an unbreakable one, which none of us would have dreamed of contesting since it was completely without rhyme or reason. One might say "Delighted to be here," "What a delightful ambience," or "You are delightful," but certainly *not* "delighted." Like the verb "to eat," unthinkable when used intransitively ("What are we eating?" or "I've eaten well"), whereas "I'm eating some chocolate" was perfectly fine. Or the word "flute" when used to offer champagne, brimming with inelegance in the expression, "You'll have a

---

1 In French, *"Enchanté"* may be tackier than *"Delighted"* is in English.

little flute?"—a massive no-no, unlike "A glass of champagne?" or "Some champagne?" which went down as smooth as silk.

As for his "Madame Ettinguer," it was a double faux pas. For although his use of "Madame" was timely and even welcome, the addition of our family name was jarring because, according to French etiquette, it implied that my mother was his social inferior. And he had fallen into the usual trap with our name, which is written Ettinguer, but pronounced *Ettingre*, something only those in the know would know, as they know that La Trémoille is pronounced *La Trémouille*, that one says *Breuil* for Broglie, *Crouy* for *le prince* Cröy, and *Beauvau-Cran* instead of Beauvau-Craon. (Just as one should pronounce English names the English way in France, saying *Charlie* instead of Sharlie, and *Johnny*, not Zhonny.)

In conclusion, Jean-Michel had been too solemn and earnest, revealing his ignorance of the fact that elegance is created like a cake, with a mixture of varied and complementary ingredients. He had just kissed the hand of the mistress of the house and should therefore have balanced that homage with a hint of humor, the way the stodginess of a tea biscuit is lightened with whipped cream. Another point: his allusion to my mother's "invitation" was too formal, just as his "allow me" was almost emphatic. As for "I'm very happy to be here," it was a pat expression and fell flat: any sincerity in the words lost all importance, since his compliment was too obvious to sit well. He would have been better off with a gracious exclamation along the lines of, "A true pleasure!" or a seemingly spontaneous—and more difficult— casual remark like, "Such a lovely surprise: it's a marvel, this house!" All in all, he seemed unaware that he had already said too much. His clump of compliments betrayed an eagerness to please that stamped him from the get-go as a clod.

I looked at him. There was nothing special about him. No aura, no presence. He was commonplace. His eyes, his features—nothing handsome about him. Nothing ugly, either. And it was hard to tell his age, because with his helmet of hair, you would have said a choirboy or a teacher in a one-room schoolhouse. But, well, it was too soon to conclude that he had no powers of seduction, for he might turn out to be a paragon of wit, intelligence, and charm once he had stepped out of the social spotlight. And yet, the first thing that struck me about him was how carefully he was following the line of behavior he seemed to have chosen, which was to vamp my mother, and so assiduously that he had not yet even looked at my sister or me, so much closer to his own age.

Logically speaking, my mother should have cold-shouldered a nobody like him. So I was dumbfounded to hear her reply with a most unaccustomed friendliness. Now Marie and I exchanged even more astonished glances as our mother gazed benevolently at him, maternal as you please. He seemed to have charmed her, making her forget her displeasure over his tagalong chauffeur. She appeared to find him irresistible! And then I understood her delight: my mother couldn't stand that her daughters or their guests might upstage her so she was relieved to find him a clod! The only thing that would truly have upset her? If Jean-Michel Destret *hadn't* been a jerk and had instead outshone my father and her friends with his superiority and success.

Marie took the plunge: "Did you have a pleasant trip?"

My mother, however, swooped in to commandeer our guest, launching into some background about the house, as if he really had marveled at its beauty only a moment before.

"It may interest you to know that L'Agapanthe was not actually named after the agapanthus, a handsome African plant commonly called lily of the Nile, but from a contraction of three first names: those of Agathe, my mother-in-law; Patrick, my father-in-law; and Thérèse, their first daughter, who died at an early age before the birth of Edmond, my husband."

"I hope we're not going to explore the entire family genealogy before showing our guest to his room," I ventured, gently sarcastic.

"Oh, but this is interesting," Jean-Michel Destret assured me before turning back to my mother. "So it was your parents-in-law who built the house?"

"No, some people from Boston," continued my mother, with the ghost of a triumphant smile. "They called in American architects. And as you will see, the house is an exceptionally comfortable one for the thirties, very American, with its walk-in closets and pocket windows, and bedrooms all with their own bathrooms. Moreover, it was the Americans who launched the Cap d'Antibes—the Murphys, for example, the models for Fitzgerald's *Tender Is the Night*. But it was an English couple, the Normans, who discovered the bay in 1902, when they were combing the coast from Naples to Marseilles to find a place to build their house, the Château de la Garoupe, which now belongs to Boris Berezovsky."

I tried again. "Well, now Jean-Michel knows everything he needs to about the bay, so that's taken care of, and I can . . ."

Wasted irony. Ignoring me completely, Jean-Michel picked up the challenge: "As was only fitting—unless I am mistaken—because Antibes did not blossom as a seaside resort until the end of the nineteenth century with the arrival of the English and the Russian aristos. The latter, poor things, had their wings clipped with the revolution, though, which certainly turned off the faucet-gushing grand dukes . . ."

Was it his "unless I am mistaken" that pricked up my ears? Or his "faucet-gushing grand dukes," which sounded suspiciously prefabricated? I was suddenly convinced that he'd learned that little speech by heart and was gumming things up with his fake spontaneous remarks, like that "poor things."

I looked at my sister, who was clearly as dismayed as I by Jean-Michel's performance, but I didn't know if he had irritated her as well with his choice of words. His "as was only fitting" was a snobbish convention, while "did not blossom" was as precious as it was pretentious. But what I simply could not bear was the use of diminutives, those relaxed little words that ring so false. People who say "teens," "nabes," and, in this case, "aristos" strike me straightaway as suspect. People's vocabularies and ways of expressing themselves often attract or repel me more than their behavior or physical appearance, doubtless because their words reveal, better than any confessions, what they are trying to show or to hide. And I didn't have a problem with the fact that Jean-Michel was ignoring my sister and me, or that he had crammed for his visit, the way he surely prepared for everything. What bothered me was that he was incapable of taking any critical distance, unable to employ the humor that would have allowed him a breathing space, by admitting, for example, that he had done his homework before coming. Instead of which, he forged ahead.

"As you were saying, the Riviera only became really Americanized in the twenties, when Fitzgerald stayed at the Hôtel Belles Rives, which wasn't actually called that at the time. Did you know that the Hôtel du Cap was already constantly fully booked? That water skiing was invented at Juan-les-Pins, and that La Garoupe was awash in bathing huts?"

Internet, travel guide, or chamber of commerce brochure? I wondered, gazing heavenward for the benefit of my sister, I was *that* ticked off by his patter. Entranced by his erudition, my mother had stopped pretending to be impressed and had sincerely succumbed to his charm.

Resignation gave way to fascination as Marie and I watched Jean-Michel and our mother together, spreading their tail feathers for each other like peacocks. We didn't want to miss a second. After all, we had the entire weekend to have a go at the fellow. And if it amused them—Jean-Michel reciting his homework, hoping to shine, and our mother poaching our Honored Guest— then so much the better. Making faces, my sister and I would look over at each other occasionally, on the verge of hysterical laughter, while teatime became the cocktail hour before we'd even noticed. Guests in Bermuda shorts, sarongs, or dressing gowns, fussing around teapots of beaten silver, slices of pound cake, cherries, and pistachio macarons, had discreetly slipped away in relays to go change. Suddenly we found ourselves surrounded by women in cocktail frocks and men in bright jackets ordering pink champagne, mojitos, or cosmopolitans while nibbling on fresh almonds, black Nice olives, and peanuts. It was Marcel who roused us from our torpor by offering us champagne.

"Heavens, whatever time is it? Marie, take Jean-Michel up to his room so that the poor man has a few moments to settle in before dinner!" exclaimed my mother, leaping up, while Marcel came over to let me know that the new head butler was asking to see me.

*Friday, 8:oo p.m.*

"Does Madame wish me to serve *à l'assiette?*" he asked me pointedly when I entered the butler's pantry.

Marcel and I exchanged pained looks; Gérard was way off the mark. *Le service à l'assiette* was the least of our preferences for serving at table, far behind the already debatable *service à la Beaumont* (named after Jean Beaumont, who laid claim to its invention), in which the attendant presents the serving platter between two guests, who must serve themselves at the same time. The rule on this point is very simple, however: this service is all the less elegant for being the most practical method and requiring the fewest servants. The most refined and, moreover, the most convenient service for the guest therefore requires the attendant to present the platter on the guest's left, unlike *le service à l'assiette*, in which serving and clearing are done on the guest's right.

"Gérard—it is Gérard, is it not? Perhaps it would be best for Marcel to explain to you our way of doing things . . ."

"It's just that that's how I served at the Khashoggis'. Adnan Khashoggi,[2] I don't know if you know him?"

---

2 Adnan Khashoggi is a famous Saudi Arabian arms dealer.

Shamelessly tossing out the name of a former employer like that was just not done! Gérard was decidedly lacking in judgment, citing an arms merchant as a reference on questions of taste! Given the circumstances, however, I couldn't pick and choose. After ascertaining that he had been shown his room and introduced to the staff, I left him to muddle through and hoped for the best.

Marie and I met for a moment in my room.

"Are you sure we should go through with this?" I asked.

"Listen, we said we would, and we will."

"Yes, but how?"

"*Surely* you don't expect me to explain to you . . ."

"What—that seduction isn't rocket science, that it's a question of *feeling*, right? But I'm too nervous for that to work, so help me out."

"Well, we start by dolling up. You swan out in décolleté, while I convey the idea of smoldering passion beneath my icy exterior. That way, there'll be something for everyone. And then we'll see!"

"Fine, but we stick together, right?"

"Obviously!" replied Marie. "Would you be a dear and keep an eye on Mummy's seating arrangements while I go dress, because she's quite capable of putting

Jean-Michel right next to her, with Gay on the other side. I'll come relieve you as soon as I'm ready."

I knocked at my mother's door: "Would you like any help with the seating arrangements?"

It would be a seated dinner, with assigned places, at two candlelit tables on a terrace used as a summer dining room. Such seating arrangements, along with responsibility for the menus and dealing with the staff, comprised my mother's essential concerns as the mistress of the house. She usually sat in her bathroom and made her seating charts while doing her makeup, quickly sketching two circles on a notepad—one for my father's table, the other for hers—before writing the date, the guest list, and rotating everyone in such a way that they would sit between different people every evening.

"Do you want me to put Jean-Michel next to you?" she managed to ask through lips clamped around hairpins, which she was slipping into the low, tight chignon she preferred for evening dress.

"Yes, if you like."

"Then I'll take the other one, what's his face, Braissant; I haven't said a word to him yet. And he looks like a tough one, too. In any case, I'm going to stick his wife with your father. What's he like, the new head butler?"

"Not great, you'll see. But better than nothing."

"Bring me my dress, will you . . ."

"Which one?" I shouted from her dressing room, standing before an entire closet of evening gowns.

"Right under your nose!" she replied testily. "I'm sure Pauline has laid it out for me already."

"If only," I muttered. "What do you want: yellow chiffon, gold lamé, or duchess satin?"

"No," moaned my mother: "It's black, lace, an Oscar!"

"Got it!" I cried, bearing my trophy triumphantly into the bathroom, where Marie had just made her entrance.

"Wow, you look stunning!" I whispered to her, admiring her palazzo pants and red bustier.

"Am I too late for the seating rodeo?" she exclaimed, winking at me in thanks.

"No, you're just in time. And I'll leave you with Mummy, because I really must go change."

Daylight was still lingering. Glimpsed through the pines, the moon seemed a touch early, suspended in the sky by an overzealous stagehand. The night-blooming jasmine, however, had followed her cue by perfuming the salty sea breeze, breasted from time to time by a flight of seagulls, whose cries drowned out the shrill sound of crickets. I went down to the terrace, where I found Odon Viel and the Braissants.

"Odon, how are you? I see you've met Bernard and Laetitia," I said, receiving the distinct impression that I had just plunged into a chilly mountain stream.

Admittedly, Bernard Braissant and our nattily attired astrophysicist had nothing in common. And yes, our cocktail ritual did sometimes smack uneasily of the waiting room. Like patients sitting around in a doctor's office, our guests examined one another discreetly and with more or less goodwill, sitting in a circle around a table bearing olives and peanuts instead of tired magazines. They stared shamelessly, however, at every new arrival emerging from beneath the arches of the loggia, who approached with a composed spontaneity with one eye on the uneven stones of the terrace, to avoid catching a heel, while the other eye braved the glare of the audience's gaze.

This Jean-Michel learned to his cost when he realized what a stir he had created by appearing in salmon slacks and a matching shirt, an outfit in which he seemed much less at home than in his CEO suit. Was he already regretting this summer outfit for a bourgeois conqueror, so ill suited for his nerdy physique? The childish pastel color made him look like a chubby baby, anything but sexy, and frankly I wasn't at all sure I felt up to making a pass at him. Without giving me a moment to consider him from that angle, however, he reprised his role as the model guest.

The first thing he did when my mother appeared was hand her a gift. As a precaution, she went into ecstasies over the wrapping, in case she couldn't compliment him on his present, so she was pleasantly surprised to unwrap a framed photo of General de Gaulle on the beach at L'Agapanthe during the winter of 1946, when he had come here to consider his options before giving up power and retiring to Colombey-les-Deux-Eglises.

"Jean-Michel, you couldn't have given me anything that would have pleased me more! I did know that the general had come to L'Agapanthe. But to have actually unearthed pictures of his stay . . . How did you find out, how did you manage?"

"You're too kind, Madame, really, it's nothing . . ."

"Oh, please, call me Flokie!"

Arm in arm with my sister, Frédéric had just arrived, and he murmured in my ear, "It's unbelievable—he's a total suck-up, your guy!"

Marie leaned close to my other ear, as I bit my lips to keep from laughing. "Frédéric is right, and our boy's beginning to piss me off with this eager-beaver crap. What about you?"

"And how!"

"Mind you, so much the better, because the Queen of the Night is waltzing off with him right before our eyes," she added, while our supposed suitor warmed to his task.

"I looked into a few things when I learned that you'd been kind enough to invite me here. And I found out that the bay had been recommended to the general by unusually choice word of mouth, because it was through Churchill, alerted to the charms of the place by the Duchess of Windsor, that Eisenhower came here in 1944 and 1945, after having requisitioned the house, which was American property. He then urged de Gaulle to come here for a quiet stay in 1946, when the house was requisitioned by the French government."

"You're a darling!" gushed my mother, suddenly eager to thank him once and for all.

Had she had enough of billing and cooing with him? Or was she changing the subject to avoid embarrassing the Braissants, in case they'd brought her only chocolates? Because she had no doubt whatsoever that Bernard and Laetitia would now offer her something. Was it not customary for a guest's visit, like a citation framed by quotation marks, to begin with a gift and conclude with a thank-you note? The Braissants, however, just kept sipping their champagne. The idea of bringing a hostess gift had clearly never crossed their minds. Nonplussed, my mother took another tack.

"Can anyone tell me why the Bellini at the Hôtel du Cap, made with peach purée, is not as good as the one at Cipriani's in Venice, where they use peach extract?"

Coming out of the blue, her question seemed enchantingly frivolous to me but shocking to Bernard and Laetitia, for I caught a pained look exchanged between them. What right had they to judge my mother? That was *my* prerogative, and I couldn't bear it when others did so in my place, especially pretentious people who confused prejudices with convictions, disdain with clear-sightedness.

Just then Gay sailed in, spectacular in a femme-fatale lamé sheath and holding a yellow plastic toy that Popsicle was trying to snatch away by leaping in every direction, but my mother serenely pursued her train of thought.

"Anyway, the hotel bar no longer even has splits of champagne. Impossible to fix your own cocktail anymore! It's so much less jolly . . ."

"No!" Frédéric exclaimed indignantly, torn between solidarity and sarcasm.

"Oh, yes, and just imagine, now they serve sushi in the restaurant near the swimming pool. This mania for raw food—wherever will it strike next? Sushi in the Midi! It's ridiculous."

"Ridiculous," agreed Laszlo Schwartz, sitting down on the low wall overlooking the lawn.

My mother's face brightened.

"Laszlo! But you haven't yet met my daughters' friends. Here are Laetitia and Bernard Braissant, and Jean-Michel Destret. Laszlo Schwartz."

Jean-Michel almost fainted when he heard Laszlo's name. At sixty-two, the German painter was indeed a star of the contemporary art scene, whose exhibitions at the Grand Palais and the Guggenheim in Bilbao had been highlights of the season. And one of his paintings had sold for two and a half million euros a month earlier. Even the Braissants looked impressed. Laetitia, who hadn't bothered to open her mouth until that moment, crinkled her eyes and cranked up a smile in an obvious effort to charm.

"I read in the papers that you live in Le Gard . . ." cooed Jean-Michel.

"Yes, I have my studio in Barjac, not far, in fact, from Kiefer's La Ribaute, but I've been thinking about going abroad."

Practically gurgling with delight, nodding at everything he said, Laetitia seemed almost ready to dissolve, so keen was her absorption in his presence. In any case, she had definitely ditched her leftist intellectual's contempt for my oh-so-bourgeois mother, whom she now treated obsequiously, having understood her bond with the famous artist. Bernard, evidently on the same wavelength as his wife, now tried to establish direct and gratifying contact with the great man.

"Did you know that Jean-Michel is a passionate collector of your work?"

"Oh, really? I'm flattered," replied Laszlo.

And yet, I would have sworn that he found them irritating, these newcomers whose sanctimonious admiration appealed to his weaknesses, pushing him to conform to their image of him. Because he already knew that he would play the great man to please them, the way people mimic sadness at the funeral of a relative whose death leaves them indifferent, and he felt pained at this impending imposture.

"And what do you do?" he asked Jean-Michel, to change the subject.

Marie and I had been flitting about, chatting, but now we fell silent, suddenly attentive to a conversation that might prove instructive regarding our "blind date."

"I'm the director of a company that deals in arms and audiovisual equipment."

"Good Lord! And I gather that you're a prime example of the French self-made man?"

"Yes, well, that's what the press says. Unfortunately, there aren't enough of us. It's becoming harder and harder to make it on your own. Passing exams isn't enough anymore to guarantee entrance into the corridors of power—you must have several generations of success under your belt. Consider the fact that the CAC 40, which lists the top forty companies on the Paris Bourse, is the European index that comprises the greatest number of family firms. As in India."

Not too bad, I thought, reevaluating his rising stock value, as if he'd been undervalued but was suddenly showing potential. What he'd said was articulate, perceptive, fair, reflecting no class resentment.

"There's nothing hereditary about good business sense, though. You know the Bamileke proverb: The father was a fortress, the son, a buttress, and the grandson, a butthole!"

"I'm not familiar with the Bamileke, but they're forgetting that a solid network of contacts makes up for many things."

"I saw your girlfriend!" Bernard broke in, flashing a naughty smile.

To general astonishment. Because his nonsensical

interruption couldn't have come at a more awkward time, right in the middle of the discussion. Still, now we were curious: Whom did he mean? And what connection could that person possibly have with what they were talking about?

"Who's that?" replied Jean-Michel, clearly annoyed.

At this point, in spite of Jean-Michel's less than captivating manner, I'd have bet that Marie was on his side and feeling as annoyed as he was at Bernard.

"Françoise."

"Françoise *who*?"

"Françoise Hardy."

"The singer? Who's married to Jacques Dutronc? But I hardly know her! I only met her that one time, and she was with you!"

It took us all a moment to recover from Bernard's incredible gall. Name-droppers usually try to take part in a discussion and show a little finesse, leading the conversation in a convenient direction before they make their move, thus posing as people with important connections and clout. Bernard had simply skipped all that.

He really had some nerve, and my indignation made Jean-Michel more sympathetic in contrast. I was almost looking forward to sitting next to him at dinner.

Instead of making his announcement correctly, in a dignified manner, the new head butler let out a shout: "Dinner is served, Madame!"

My mother glared at me for a microsecond before saying lightly, "Girls, time to fetch your father. He must still be on the phone with Sotheby's in New York, in the library with the Démazures."

"Where *did* you dig up the hog caller?" said Marie sweetly as we set out on our mission.

"Watch out. I'd advise you to put a cork in it, because I could return the compliment with those brown-nosing Braissants!"

# *Dinner, Friday, July 14*

## THIRTEEN PERSONS

| MEN | WOMEN |
|---|---|
| Edmond Ettinguer | Flokie Ettinguer |
| Frédéric Hottin | Laure Ettinguer |
| Odon Viel | Marie Ettinguer |
| Henri Démazure | Polyséna Démazure |
| Laszlo Schwartz | Gay Wallingford |
| Bernard Braissant | Laetitia Braissant |
| Jean-Michel Destret | |

| SEATING:<br>EDMOND'S TABLE | SEATING:<br>FLOKIE'S TABLE |
|---|---|

|         | Laure          |        | | Henri | | Frédéric |
|---|---|---|---|---|---|---|
| Jean-Michel | | Laszlo | | Marie | | Polyséna |
| Laetitia | | Gay | | Bernard | | Odon |
| | Edmond | | | | Flokie | |

# MENU

*Gazpacho*
*Grilled Sea Bass with Fennel*
*Risotto with Morels*
*Salad and Cheeses*
*Crêpes Royale*

Marcel and Gérard were standing at benevolent attention on the covered terrace outside the winter dining room, like parents supervising a sandbox where their children are busy playing. On tablecloths of orange and fuchsia linen strewn with white orchids, silver candelabras and crystal glassware reflected the flickering candle flames onto charger plates by César, signed with golden grooves representing the sculptor's fingerprints. The effect was so lovely! No one else took this much trouble anymore over the décor for a dinner party, I thought proudly.

My mother called over the guests seated at her table. "Odon, Polyséna, Frédéric, Henri, Marie and Bernard, you are with me."

"Doesn't this remind you of school, when the teacher gathers her students on the first day of classes?" quipped Frédéric, to ease the newcomers into our protocol.

"Odon, you're on my right; Frédéric, Marie, and Polyséna—do please stop chatting, naughty, naughty! Bernard, sit on my left. And Henri, between Marie and Frédéric."

Inheriting those who hadn't been summoned, my father solemnly brandished the paper on which his table seating plan had been scribbled.

"Here we all are in the same boat, cast adrift by Flokie," he announced facetiously.

For just as my mother fulfilled her duties as hostess with the utmost devotion, my father took equally seriously his role as the class clown.

"Let's see," he murmured, slipping on his glasses. "But I *can't* see a thing with these! I must have left my reading glasses in the library. Laure, dear, would you do the honors?"

"I've got the thumb!" Gay crowed triumphantly, having turned over her César plate to check.

"Oho! Much better than getting the finger!" Frédéric called over gaily from the other table, and the two friends exchanged fond smiles.

Jean-Michel was on my right. Without any misplaced pretensions, I naturally assumed that he would strike up a conversation with me, if for no other reason than that he had clearly been trying to bone up on the appropriate social conventions. He would thank me for his invitation to L'Agapanthe as a lead-in to some friendly or simply polite chitchat. He did nothing of the kind, however, and merely smiled at Laetitia, seated on his right. When I recovered from my surprise, it dawned on me that he had been avoiding my sister and me ever since his arrival. Of course I had noticed how he'd been all over my mother, but that was quite probably his idea of the proper courtesy due the mistress of the house. And I had the impression that flattering his "elders" was right up his alley, but so what? That was hardly a dishonorable means to achieve social success, after all. But between that and imagining that he was really trying to avoid Marie and me . . . His stubborn silence was suggestive, though; still, I really couldn't see myself having such an effect on a supposedly intelligent man, so I wondered: was he nervous at the prospect of speaking to me, or simply worried that he would commit some gaffe?

Jean-Michel seemed to be studying the napkins and bread and butter plates next to the chargers by César, which we were discussing as the butler replaced them with soup plates of marbled yellow-glazed faience from Apt. In matters of etiquette, I would have been glad to whisper advice to him, but everything in his manner indicated that he would take my kindness for condescension. Too bad! He could just wonder away. As he would surely do throughout the entire dinner.

Debating, for example, when to begin eating what was on his plate. And he would discover that unlike in the United States, where it is customary to wait for everyone to be served before picking up one's fork, it is the mistress of the house or the most prominently seated woman at the table who gives the signal, even before all the gentlemen have been served. Sitting on my father's right, Gay would thus be our "hostess." The butler would then serve the men, and my father last, who might be left on short rations, moreover, for the platter sometimes offered only slim pickings by the time it reached him.

In the same way, Jean-Michel might well be perplexed by the semicircular salad plates, or the dessert plates that would presently appear with a silver-gilt fork and spoon, along with a finger bowl to be placed with its doily to the left of his dinner plate.

*Too* bad for him, I thought again, and then my generous nature recovered its aplomb and made me fiddle with my bread-and-butter plate, on my left, to show him innocently which was whose.

Laszlo, meanwhile, was grimacing as he bent down sideways and exclaimed, "Can someone enlighten me as to why mosquitoes always attack your ankles? And aren't they unusually ferocious this year?"

"You're telling me," replied Jean-Michel, who started scratching in turn.

Ah, now I've got it, I thought, since Jean-Michel obviously had no difficulty smiling and talking with anybody but me. I then put him to one last test, handing him a small bottle of mosquito spray I'd taken from my little evening bag.

"Here, it's my constant companion. What can I say? Mosquitoes adore me."

Nothing. No reply. Aside from a feeble smile of thanks before using my spray.

Having no doubt observed my mounting irritation at Jean-Michel's awkwardness or rudeness (and frankly, at this point I didn't care which), Laszlo jumped in to rescue me from the lengthening silence. "But the worst time is at night!"

"That's because like all insects, they don't sleep," observed my father, a fountain of information on all creatures great and small. "Sleep only becomes possible when the brain has reached a certain size. Butterflies, for example, do not sleep, whereas whales, orcas, and dolphins sleep with just one brain hemisphere at a time, which allows them to swim without ever stopping."

"Perhaps he doesn't like me?" I wondered. But after all, that wasn't any reason not to speak to me! Just look at that stuck-up stick Laetitia, whose hitherto unsuspected passion for nature documentaries was making my father happy to chat with her. Oh, well, as if I gave a damn! Why should I let a moron like him bother me? I decided to ignore Jean-Michel and join the conversation Gay was whipping up about Marie Antoinette.

"I'm reading a most amusing book by Caroline Weber about Marie Antoinette called *Queen of Fashion*, in which she describes how the young queen used her opinions and prejudices about dress to demonstrate her influence on the court, which she systematically challenged in the realm of fashion."

"Isn't that what Louis XIV had already done?" I asked.

"True, and Marie Antoinette was in fact greatly inspired by him. But she *democratized* fashion. First with her overdressed and even over-the-top style with those coiffures, the utterly insane bustles, which had such a success that she made the hairdressers and couturiers of that era rich. Then she turned fashion completely around with the simplicity of her shepherdess period at the Petit Trianon, inventing the minimalist white muslin dress worn without a corset—which became all the rage, just like Coco Chanel's famous little black dress did."

"Have you read Antonia Fraser's book?" Laszlo asked.

"No, but I did see the Coppola girl's movie."

"Oh, a disaster!" he replied.

"I thought it rather pretty, with all those candy colors," I said.

"So did I," Gay chimed in. "Everyone jumped on her. But the film wasn't pretending to be historically accurate. And it was full of familiar faces."

"Such as?" Laszlo prompted.

"Natasha Fraser, Antonia's daughter; Hamish Bowles, a *Vogue* editor; the socialite Pierre Ceyleron . . ."

"I'm sure they're all wonderful people, but they proved unable to save that insipid excuse for a movie. Besides," Laszlo concluded, "I don't think anything can top the biography by Stefan Zweig."

Gérard began to serve the main course, sea bass grilled over fennel, and I still hadn't exchanged a single word with Jean-Michel. Since my decision not to let that bother me, however, I had made some progress on this question. And I had understood, after trying to put myself in his place, that he was able to chat with Laszlo or my father because he felt all of them were on the same ladder of financial and professional success, albeit at different levels. He could not, however, carry off a casual conversation or exchange with me or my sister because he was lost and had no frame of reference in our house. Wasn't that why he'd insisted on bringing along his car and driver? To carry with him a bit of his world and a token of his success, to help him confront "the upper crust" of which Marie and I, with our pedigrees, were the incarnation? Because with us he must have felt lacking in something essential, an ease and elegance of being that requires generations to breed true.

And he was doubtless right. Not everyone has enough brio to show, as Laszlo did, that one can be a little Hungarian Jew from the gutter—as he described himself—and dazzle the most snobbish and intolerant people. Jean-Michel's manners, for one thing, distressed me in spite of myself: his way of saying *bon appétit*; his elbows on the table; his knife and fork laid obliquely on either side of his plate, like the idle oars of a drifting boat. I could tell myself all I wanted that this wouldn't have irritated me had I found him attractive, but I wasn't sure it was true. Because I was conditioned by my upbringing, even though I found such conventions absurd. (As a proper Englishwoman, for example, Nanny had set our table with glasses to the right of the plate, forks placed tines up, knives with

the cutting edge facing right, and she had constantly reminded us, *Hands under the table!* Then my mother would
visit us. Shifting the glasses to a position above the plate,
turning the forks tines down, and the knives, cutting edge
left, she would order us to keep our *Hands on the table!*)

In any case, given the simpleton sitting next to me,
what did it matter? I was hardly likely to experience a
soul-wrenching conflict between any personal attraction
to him and the repulsion I felt for his disappointing behavior. And I had decided not to take offense at his silence,
which was a small thing, after all, to one as experienced
as I in making conversation and coping with the vicissi-
tudes of formal dinners, where I had once actually seen a
dinner companion fall asleep and another choke to death.

I learned the art of conversation at an early age.
Mother would invite my sister and me to eat with her
from time to time, for fun, as she said, although she actually had no idea what that word meant. The upshot is,
now I feel capable of getting anyone at all to talk.

I have a few simple precepts. I talk about what interests the other person. And since people like to talk about
themselves, I ask them questions, avoiding as much as
possible anything concerning their professions. I would
rather ask them if they are afraid of flying, if they've ever
talked to a stranger on a train, if they think women should

ever make the first move, or if they're men, I ask if they're attracted to women who are clinging and needy. Or I toss out something trivial: Do you like baths or showers? Tea or coffee? Monet or Manet? The sillier the question, the more interested I am in the answer. But no matter what people say, I make sure to seem fascinated by their observations and impressed by their wit, without seeking to impress them myself. Or discreetly, in a very low-key manner (just in case my audience has nothing to bring to the table), I announce, let's say, that I have never been to Venice. Then I sit back and enjoy the *ohs* and *ahs* my admission invariably provokes. Or I put their kindness to the test by pretending to be shy. In short, I follow to the letter the old adage advising us to speak frivolously of serious things and seriously of frivolous ones—even if that doesn't suit everybody, in particular the crashing bores who join a discussion only to show off their knowledge of history, politics, or philosophy, and who like nothing better than to trip you up over some mistake.

And conversation at our table was languishing, so I turned to Laszlo, who was serving himself seconds of the risotto and morels.

"I'm bored," I whispered. "Tell me again about the time you mistook Ungaro, the couturier, for Trichet, the governor of the Banque de France."

"But you know that story by heart!"

Instead, my father revealed his own worst blunder.

"Last December, I gave one of those end-of-the-year speeches I deliver at my company's Christmas party, when I convey my best wishes for a happy holiday to the personnel, with respectful mention of the year's deaths and retirements. So, after the jolly bits, and armed with a list of the deceased's virtues (drawn up by my secretary), I assume a dignified expression and solemnly intone, 'I would now like to invoke the memory of Monsieur Puchet, and to pay tribute to a man whom we all knew and appreciated, who died this year.' I pause for breath, and out of the audience comes a voice, loud and clear: *Oh no, I didn't!*"

Laetitia, Gay, and Jean-Michel crack up. Pleased with his success, my father forges ahead.

"Dreadfully embarrassed, I try to smooth over my blunder by saying cheerily, 'This is excellent news indeed, and we all fondly hope you will remain with us for a good long time.'"

Laszlo leaned forward eagerly. "And then?"

"And then—just imagine!—the voice pipes up, very cordially: *Oh no, I won't. I'm looking forward to retiring at the end of this week!*"

Our screams of laughter plunged my mother's table into an envious and admiring silence. I, however, had achieved my goal: Jean-Michel, feeling more relaxed, found the courage to speak to me.

"And what is it you do in life?"

Too bad he picked that to start with, I thought.

"I'm a psychoanalyst."

I knew that this confession would stop our budding relationship cold. And even though Jean-Michel wasn't attractive enough for me to regret this, I was irritated to have hit another wall in my efforts to loosen him up. My profession provokes two reactions. People sometimes flee as if I were an X-ray machine intent on snooping around in their dark corners, like my dinner companion last week, a charming guy in advertising, who made me laugh and laugh and with whom I'd gone out on a balcony for a smoke. Upon learning my profession, he'd replied, "Never, ever, say that. Tell people instead that you're in communications." Then, without another word, he turned his back on me and stole away like a thief. The other thing men do is dredge up intimate details about their relationships with their sisters, mothers, or wives in an effort to extract as much information as possible from me without having to go into therapy.

As for Jean-Michel, he asked, "Are you going to analyze everything I say?"

"Only if you pay me." I laughed.

"But could you?"

"Could I what?"

"Interpret what I say, what I do."

"Let's say that I'll be making suppositions. If I'm dealing with someone extremely talkative, driven by distress, I'm not going to say to myself, this person's mother must be dead, or this person has been raped. I would have to determine some contours. For example, instead of seeing gaiety in someone who laughs all the time, the way most people would think, I'll see suffering, but I wouldn't be able to describe its source. I'm not Madame Irma the Mind Reader. We don't invent, we don't guess, we need something to work with."

But Jean-Michel, as I expected, turned away from me. I hadn't expected what came next, though: he committed conversational hara-kiri with my father.

"Have you ever been tempted to sell your house?"

"Uh . . . no, why?"

"You might have been thinking about buying one somewhere else, I don't know . . . in Saint-Tropez, for example."

How could this apple-polishing arriviste have been so clumsy? Didn't he understand anything about the very essence of a family house, and people's attachment to their childhood home? Stunned by his misstep, I saw in my father's face how it pained him to realize that his guest was clearly incapable of appreciating the subtle grace of L'Agapanthe, or the old-fashioned splendor of the Cap d'Antibes, so lacking in the glittering tinsel of cheap seduction. Jean-Michel was, quite simply, amazed that an important man like my father would be content here, since our guest considered the easy glamour of Saint-Tropez the very acme of perfection.

My father's character was rather well reflected in his opinion of Saint-Tropez. He was amused by the kitschy lifestyle of its summer visitors, whom he would never have thought to call vulgar because he was so impressed by their energy. Just think about it! All those young people—popular actors and singers, reality TV stars, gallery owners, artists, fashionistas and jet-setters— dancing like crazy in wee-hours clubbing, fornicating their brains out, then dashing off in boats to drink and screw some more beneath the blazing blue sky. No need to worry about sunburn, stomachaches, doubts, inhibitions. What glorious good health!

But my father was impervious to the attraction of a place where the height of snobbery was to dress like the locals and buy firewood or vin rosé where the garage mechanic does because it's cheaper and you have to look authentic, just plain folks, in the eyes of the native

Tropezians, so you'll fit in. Nothing annoyed him more, in fact, than people who went on endlessly about their passion for authenticity. Whatever were they trying to prove? That they were the salt of the earth? Close to the people, to nature? There was something fishy about it. About that whole business of proclaiming one's conjugal love, fidelity, attachment to family values, whatever. Why should a man on vacation have to dress up in overalls, a straw hat, and espadrilles so he can look relaxed? Especially since these poets of authenticity were stuffed with prejudices, singularly intolerant, and often contemptuous of the common people, because how else would you qualify their condescending efforts to "talk country": "Hey there, M'sieur Menant, still happy as a pig in a puddle?" And such people were especially dismissive of my father, whom they considered an uptight snob. Accused of being a freak, and called upon to justify himself, he was expected to explain why he'd never worn a pair of jeans in his life, *always* wore a jacket for dinner, and couldn't imagine entering a capital city without a tie. Marie and I even used to tease him: "Aix, candy capital of the *calisson*! Papa, your tie!" Well, he found it extraordinary that those who preached authenticity to him reproached him for his own natural style!

The dinner was coming to an end. Jean-Michel and Laetitia ate their dessert with spoons without realizing that we considered this a faux pas. Then, barely had we left the table when Gérard, who had made one mistake after another throughout the meal, interrupted us to ask whether we wanted herbal tea, coffee, brandy, or a liqueur.

My father and Jean-Michel: what a difference between these two men, I thought! A stickler for formalities, my father had the humility never to question what "just isn't done" because he knew that appearance and foundation are frequently in league with each other, and that these codes often support the most elementary rules of morality. But he also employed an exceptional freedom of thought and manner to apprehend or judge the world. Jean-Michel was just the opposite. Presenting a facade of easygoing self-possession, eager to appear young, cool, cutting-edge, he was a self-righteous conformist through and through: an altar boy in predistressed jeans. Hoping to be taken for a politically correct nouveau bourgeois instead of a nouveau riche, he was a dud not only socially but as a human being as well, because he had just wounded my father without even realizing it, so sure was he of himself, certain of knowing what's good and what's bad, and of his ability to do well thanks to this crude filter.

The evening ended without any surprises. My father excused himself to bid on his painting on the telephone.

"I got it!" he announced joyfully when he returned. Mother's "little band" congratulated him on his triumph as if he had scaled Everest, while Frédéric pretended to protest: one shouldn't pat a fellow on the back for tossing money out the window! Polyséna didn't appreciate his humor: doesn't he know that one needs a good eye and cultivated taste to appreciate a work of the quattrocento! But Papa, oblivious of the bickering, simply seemed thrilled with his acquisition. At moments like those, I loved him all the more.

"Shall we do the fridge tonight?" Marie whispered to me, under cover of the general chatter.

Like our midnight swim, this was one of the rituals we performed religiously at least once every summer, a way for us to revive the blessed intimacy of our childhood. We observed these rites with pleasure, just as we seized on the slightest opportunity to repeat to each other the gems once periodically produced by our kindest but least educated governess. "The sky is befuddled with stars," she would say with a sigh. Something elegant was "of a great refinery." Once she huffed—instead of "onus"—"The anus is on him!" and such slapstick delights formed the repertoire of our complicity, like the languages invented by certain real twins to communicate secretly through shared references, which we recited fervently, like incantations.

As for the fridge, it wasn't hunger that drove us, of course, but the tantalizing prospect of snooping in the pantry and kitchen deserted by the staff. What would we find there? Instructions as mysterious as hieroglyphs jotted down on scraps of paper left by the pantry phone? Or would we come face-to-face with a headachy guest searching for aspirin? On the alert, our senses heightened by misbehavior, we felt wonderfully alive. Happy and relieved at being just the two of us, sans parents, sans staff, enjoying a well-being like that achieved by taking off a girdle, which might seem mystifying to anyone unfamiliar with the way we lived in thrall to codes and constraints.

Our behavior was in fact inevitably affected by the presence of servants, which demanded a formality that pervaded our lives. How could we slump and slop at a meal served by gentlemen wearing white jackets and ties? Impossible, even if our parents were away, and Marie and I were alone in the house! Just try to act supercasual in front of someone who is addressing you in the third person: "Would Madame Laure and Mademoiselle Marie prefer to dine in the loggia or out by the water lily pond?" Such an idea would never even have occurred to us, in part because the disapproving staff, silent witness to our transgressions, might have subtly betrayed us to our parents, but chiefly because it was more difficult for the servants to perform their duties "informally" instead of waiting on us at the table.

Which ruled out, for example, the incongruous idea of a picnic on the beach. "At what time?" would have been their first concern, in complete contradiction with the very principle of an impromptu supper. And never mind trying to fob them off with the likes of, "Don't worry, we'll take care of everything," because they would have felt obliged to leave the picnic spot spick-and-span and wash our dirty dishes before going to bed. Not to mention that having to lug down to the beach all the items indispensable in their eyes to a proper meal—the silver salt cellars, water tumblers, wine and champagne glasses, finger bowls, and other impedimenta—would have taken them forever and proved much more exhausting than serving us at the table, even from heavy platters while bundled up in the most uncomfortable outfits in the world. Besides which, the caretaker would have had to wait until it was all over before turning on the outside alarm.

So Marie and I had taken to giving the staff the evening off on those occasions, pretending that we were dining out at a restaurant or in the home of some friends. We'd hide somewhere in the house until everyone went off duty, and as soon as they sat down to supper in their dining room, we'd sneak off somewhere to quietly eat the sandwiches or pizza we'd discreetly bought in town (since we couldn't raid the kitchen), taking care afterward to dispose secretly of the wrappers that might have betrayed us the next day.

We censored our conversation as well, hesitating, for example, to discuss homosexuality in front of a butler with a preference for men, and avoiding any talk of money save through allusions, so as not to shock or wound employees whose income was in no way comparable to ours. When describing a millionaire, we'd simply say, "He has a lot of money," and leave it at that. Whenever possible we minimized the attributes of wealth, so if someone said, "He had a lovely house" or "It's a handsome picture," you could be sure the item in question was a castle, a palace, or a priceless masterpiece.

In the same way, we found it unimaginable, living as we did under the constant observation of our staff, to squabble *en famille*, gobble our food, or get drunk. Asking for a second go-round of the cheese platter or another drop of wine was actually so awkward that we only rarely indulged such whims—even if it meant waiting, when the wine was exceptional, for the servants to head back to the kitchen so we could jump up and quickly serve ourselves on the sly from the bottle sitting on the dining room sideboard.

We'd been conditioned from childhood to temperance and the good manners de rigueur before servants, so their presence seemed nowhere near as oppressive to us as it did to novices. Still, after the butlers had served the liqueurs and wished us good night, there was a subtle relaxation in the atmosphere all around, as if we'd been aware of suddenly recovering a liberty all the more precious for being rare.

And so at midnight, we found ourselves at the head of the stairs leading to the kitchen and pantry, ready to "do the fridge."

"That's an invitation to rape, your little shorty pajama set," I joked. "I hope we don't run into anyone!"

"Look who's talking—your peignoir's *totally* transparent."

That was enough to set off our first fit of giggles: a Pavlovian reflex, fueled by the delight we always took in this ritual expedition. Down in the kitchen area, feeling around in the shadows for the light switches, we experienced the same thrill of fear we'd felt when playing hide-and-seek in the dark and sparked our second giggling fit by trying to frighten each other.

"Don't these huge deserted kitchen rooms sort of remind you of Kubrick's *The Shining*?" I asked Marie.

"Oh, stop, you're really making me nervous! And *you'd* better be careful you don't lose a finger on the ham slicer."

Once we'd found the light switches, located in the most improbable places (inside cupboards or behind glass doors), the ambiance changed completely, but we pretended to still be afraid just to prolong our pleasure.

"What was that noise?" I asked sharply. "Did you hear it?"

"No, I didn't hear a thing, cut it out."

"Look, there's nothing but consommé in this fridge! I can't believe it! The consommé consumption in this house must be e-nor-mous!"

"You mean you've really never noticed that almost every luncheon dish is swathed in aspic?"

"Ooo, you're right: the ever-popular rabbit terrine, cold jellied chicken, what else . . ."

"Who cares? At the moment, if we want a decent snack, we're going to have to do better than jellied consommé, veal stock, and some choux pastry!"

When we finally sat down at the pantry table with a cheese plate and some *olives de Nice*, I got straight to the point.

"He's a total disaster, isn't he, this Jean-Michel Destret."

"That's for sure," Marie replied morosely, "since I don't like him any more than you do."

"Mind you," I admitted, "the least we can say is that he doesn't much care for us, either. He only has eyes for our dear mother."

"Yup, it's a complete flop! Even a fiasco—he seems scared stiff of you. I was watching him at the table. But I didn't do too much better after dinner when I tried to thaw him out."

"Yes, I caught your number as the modest and meritorious interpreter: 'I get by rather well, although my linguistic repertoire is nothing out of the ordinary, since I grew up speaking French and English, then added Spanish, Portuguese, and Italian as backups . . .'"

"That's it, dump all over me!"

"No, no, you were right to play the good little girl, seeing as my low-cut-and-liberated shrink persona flipped him right out!"

"Except that I flopped just like you did."

"Right," I agreed, "but now let's think. What do we want? What are we looking for? How far are we willing to go? We really didn't consider things properly when we became involved in this whole business."

"What do you mean?"

"Listen, Jean-Michel Destret has done us a huge favor by taking a pass on us instead of making a pass at us. I mean, imagine, a clunker like that! We're not really going to turn into high-class anything-goes whores just to bag a total *sucker*! We have to like the guy a *little* bit, right?"

"Yes, okay, but what is it you're expecting from this guy? Give me just one or two vital qualities, no more, because the whole Prince Charming thing is really useless here."

"Hold on. We are *not* going to sacrifice our romantic dreams in order to save the house!"

"Oh, enough already. But you're right. So?"

"He has to be nice," I began.

"Wait: that's your prime requirement?"

"Precisely. Nice, and intelligent."

"Even if he's crummy looking? I couldn't handle that."

"Even if he's crummy looking, absolutely. I've got nothing against ugly people. I even think they're in at the moment—look at all those glamorous actresses with homely guys. Plus, remember, I already did my bit when I married a real looker. That was enough for me."

"Well, okay, I've already had *serious* exposure to gorgeous lovers and I'm still eager for more, I can tell you!"

"That, we can talk about later. Oh, one last quality," I added. "He has to be entertaining."

"Entertaining? You mean funny?"

"No, more like lighthearted, open to imagination and gaiety."

"It's my turn, said Marie eagerly. "Me, I'd like him to be handsome, fantasmic, and prefer me above all other women."

"Fantasmic? Meaning?"

"Seductive, charismatic."

"In other words, that he's a fabulous success, like a movie star or a business whiz, or that he's magnetic in a sexy way?"

"Why not the best of both worlds?" Marie asked brightly.

"Ah, I see. Well, I have to tell you, we're not there yet, not by a long shot. So now what do we do?"

"About what?"

"We're not going to overexert ourselves, are we? Either we fall in love, at least a teensy bit, or it's no go?"

"That works for me."

My sister and I had obviously only skimmed the surface of the problem. The deeper truth was that I had been avoiding tackling the thorny subject of men ever since my divorce. I agreed with all my single friends who had looked around without finding anyone seriously desirable, and I had taken up their mantra: "Where are all the men?" As far as I was concerned, the answer was "Wyoming!"—and only half in jest, because on a trip there I'd seen lots of men who seemed completely well-adjusted, perfectly happy with their horses, their cowboy duds, and their outdoor life *right where they were*—so that was the end of that.

I used to say that I loved men but not unconditionally. I wanted them to be, in descending order of importance: nice, intelligent, ready to be happy, forgiving of themselves and others, generous, and wise. They had to have no fear of women, be virile, fond of making love but at the same time past the frolicking-with-bimbos stage. I'm demanding, I know. Especially since they had to be successful in their careers; otherwise they were bitter or limited in their outlook on life. They couldn't be hungry for power and honors, however, because too many of such men feel empty inside, buffeted by anxiety, and seek to fill that void with the trappings of greatness. And they often bring home the habits of their workplace, namely, their bullying mistreatment of others. No matter how seductive and successful they appear, they are hollow promises, because they are immature, lacking in humanity, and care only for themselves.

It was also true that I had buried my romantic aspirations in the absolute love I devoted to my son. And I was so fulfilled by him, so involved in the care I took of him, so captivated by the act of nourishing him, watching over him, loving him, that my sexual desire had largely disappeared and I no longer wanted to find someone else. I had had a few affairs, of course, but had even let go of the idea of romantic love, which now seemed like an illusion, a preoccupation for those who had no children, no one close to them to cherish and love. In short, I was no longer available.

*Saturday, 9:00 a.m.*

The next morning, my son sounded sad on the telephone. He missed me, found time hanging heavily without me. How I longed to take him in my arms! But I could only murmur words I hoped would comfort him, and pause to listen, gauging their effect on his mood. When his unhappiness crashed over me like a wave, I would hold my breath and bite my lips to keep silent, waiting for the moment when I could regain the upper hand before he got too carried away with sobbing. Then I would speak confidently to him, with growing intensity, as if I were turning up the volume on a radio. I'd lighten my tone with a hint of playfulness before affecting a gruff severity intended to induce him eventually to laugh. Only then could I manage to breathe normally, wiping away the tears I'd held back until that moment. And we'd joke around a little, to my relief, before I hung up, completely drained.

Then my reflexes as hostess kicked in, and I took charge of the "sports program" for our guests, who seemed to need distractions, like children at a summer camp. I reserved a tennis court at the Hôtel du Cap to keep them occupied until eleven o'clock, when a boat would pick them up at our beach to take them waterskiing.

Relieved of the obligation to be seductive, Marie seemed more relaxed. And I reflected wryly that it hadn't taken us long to disqualify Jean-Michel Destret. I couldn't feel bad, though, about anything that allowed us to renew our bond as sisters, because our complicity was worth all the lovers in the world. Besides, we still had two weekends left in which to catch up.

Marie had invited Alain Gandouin for lunch. He was an accomplished technocrat, a graduate of some of the finest institutions of the Republic, and universally acknowledged to be brilliant. He had become the power behind the throne in France, an unofficial and redoubtable adviser to business moguls and the many politicians who valued his counsel. And this in spite of the abysmal failure of several business ventures he had run into the ground. His detractors had nicknamed him "Monkey Say, Monkey Don't Do." France is the only country in the world where a reverence for words confers so much authority on those who call themselves intellectuals—and express themselves with brio and erudition—that they are *excused from everything else*, including thinking straight, and allowed to intervene and say any old thing in public debates, which are dominated in the United States by pragmatic corporate chieftains and in Italy by art historians.

Marie was constantly running into Gandouin in the corridors of power, whereas my father, who did not think much of him, kept him at a distance through courteous formalities. Although I had never met him, I knew something about him thanks to one of my patients, who worked for him and considered him a nightmare, against whom he defended himself with the help of his sessions with me, during which we sometimes wound up laughing maniacally. We'd wept tears of hilarity, for example, over Alain Gandouin's description of the ideal consultant.

"The secret lies in telling the client what he wants to hear," he'd explained to my patient. "But to do that, you must know how to listen, watch, and talk, all at the same time, so as to observe the effect of your words on your interlocutor. For example, you begin, 'My friend, your company is too small to survive in the face of the competition out there. You are thus at a strategic cross-roads. You must make a choice. Either you face the music and decide, in spite of the years of effort and energy you've put into your firm, to sell . . .' And now, while still emitting sounds that can pass for words, you study your client carefully, scrutinizing the slightest quiver of his body and face. And if you detect a tiny tightening of the jaw, a sign of protest, you segue immediately into '. . . and that's the solution most of my colleagues would doubtless recommend to you.' There you pause, to make your slowness seem solemn and thoughtful, before continuing: 'The way I see it, such a solution takes the easy way out, and I do not advise you to embrace it. You have the mettle and ambitions of a major player: give yourself the opportunity to show what you can do in a bigger arena. And let me remind you that I already have in place, twenty-four/seven, research groups that ferret out the kind of acquisitions that will raise you to the level of the market leaders.' *If*, however, your client welcomes your initial allusion to the sale of his firm with a hint of a smile, or reveals a furtive flicker of relief, your pitch should be: 'And although most of my colleagues, taking the usual tack in such situations, would advise you not to sell, evoking the years of effort and energy you've devoted to this company, my personal opinion is that on the contrary, the solution is to sell. A courageous, I would even say ambitious choice . . .'"

So we'd thought it hardly surprising both that this high-flying power player was so popular and that at the same time, since he'd never had any business ideas or even any idea what business is, he nevertheless gave bad and sometimes even catastrophic advice. Besides, the stories about him were legion. A particular favorite, set in a company where everybody relished their anecdotes about his sliminess, was the tale of how he had somehow extorted obedience from a lackey forced to alert him every time the big boss went to the bathroom, so that Gandouin could pretend to run into him there by chance. And there was the time when he finally decided to unveil the results of weeks of five-hours-a-day private English lessons, and showed off with an American client.

"Yes, I understand you perfectly," he'd said. "You want to focus on the business, you want to focus on the contract."

A reasonable statement, except that his accent was so bad that what he'd really said was, "Yes, I understand you perfectly. You want to fuck us on the business, you want to fuck us on the contract," and *that* had created a diplomatic incident of no small consequence.

But I couldn't share all these delights with my sister, unfortunately; my profession was indeed a weird one, obliging me as it did to keep quiet outside my office about what went on inside it. Sometimes I even ran into patients out in the "real world" whom I scrupulously pretended not to recognize, leaving them free to react as they wished. At the same time, I met strangers about whom I sometimes knew every detail of their lives, character, or sexual proclivities, information revealed to me by their spouses, children, colleagues, employers, or competitors.

# Luncheon, Saturday, July 15

## MENU

*Stuffed Baby Vegetables*

*Melons, Figs, Prosciutto*

*Pasta Salad with Chicken and Pignoli*

*Crab Parisienne*

*Curried Lamb*

*Waldorf Salad*

*Tomato and French Green Bean Salad*

*Cheeses*

*Coeur à la Crème with Berries*

Marie and I went back on duty with our guests only at lunchtime, in the loggia, where the view now featured an ocean liner that had appeared on the horizon, visible through the scattered parasol pines, like a toy set down on a shelf. Four round tables had been set up along the edge of the terrace. This was an almost daily occurrence, because many people considered lunch at L'Agapanthe an obligatory part of their stay in the Midi. Like the most fashionable restaurants, we were thus forced to turn people away, and for the same reasons: because it was one of *the* places to visit, where one met well-known or interesting personalities, and lunch here was something to boast about back in Paris.

Often, however, we really didn't know who was coming, because people we knew would call up to tell us they'd be bringing along however many houseguests they had at the moment, so we'd have to wait until the guests strolled into the loggia to discover who they were, like those flimsy little surprise gifts one used to find inside old-fashioned party favors.

Each household did, however, have its own brand of guests, which helped us out a little. One house might collect pretty girls; another, down-at-the-heels aristocrats or businessmen; a third would favor show people. And by ricochet, the habitués of those houses became in turn regulars at our luncheons, which wound up gathering together a breathtaking number of the most varied guests.

So we welcomed Alain Gandouin, whom Jean-Michel had sent his chauffeur to fetch at the Colombe d'Or in Saint-Paul-de-Vence, where he was staying, while our parents handled greeting their contingent of guests, among whom were the director of the Fondation Maeght; Maurice Saatchi and his novelist wife; Lord Hindlip, the former chairman of Christie's; Karl Lagerfeld; Martha Stewart, and one of her friends, a world-famous chef whose Flemish name we didn't recognize; along with François Sallois, a star in the firmament of fusion acquisitions, and his wife Héloise. My mother made all the introductions and discovered to her amazement that none of her daughters' houseguests had ever heard of Martha Stewart.

"Heavens! But Oprah Winfrey, let's say—surely that name rings a bell?" she said with gentle acidity to Laetitia Braissant, who was spending too much time simpering at my father for her taste. Whispering in my ear, she added, "The fine flower of the French intelligentsia? My eye! They've never left Paris, or what?"

Taking advantage of a lull in the cocktail chatter, Gérard announced—quietly this time, I'd seen to that—"Luncheon is served, Madame." My mother swept a few people along into the winter dining room where, like ushers stationed along the red carpet at a film festival, attendants were posted at either end of the buffet to hand plates, napkins, and cutlery to the guests who would soon be hesitating before the profusion of dishes. And in spite of this bountiful spread, my mother (who would be content with a few leaves of lettuce and a morsel of cheese) still took my sister and me aside for her ritual admonition: "I'm afraid there won't be enough, so wait until the guests have served themselves." Which suited Marie and me just fine, given the terrible impression that always came over us, after about a day and a half at L'Agapanthe, of having done nothing but eat ever since our arrival. And it wasn't simply our imaginations. On average, our guests gained from four to six pounds on each visit—as the scales in each guest bathroom obligingly pointed out to them—because it was nigh impossible to resist the excellence of the dishes prepared by the cooks and the outstanding wines that accompanied them.

My mother then undertook, from her usual table, to ensure the relaxed atmosphere of a festive luncheon in the Midi without sacrificing protocol or carefully orchestrated organization. She seated her guests as strictly as if she had set place cards on the tables, but she did so without seeming to, pretending to be suddenly inspired by whoever was returning from the buffet.

"Karl, I'm kidnapping you! Come and sit with Maurice Saatchi and me." While striking up a conversation with her tablemates, she called out playfully, "François! The girls are waiting for you at their table with Alain Gandouin!" And switching easily to English she burbled, "Martha, why don't you go sit next to Edmond and Charles Hinley—I know they'd be delighted."

She permitted her guests to dawdle and cruise around the buffet table at the beginning of the meal, to keep up the appropriate ambiance of cheerful freedom, but had them sit down as soon as possible, to be served at their tables by attendants who set the pace of the meal, so that it would not drag on interminably. Her guests were thus spared even the slightest discomfort inherent in buffets, which inspire trivial worries that would have nibbled away at their pleasure: "When should I get up, and what do I do with my dirty plate? I can't very well be the *only* one going to get some dessert! How can I interrupt my neighbor to go get more to eat? Is the cheese out on the buffet yet?" Everyone was at liberty to savor the luxury of service worthy of a grand hotel, yet in a decidedly bohemian atmosphere—even if they were (as often happened) too impressed by the quality of the food and the number of servants and important guests to even notice this. And although I teased my mother relentlessly, I was grateful to her for the trouble she took, because her refinement, all the more subtle in that it went unnoticed, implied a sense of delicacy and nuance that I found touching. How many hostesses, adding thoughtfulness and discretion to luxury, still managed to turn it into elegance?

Alain Gandouin was fat, squat, and badly dressed. He had a pasty complexion, yellow teeth, and a habit of resting his elbows on the table with his hands at right angles and then stroking the outer rim of his ear with his pinkie or ring finger. Bernard Braissant seemed enchanted to see him again. He wasn't important enough to have many chances of meeting him in Paris, probably, since his newspaper, which gave him the intoxicating illusion of intimacy with the major upheavals of the world by allowing him to take personally the liberation of a hostage or the election of a pope, was nevertheless of small circulation and not influential enough for Gandouin to bother taking an interest in him.

Frédéric, as usual, made bawdy jokes.

"Tolerance? Not for nothing do we French call a brothel a *maison de tolérance*," he sniffed to Héloise Sallois, the banker's wife, a Sunday painter whose cloying goody-goody personality had finally ticked Frédéric off.

Yet at first impression, she seemed an advantage to her husband, whom one would have expected to come equipped with a more spectacular companion, a trophy wife, as the Americans say. Short, slender, with limpid eyes, she seemed unaffectedly gentle. There was something moving and poetic in her way of wearing her age well and not striving to be beautiful. Yet in spite of her subtle, tart sense of humor, it wasn't long before she blindsided us by steering the conversation, with a contrite air, to her hiking holidays of backpacking and roughing it in mountain shelters, the significance of which became clear when she quizzed us about the meaning of our frivolous vacations. She gave the bizarre impression of conducting a catechism class polished by the practice of worldliness, and exuded a pious but petty austerity. Delighted with herself and with the way she imagined having avoided the perils of proselytism, she still came across as a self-righteous prig lecturing, out of pure generosity, on tolerance.

"Oh, well!" exclaimed her husband, with an attempt at humor that baffled the rest of us. "Entrust your wife to a Jesuit and your savings to a Dominican, but never the reverse!"

The talk at our table, turning to the CAC 40,[3] became so stodgy and off-putting that Frédéric kept stage-whispering remarks to me, hoping for a smile.

"Have you been elevated to the empyrean heights of the CAC 40?"

"Go to your CAC 40 immediately and stay there!"

"Well if *that's* the way you're going to be, I'm going home to the CAC 40!"

But for most of the luncheon, our table watched Alain Gandouin and Jean-Michel Destret seducing each other. Jean-Michel, who hoped to demonstrate his status as a captain of industry to the prestigious consultant, with whom he'd had little contact until then, used the occasion to reveal his talent for running the gamut of

---

3 French stock market index.

emotions. As cunningly as an old gypsy violinist bringing tears to a crowd's eyes, he played his listeners like a baby grand, shamelessly.

Which now lent credence to all those press cuttings hailing him as a showman who could galvanize his audience at the shareholders' meetings of his firm. Still, his vocabulary struck me as ridiculous and as conventionally pretentious as the feel-good emotions he was trying to tap into at every turn. He claimed to have been not "changed" but "tempered" by success. He "spent time with" ideas, including the rather obscure one of "corporeity," and trotting out some cheap poetry, he confessed that he had "too much living" behind him and sometimes had to pull himself together "by fighting through fits of the blues," followed by "splashes of sunshine" in his soul. I was aghast.

As for Alain Gandouin, he went all out to dazzle Jean-Michel on the hot-button topics of the moment, not just because he was an exhibitionist and enjoyed demonstrating his gifts at analysis but also because he wouldn't have minded picking Jean-Michel up as a client, either. He seemed to have his technique down pat. Once he'd established the superiority of his intellect, he tossed out two or three anecdotes intended to prove that he had no qualms about taking on powerful people.

It was Gay who had the last word. Primed by a few glasses of vodka, she amused us with sallies along the lines of, "I was so lovely you could hear silverware clattering onto plates whenever I entered a restaurant." And *her* coup de grâce took the cake. Noticing that the banker's wife, Héloise, had a scar on one leg, she asked impertinently, "Shouldn't someone tell her she has a run in her stocking?"

As often happened, we had a world of trouble getting rid of our luncheon clients, who were enjoying themselves so much that they would willingly have stayed all afternoon to take advantage of our beach, whereas the rest of us could think only of quietly retreating to our rooms with a book, or of diving headlong, without them, into the sea.

Laetitia wanted to visit the Fondation Maeght but didn't feel like going there by herself, so I came loudly to her rescue by suggesting various departure routes to our guests and asking if anyone needed a ride home. Jean-Michel offered his chauffeur around, for which I thanked him effusively, and it was past five o'clock when Bernard and Laetitia took their seats in the back of Jean-Michel's Safrane to go to Saint-Paul-de-Vence, followed down our drive by a Hummer, a Maserati, a Bentley, a Twingo, and a Ferrari.

"Oof! It's about time," we all exclaimed and headed for our rooms.


*Saturday, 6:30 p.m.*


I wasn't tired. But I was curious: someone somewhere was running sound checks on an orchestra tuning up. I could hear the noise in my bedroom, along with the throaty rumble of outboard motors and the harangues of ice-cream vendors crisscrossing the bay in little boats, hawking their wares to the pleasure boaters. I went down to the beach.

# The beach in winter

*January 2000*

*I am twenty-three years old.*

    *The olive trees seem clothed in their Sunday best, tucked into their ermine muffs of snow. I walk across the lawn, crackling with frost, and pause at the top of the stairs leading down to the beach. The mistral has already swept away the scumbled fog of winter. The contours of the bay are now clear, the colors crisp and gleaming. I descend the staircase carved into the rock with the sensation that I will enter and be embraced by the blue of the sky, but the sky retreats as I advance, as if content simply to cover the landscape with a sheet of blue. Squinting, I look at the ruffled sea, frosted over by the wind.*

    *Solid patches, flecked with foam or wrinkled with streaks of dull white, rise up to lick the rocks and then submerge them.*

*I take off my clothes, place them on a tumble of rocks the color of raw silk. Compact and frothy, the edging of foam fades into lacy lines around me before pulling itself together and rejoining its race with the waves, as mighty as a waterfall.*

*It's cold.*

Since Marie was taking a nap, I had to stroll around outside on my own, which entailed certain risks, in particular that of bumping into Destret, whom I could definitely have done without for a few hours. I might also be waylaid by Odon Viel (who was always ready to tell me about particle physics or the density, luminosity, temperature, and chemical composition of the stars, planets, and galaxies), or even worse, by the Démazures. Especially since I knew that Polyséna wanted to talk to me about her precocious daughter. I was fairly sure, however, that all she wanted was to sing her child's praises under the pretext of asking my advice. And so I spent the afternoon, or what was left of it, trying to avoid everyone, treated all the while to the noise of the orchestra set up on the Russians' beach, where preparations seemed to be under way for a truly hellish party.

"One . . . two, one . . . two," a man kept repeating into the mike.

By zigzagging between the beach and the swimming pool while carefully avoiding the loggia (which was too dangerous, especially at teatime), I almost succeeded in my evasive maneuvers. Then, while coming up from the beach, I let myself get trapped like a rat when Polyséna pounced on me from the guests' shower tucked under the steps leading from the lawn up to the house.

"Come down to the beach with me," she said. "Everyone's inside, so we can talk privately."

It must have been seven o'clock, meaning that if I wasn't careful, I could get stuck with her until dinnertime. Things took an unexpected turn, though, because in fact Polyséna had real questions on her mind, and as usual when someone speaks frankly to me, I was touched and eager to help. Her problem was not very serious after all, and after twenty minutes of discussion she announced that thanks to me, she understood things ever so much better now. She was beaming, and her palpable relief cheered me, gratifying my deep need to be of some use and assistance in this world, which is, along with my son, the only thing that gives meaning to my life. I was happy. We were about to return to the house when we froze, startled and intrigued by the sound of a propeller.

A helicopter was circling over the Russians' beach, now awash in tuxedos and evening gowns! Absorbed in our conversation, Polyséna and I had not even noticed how these guests, competing with the crickets' chirping, had gradually replaced the background noise of the orchestra's sound testing with their lively chatter. There looked to be about fifty of them, neither young nor old, but more stocky than not and somewhat provincial in appearance, judging from the slightly outdated style of the dresses and awkward cut of the dinner jackets. They squinted against the blast blowing their hair in every direction as the helicopter came in for a landing, its propeller blades so menacing that even Polyséna and I ducked instinctively.

As soon as the craft had landed on the beach, however, the guests crowded together into an audience that raised their glasses as one to salute the three disembarking passengers. Was it the raincoats they wore, the attaché cases they carried, or the zeal of the welcoming delegation that rushed forward to greet them with a toast? Something about the scene was definitely disquieting.

While Polyséna and I were wondering whether the new arrivals were Russian, Georgian, or Albanian, one of them stepped forward with the composure of a movie Mafia don. He said a few words and was vigorously applauded by the throng, into which he plunged as if diving into the sea, clapping a few men on the back and greeting others with a manly embrace, before leading his two acolytes back aboard the helicopter, which immediately took off.

"Did you see that? I don't believe it!" we kept repeating in a daze, while Frédéric and Marie, attracted by the commotion, came rushing down the steps.

"Are we too late? What happened!"

For a few minutes Polyséna and I had their full attention.

"What did he look like? Was he handsome?" Marie asked eagerly.

"Oh, please! You're such a nympho! No, he was completely blah," I told her.

"Meaning? Tall, short, fat, skinny? Come on! Details!"

"He was completely bland, that's the best I can do. Polyséna, you tell her."

But having just realized that Frédéric and Marie were dressed for dinner whereas she was still in her bathing suit with wet hair a half hour before dinnertime, Polyséna was in a flap.

"Hurry back to the house and change, while I deal with these two scatterbrains!" Frédéric urged her, then whispered to me, "Stay, I've got a serious scoop."

"What's up? Tell me," I said as soon as Polyséna had gone.

Now Frédéric had the spotlight, but he wasn't a playwright for nothing and he knew how to pace his effects to keep an audience on tenterhooks. His bedroom happened to overlook the servants' dining area, and when he'd heard them howling with laughter at the table, earlier in the afternoon, he'd listened in, finally piecing together what was so funny.

After knocking on the door of the Yellow Room, for which she was responsible, Colette, the chambermaid, had not heard any reply. Upon entering she had found Jean-Michel lying on the floor, up against the baseboard, with his head wedged in a corner of the room and his ear glued to a cell phone connected to a charger with a cord so short he had to stay right by the wall socket into which it was plugged. Rolling his eyes in embarrassment at being surprised in such a posture, he nevertheless continued his business conversation while making gesture of helplessness in Colette's direction.

"I don't get it," I admitted. "What was it he was doing down by the baseboard?"

So Marie explained it to me again, while Frédéric delivered the chambermaid's imitation of Jean-Michel for the staff, all convulsed with laughter: "You have certainly been following recent developments in the business sector and seen that Femo has launched a hostile takeover of Ymex. I can't really speak to you as frankly as I would like because I'm in a meeting, but I *can* say that I am concerned. So much so that, to tell you the truth, this morning I put together a team in Paris to study the question, devise a suitable strategy, and allow us to go forward with the appropriate action . . ."

"No!" I gasped, torn between laughter and pity. "The poor guy, can you imagine! It must have been a nightmare!"

I could tell they were disappointed with my reaction and thought I hadn't truly appreciated the importance of the hot news flash they'd just delivered, but it was already ten minutes to nine and I had just time enough to dash back and slip into a dress, a marvel of Parma violet chiffon that had cost me a tidy fortune, and tuck my hair into a low chignon like my mother's before going down to dinner.

Jean-Michel didn't deserve so much consideration, however, because he behaved disgracefully when he discovered that Frédéric knew all about his misadventure.

"What room are you in?" Jean-Michel had asked him with studied casualness.

"The Chinese Room, which, like yours, overlooks the staff dining room," Frédéric had replied, to allow him to tell his story himself and put all those laughing on his side.

Instead of which, Jean-Michel, who was trying to bamboozle him and assure himself of Frédéric's discretion as quickly as possible, clumsily attempted to establish a relationship of complicity with him that was based on some very ill-advised remarks.

"Don't you think it's strange, how we're all obliged to live cheek by jowl here, in a villa of this size?"

Then, assiduously mongering his little scandal, he explained in a confidential tone that he'd been disappointed in this house, which he'd imagined was quite grand, having heard so much about it, because an invitation to L'Agapanthe was a social coup much prized by regular visitors to the house as well as by any fortunate occasional guests. But, well, he'd been forced to admit that it really wasn't much to write home about. He, for example, wouldn't have hesitated one second to enclose the loggia with glass walls.

"It would help with the mosquitoes and allow the area to be used year-round, as a kind of winter garden. Don't you agree?"

"An excellent idea! You should just have a word or two with Flokie about that," Frédéric replied treacherously before turning his back.

# *Dinner, Saturday, July 15*

**THIRTEEN PERSONS**

| MEN | WOMEN |
|---|---|
| Edmond Ettinguer | Flokie Ettinguer |
| Frédéric Hottin | Laure Ettinguer |
| Odon Viel | Marie Ettinguer |
| Henri Démazure | Polyséna Démazure |
| Laszlo Schwartz | Gay Wallingford |
| Bernard Braissant | Laetitia Braissant |
| Jean-Michel Destret | |

| SEATING: EDMOND'S TABLE | SEATING: FLOKIE'S TABLE |
|---|---|
| Laure | Henri      Laetitia |
| Bernard          Odon | Marie          Frédéric |
| Gay          Polyséna | Jean-Michel      Laszlo |
| Edmond | Flokie |

# MENU

*Consommé*
*Seven-Hour Leg of Lamb*
*Salad and Cheeses*
*Red Currant Pie with Custard Sauce*

Jean-Michel was truly hopeless, since he seemed to disapprove of his dinner as well, so much so that my mother, sitting next to him, felt obliged to explain that the lamb, far from having been overcooked, had been caramelized for seven hours to become so delectably tender that we could have eaten it with a spoon, had the rules of etiquette so permitted. In the same way, he downed his Cheval Blanc 1961 without a thought, while the other guests were in raptures over its charms.

At our table, Odon Viel had us in stitches with the description of his train trip from Paris and his discomfort at the behavior of a group of young people, in particular some lovebirds sitting across from him in his compartment, who had spent the entire trip in energetic liplock.

"But that's all they did, the whole time! Like those endless train picnics in earlier days, with *pâté de campagne* and orange peels flying everywhere."

Polyséna talked some more about her book on portraits, and about the game of matching up "twins" from among the subjects in great portraits and the celebrities of today. Which led Odon to bring up Proust.

From there the conversation drifted onto art and the "repudiation of realism" offered by René Huyghe, the way that painting, which once strove to "transcribe physical or psychic reality," has "purified" itself ever since Mondrian, throwing off the weight of "everything that is not strictly within its nature" to eliminate all traces of tradition and the past, and to embrace "a new enlightenment."

"Ain't No Sunshine" by Bill Withers; "I Will Survive" by Gloria Gaynor; "Strong Enough" by Cher; the Beatles' "From Me to You"—the orchestra at the Russians' party was playing one golden oldie after another, making me just itch to jump up and dance, so when dinner was over I suggested going down to the beach for a musical midnight swim. Marie had been so excruciatingly bored, sitting between Henri Démazure and Jean-Michel (who was still refusing to lighten up), that she leaped at the opportunity.

"Oh, absolutely! I'm going to go change."

"Good idea," chimed the Braissants in unison.

Which forced Jean-Michel, who had no desire to be grilled on his knowledge of art history, to go with the flow.

Down at the beach, the moon glowed russet red, throwing a veil of mist over a gleaming jet-black sea. It was beautiful, but spooky, and pausing at the water's edge, in fact, all I could think of was sea monsters, giant octopuses bristling with tentacles, and marauding sharks. My brave smile quickly began to fade.

"Don't worry, shivering is part of the exercise!" exclaimed my sister. "I'll go in with you."

We were standing in our bathrobes at the foot of the ladder, while near the grotto, a little farther up, our guests were chatting with a conspiratorial air that left no doubt they were slamming us, or running down our parents, the house, or the way we lived. We couldn't have cared less: "Black and White Eyes" by Syd Matters had put us in a deliciously nostalgic and sentimental mood.

"Can you tell me what the fuck we're doing with jerks like them," I asked Marie, "when we could be with perfectly wonderful guys?"

"Have you been drinking, or is it James Blunt?"

And she was right: "One of the Brightest Stars," which the orchestra was now playing, was having a romantic effect. As were the shouts and laughter coming from the neighbors' place, despite the fact that the seriously unhip Russians and mafiosi were taking time out from dancing to grope one another like Odon's amorous fellow train passengers.

Mungo Jerry's "In the Summertime," then "Soul Bossa Nova" by Quincy Jones—the quarter-hour of languorous music seemed to have come to an end. And our companions suddenly realized that it would be polite to join us. So, in a hearty voice intended to gloss over the nasty things they'd just been saying about us, Bernard cried, "Wait for us, girls!"

But Marie and I were already swimming toward the festivities, spreading our fingers slightly in the water to create streams of starry reflections.

"Great," I thought, "now he's trying to be the life of the party!"

And my worst fears were realized: diving showily from the board to attract the attention of the group watching us from the Russians' dock, Bernard quickly caught up with us in a fast crawl.

"A little passé their little soirée!" he announced loudly.

"In any case, their orchestra is incredible," I replied, but he was shouting to the people on the dock.

"Having fun?"

"Leave them alone!" Marie told him. "Anyway, they don't speak French."

At this, he yelled in English, "Are you having a good time?"

"Yes," answered a man in a calm voice that contrasted strongly with Bernard's blustering.

"Would you please stop?" I begged Bernard, horribly mortified, and I started nervously side-stroking in little circles.

But Bernard, who'd been joined by Laetitia and Jean-Michel, was all keyed up, as if he'd found a way to act out in revenge for a weekend during which he'd felt confined to playing a bit part.

"You should come visit us! We have a better beach, better food, and better company!"

"Have you gone crazy?" I hissed at him. I was furious.

"Totally insane!" agreed Marie, who swam over to Bernard and told him firmly in a low voice, "Didn't it ever occur to you that we might want to avoid our Mafia neighbors?"

"Why don't you come over here?" asked the mystery voice.

"We weren't invited, that's why. But have a wonderful evening, sir!" replied Marie, hoping thereby to put an end to the scene and prompt everyone to begin swimming back to our beach.

But Bernard, spurred on by the giggling of Jean-Michel and Laetitia at his side, simply upped the ante.

"You should listen to me! You seem like an adventurous guy, and you'd be a fool to miss out on meeting my girlfriends here, who happen to be the best-looking women I ever met!"

"Wait a minute here, hold on!" Marie said with a laugh. "That's like putting a price tag on us!"

"She's right, you've got some nerve!" I huffed and turned to Laetitia, but she didn't think Bernard's joke was funny anymore.

"Oh, shit!" she cried. "He's taking his clothes off!"

"What?" I craned to see where she was looking and saw our mystery man on the Russians' beach doing a striptease to Jimmy Cliff's "Many Rivers to Cross."

"Oh, God." I sighed, and we all raced back to our beach.

The figure dressed in black slowly grew lighter. First the white shirt appeared from under the dinner jacket, then the bare skin. Laetitia, Marie, and I watched with sinking hearts, while Bernard acted nonchalant to hide his surprise and perhaps even his dismay at thus having the spotlight stolen from him by a stranger whom he'd never imagined might take him up on his invitation.

"Wait a minute," he asked suddenly. "Do we at least have something to offer him to drink, now that I've boasted about our wonderful hospitality?"

"Not to mention the beauty of your female company!" added Laetitia, frankly worried about disappointing our unknown guest in that department.

"Well, thanks!" I said haughtily, to ease the tension, and headed for the shower in the grotto to rinse off the salt.

Marie had joined me there, and as we toweled off walking back toward the others, we looked over at the stranger who was about to dive into the water.

"Do you think he'll be handsome?" she asked.

"That *would* surprise me, but it doesn't that you're fantasizing already!"

"Why? You're not?"

"Well, sure, actually I am. You're right! I hope he's divine."

"Aha," Bernard said acidly, eyeing his studiously indifferent wife. "So that's how it is!"

Riveted, Marie and I followed the progress of the stranger swimming toward us to the strains of a Nino

Ferrer hit single, *La maison près de la fontaine*, while we sang along at the top of our lungs.

Jean-Michel, however, standing silently by, seemed suddenly to have realized from our excitement that we'd never shown that kind of feminine interest in him. And he had realized as well that although he hadn't wanted to arouse such interest, he now felt disappointed and irritated at being left out.

The mystery man emerged from the waves to the accompaniment of Nancy Sinatra's "Bang Bang," climbed the steps to where Marie and I were standing, bowed smartly from the waist to kiss our hands, and introduced himself.

"Rajiv Kapour, how do you do?"

Marie quickly handed him a towel, and then we took a closer look at him. Young, about thirty, he was amazingly relaxed and graceful for someone standing in sopping wet underpants in front of perfect strangers. Self-possessed, I thought. And I found his serenity immediately seductive. As were his black eyes with their long, silky lashes.

Bernard, who had unearthed some vodka in the freezer of the bar in the little cave, handed around the drinks while we pulled up some beach chairs.

When we were all settled, Marie did the honors. "I'm afraid my friend Bernard has enticed you here under false pretenses, but we're very happy to meet you."

What was it about her behavior that gave me a jolt? Something lordly, imperious, something both irre-proachable and robotic, something I felt so strongly that it seemed to exclude me and deny our affectionate intimacy. Then I realized what it was: she was playing mistress of the manor, putting herself forward as the spokesperson for us all, a queen surrounded by her fa-vorites. My resentment at that dominant, arrogant note in her voice was something I hadn't felt since childhood, and it stabbed me to the heart. Everything in her atti-tude was reclaiming her rights as the elder sister, the pretty girl who condescendingly dominates her younger and in every way less favored sister.

With a sudden pang of dreadful sadness, I felt alone and troubled by a sense of not loving Marie at that mo-ment, of feeling neither tenderness nor admiration for her. Was I jealous of my sister? Did I want to attract this young man's attention away from her? Judging from the glances he'd been giving me since his arrival I thought that was already a fait accompli. Because he was actually studying me intently while simply replying cordially to Marie.

Faced with this situation—which I couldn't explain, since I thought Marie much the lovelier of us two—I reflected that I had never yet witnessed the beginning of any of her love affairs, and had never placed myself in competition with her, because not only would I have felt condemned at the outset to failure but I could never have handled a triumph, either. I probably had some confused intuition that Marie, more fragile than I was, would have taken defeat very hard, since she was used to winning contests of beauty and seductiveness, whereas I was used to walking away.

Meanwhile, lost in her performance as a perfect hostess, Marie did not pay attention to the fact that Rajiv and I were engaged in conversation. I quickly found out that Rajiv was an economist close to Amartya Sen, the Nobel Prize winner whose ideas on human development I was familiar with, and that he was a microcredit specialist. Finally somebody interesting! I said to myself, not quite realizing that the Indian man had done more to me than simply capture my attention. Because, in spite of my sadness over Marie there was a definite current of desire flowing between us, invisible perhaps, but palpable, and I felt it sweep over me in unwelcome waves whenever he looked at me. The ache deep in my belly was so violent that I would really have flinched if I hadn't spent my life learning how to keep even my strongest feelings hidden behind a diplomatically impassive facade.

As "Tears and Rain" by James Blunt, Otis Redding's "Sittin' on the Dock of the Bay," and Lenny Kravitz's "Stand by My Woman" were played, we learned that Rajiv was from Bombay and was a friend of Tatiana's, the daughter of the owners next door, who had studied with him at the London School of Economics.

"I'm starting to feel cold," remarked Jean-Michel.

"Me, too," admitted Laetitia.

"Well then, I'd better be going," Rajiv observed, giving me a long, lingering look that seemed to suggest he was trying to figure out a way of maneuvering himself into being alone with me.

Since all five of us saw him off, to the accompaniment of Janis Joplin's "Cry Baby," there wasn't much he could do, however, except declare that he'd be delighted to return our hospitality one day if any of us ever happened to be in London.

The party next door found its second wind as we trooped back to the house; I even found myself humming along to David Bowie's "Ashes to Ashes" as I was going to bed. But what really preoccupied me before I fell asleep, aside from my fresh anxiety over what I now saw as the considerable risk involved in Marie's and my plan to seduce a possible future husband, were the spasms of desire I was still feeling for Rajiv. And as I dropped off I wondered if I would ever see him again, or if he would join the list of what I called my "might haves," as in, "It might have worked between us," those men who had courted me or whom I had desired, with whom I would have liked to have an adventure if things had turned out otherwise—if they had dared, if they hadn't been married and faithful, if I had given in when it might have been possible, if only . . .

*Sunday*

The next day saw the departure before lunch of Jean-Michel and the Braissants, who left for Aix in Jean-Michel's car (the usefulness of which I now finally grasped) to attend some festival or other they needed to get to before the end of the day. Another highlight was my realization of the effect I was having on men ever since Rajiv had set my sensuality on fire. I must have had bedroom eyes, because I proved indecently popular with men at luncheon that day—a development I instinctively took care to conceal from my mother and Marie. Our male guests seemed to grow shy, blush, or make sheep's eyes at me upon approaching, when they weren't simply proposing a quickie in the bathroom, like the ruddy-complexioned fellow with hairy nostrils and ears, a curator from some provincial museum, who seriously thought he might carry that off by murmuring to me that I made the other women present look like goats.

# *Luncheon, Sunday, July 16*

## MENU

*Onion and Tomato Tart Niçoise*
*Corsican Charcuterie*
*Crudités*
*Rabbit Terrine with Prunes*
*Lobster Fricassee*
*Saffron Rice*
*Zucchini Flowers*
*Cheeses*
*Melon Surprise*

Even if I found it impossible to suppress my sensual awakening, which sprang from something too primitive to be denied, I could resolve to forget the thoughts and feelings about Marie that had so pained me the previous evening. And this I tried to do all during that last day before our return to Paris. Because there was no question of my allowing the slightest distance to grow between us, still less when we were already committed to our project, even if it was absurd.

*Three*

# WEEKEND OF
# JULY 21

# Weekend of July 21

## THE FAMILY

Marie Ettinguer

Laure Ettinguer

Flokie Ettinguer

Edmond Ettinguer

## THE PILLARS

Gay Wallingford

Frédéric Hottin

## THE LITTLE BAND

Odon Viel

Henri Démazure

Polyséna Démazure

Laszlo Schwartz

## THE ODDBALLS

Georgina de Marien

Charles Ramsbotham

## THE NEWCOMERS

Béno Grunwald

Mathias Cavoye

Lou Léva

# SECRETARY'S NAME BOARD

M. and Mme. Edmond Ettinguer     Master Bedroom

Mme. Laure Ettinguer     Flora's Room
(*Arrival from Paris Air France Friday 5:00 p.m.*)

Mlle. Marie Ettinguer     Ada's Room
(*Arrival from Rio de Janeiro Friday 6:00 p.m.*)

Lady Gay Wallingford     Peony Room

M. Frédéric Hottin     Chinese Room

M. Odon Viel     Turquoise Room

Count and Countess Henri Démazure     Annex: Coral Room

M. Laszlo Schwartz     Lilac Room

Viscountess de Marien     Annex: Peach Room

Earl of Stafford (Charles Ramsbotham)     Annex: Lime Room

M. Béno Grunwald     Yellow Room
(*Arrival helicopter?*)

M. Mathias Cavoye and Mlle. Lou Léva     Sasha's Room
(*Arrival EasyJet Friday 7:00 p.m.*)

The plot thickened the following weekend, when some friends of my father, Georgina de Marien and Charles Ramsbotham, arrived at L'Agapanthe. My mother called them the Oddballs and found them so tiresome that she regretted not having argued more firmly, at the moment of sending out her invitations, against their coming. She'd been particularly set against Charles Ramsbotham, who, although tremendously rich and upper-crust (being a lord, the seventh Earl of Stafford) did not "play the game" with the culture and refinement she had expected of him.

Charles was, it's true, surprising in every way, beginning with his looks. Through a laudable desire to take care of himself, this middle-aged man had concentrated all his attention on his face, but since he had no taste whatsoever, he'd had his hair dyed as black as shoe polish. More or less insensitive to pain, he'd gone the whole hog: botched eyelid surgery had left his eyes in a permanent state of astonishment, while his skin—no doubt pockmarked even before his several face-lifts—had the texture of sandpaper and the color of a pear way past its prime. Through an inexplicable paradox, however, he had completely neglected to keep physically fit. He was fat. Quite fat. Which didn't seem to bother him, but my mother couldn't get over it, as if he'd meant his waistline to be a personal affront to her. Why else did he merrily stuff himself at every meal instead of being ashamed of his girth and trying to slim down?

The other game Charles seemed unable to play was the art of dressing stylishly. His own codes and predilections, for example, allowed the wearing of polyester shorts and a leopard-print short-sleeved shirt with an elastic bottom hem that puffed out over his paunch. And taking my mother's suggestion of "casual" attire too literally, he could turn up for breakfast in a canary-yellow tracksuit he'd personally ordered from an Italian couturier shortly before the man was assassinated. In other words, Charles was *the* client for men's ready-to-wear, of the kind one would have thought had long since vanished from this earth.

So he stuck out like a very sore thumb at L'Agapanthe, a temple of graceful conversation, and adding insult to injury, he was utterly indifferent to the charms of the mature women who formed the core of the feminine contingent there. The only women who interested Charles were breathtakingly beautiful prostitutes—or fighter pilots! And he made no effort to speak to my mother or her women friends at meals, except when he interrupted their noble attempts to entertain him by asking them to pass the salt, tell him the time, or inform him what make of car they drove. Because Charles really cared about only two things: automobiles, about which (delighted to be an expert at last on at least one subject) he loved to know and understand everything, and gorillas, which he truly worshipped. To the point of building more than a dozen supersophisticated cages for them at his home in Gloucestershire.

All this made it hard for my mother to put up with this boor whom she considered shallow and uncultivated and who did not blend in with her "little band," like a gladiolus stuck in among orchids. And aside from her displeasure at being invisible to him, she found fault with Charles for the admiration he aroused in the imbeciles who, eager to appropriate some of his originality, made much of the funny stories he told about his gorillas. My mother therefore felt within her rights to expect that her faithful friends should openly share her disdain for Charles, whose shortcomings she pointed out at every opportunity.

Frédéric was always the first to oblige, with brief remarks that both soothed and enchanted his hostess, quips along the lines of, "So when may we expect him, our Goat's Butt?" For nothing amused him more than to indulge his passion for nicknames, which he invented by translating or deforming the real name of his victim. "And George?" he added, meaning Georgina de Marien.

Georgina was my father's acknowledged "platonic girlfriend," and my mother had nothing nice to say about her, either. For at least ten years now, my mother had been in the habit of inviting a woman who would prove an amusing companion for her husband, since she had little time to pay attention to him herself, given that L'Agapanthe was as difficult to run as a busy hotel. The ideal woman for this task had to please my father, which implied gaiety on her part, good looks, and the ability to accompany him on his long swims in the bay. This lady friend should also, however, suit my mother, by not harboring any desire to flirt with my father for real or play at being mistress of the house—so she had to be astute enough to understand any such obvious prerequisites.

Well, such a pearl doesn't turn up every day. So once my mother had assured herself that Georgina was not an adventuress, she assigned her the part.

The drama in question had been running for a long time, though, and my mother shared the philosophy of one of our neighbors, who made it a rule never to rent her house more than three years in a row to the same person, to make sure of remaining the lady of the manor. My mother was therefore preparing to banish Georgina from L'Agapanthe once she had laid the groundwork with enough cutting remarks in that regard.

And yet Georgina was a nice person, who never spoke ill of anyone or had any intention of vamping my father. She would naturally have loved to have a touch of romance in her life, but she wasn't prepared to go to the mat over it with my mother, whose temper she feared as deeply as she appreciated her hospitality. Besides, she was independent and happy to be so. Born Miro Quesada, she was the daughter of a man known as the Guano King, just as Patiño was the Tin King. A Peruvian, she came from a family that had Spanish roots and numbered among its members two presidents, many intellectuals, some newspaper magnates, and one hero of the hostilities with Chile during the War of the Pacific. With no need to work for a living, Georgina de Marien began traveling after the death of her husband, but she neither went off to spas nor embarked on short cruises. Rather, she traveled like a diplomat sent from post to post and had gone in succession to London, Rome, Barcelona, Hong Kong, and New York.

*Friday, 6:00 p.m.*

Hidden behind his *Paris-Turf,* Frédéric greeted me when I showed up at L'Agapanthe that Friday like a puppeteer announcing the arrival of Punch and Judy, with a jolly "Are we ever going to have fun!"

Charles Ramsbotham, who had shown up shortly before I did, had just broken all the rules in the book by giving my father a Jet Ski, even though he knew perfectly well that all guest gifts ought to be purely symbolic gestures.

A man of concrete and practical mind, Charles could never remember any of these rules of *savoir vivre* for very long, for he had no patience with such subtleties. As a guest, he thought it shameful to offer what he considered "crud," which was doubtless suitable for the impecunious friends of my parents, but not for him, for his lifestyle was so opulent that one might well have thought him even wealthier than he was. Indeed, his generous character and personal ethics impelled him to treat his friends with the same lavish generosity with which he indulged himself. This led him, every year, to offer my father some costly gadget such as a GPS or a satellite telephone with worldwide coverage, a device that had the considerable merit of keeping Charles temporarily occupied (until he had mastered the operating instructions and tested his gift for his hosts) in a house where he was bored stiff.

"This is too much, simply *too* much! Just because this idiot charters private planes and helicopters to go have coffee in the Dordogne or in Moldavia where he requisitions entire hotels and dislodges all their clients, that doesn't give him the right to do as he pleases!"

My mother was letting off steam in her bathroom, where she had taken refuge to explode in private.

"Don't work yourself up into such a state!" pleaded my father, trying to calm her down.

"No, I mean *really*! That thing is expensive, the exhaust stinks, it makes a hellish racket, and it's dangerous. Who knows if it's even legal in the bay!"

"You know perfectly well that this Jet Ski will end up in the cellar, with all the rest of Charles's presents. You can't really see me revving up the motor just for fun!" my father replied, at which point I joined their company and added my two cents' worth.

"At least that contraption might bring us more in line with our neighbors, because what do we look like, with our plastic kayak-canoe from the toy store in Juan-les-Pins, bobbing around next to their cutting-edge playthings?"

And it was true that wherever we went in the bay, we now seemed like amateurs in a world of professionals. Take children's games, for instance. While we were satisfied with a sandbox on the terrace above the staff beach, our Russian neighbors provided their offspring with a miniature golf course, a go-cart racetrack, and inflatable castles featuring hiding places and slides worthy of an amusement park, all installed on a lot purchased for that purpose. It was the same situation with our antimosquito strategy, because our Saudi neighbor deployed extermination on an industrial scale with machines diffusing a blue light that vaporized the insects with ghastly zapping sounds, while we persisted halfheartedly in setting out yellow bug lights and saucers of citronella.

It was in the security department, however, that we failed the most ignominiously, since our alarm system, which we found perfectly satisfactory, looked ridiculous next to the armed guards of our neighbors and the motion detector lights that broadcast a booming electronic voice to explain, in a menacing tone and several languages, what dangers awaited any feckless fool who persisted in violating the perimeter of the property or its offshore stretch of bay.

And if you also considered the yachts at anchor, the Riva speedboats, plus the floating docks and rafts that formed ramparts around our neighbors' beaches against intruders of all kinds, we had by some strange paradox become the only wealthy residents on the bay on whom it was physically possible to spy.

Which was precisely the mission of the yellow boat out of Juan-les-Pins that crisscrossed the bay every hour under the clearly feeble pretext of studying the underwater scenery, thus allowing its passengers to examine us as if we were exotic fauna for the sum of 12 euros per adult and 6 euros per child (between the ages of two and eleven). Hugging the shore wherever possible, this boat actually came right up to our beach ladder, meeting with a reception that depended on our mood. Although we usually sheltered behind our books or newspapers to avoid the gaze of these vacationers who, camera in hand, hoped to grab a photo of some famous face or silhouette while snatching a glimpse of how the *beautiful people* live, we might also decide to wave cheerily at them, or hide in the grotto and launch a squirt gun attack.

My silly joke about the neighbors did nothing to cheer up my mother, of course, but she was not the only person whose patience and good humor were in short supply that day. I'd had a hard week in Paris. Too many patients, but above all I was missing Félix more and more as his month with his father dragged on. And I was worried about my ex's mood swings and irresponsibility. To crown everything, Marie had gone off to who knows where to some conference or other, with a time change that meant we'd hardly spoken to each other since the previous weekend.

Frankly, I was in a tight spot, because my guests weren't the kind to outshine Charles Ramsbotham. In fact, Mathias Cavoye was a walking cliché: a private dealer in the secondary art market, he was fifty, handsome, but getting on, with a nuclear tan and all the accoutrements of a seducer going gray at the temples but trying to look young in jeans and a blazer, with turtlenecks in the winter and colorful polo shirts in the summer.

I was fond of Mathias because he wasn't pretentious, had never tried to hide the fact that his mother had a little grocery store in the Parisian suburb of Bourg-la-Reine, and he always invited me to the parties he gave at his home to fend off ennui. Until now, however, despite the many hints he'd made, I'd been very careful not to invite him to L'Agapanthe because I just didn't trust him.

Was it because he was depressed? Hung out with celebrities? Or was constantly angling to swindle extra money out of every deal he made? I could just see him slipping coke to a pretty young thing to rev her up or keep her under his thumb. Bluntly put, with him and his pal Lou Léva, a starlet desperate to make it to the top, we were definitely in the demimonde, and it wouldn't take my parents more than thirty seconds to figure that out. They would then conclude that I must have fallen on my head and lost all my bearings. Beyond the distinction they made between chic and cheap, my parents divided society into decent, respectable people and those who were not, a criterion based on moral judgments as antiquated as they were denigrated in our café society. This was one of the things I most liked about them, and I valued their good opinion enough that their parental disapproval would upset me. Especially since I had no intention of explaining to them that the whole point about Mathias was that he was bringing us Béno Grunwald.

To my surprise, my mother quickly composed herself after my father left for the beach, where Charles was already putting together the infamous Jet Ski. Then she asked me not about Mathias, but about his girlfriend.

"So, she's an actress, is that it? Then why haven't I heard of her?"

My mother affecting a shopgirl's interest in show business, that was a new one for me, and I had to smile, given that she and my father knew nothing about *any* stars, not even the ones so famous their public appearances cause riots.

"Actually," I replied, "I'd have been astonished if you did know her, because aside from her roles in two minor films . . ."

"Lou Léva? That's her real name?"

"Of course not, what an idea! She must have chosen it carefully in the hope that the alliteration would help casting directors remember her name. But you can ask her yourself, she's arriving with Mathias Cavoye just before dinnertime."

"And young Grunwald?"

My mother invariably attached that adjective to all her close friends' children. Irritated to think that I might have felt I was about to introduce her to someone "elegant" of whom she hadn't heard, my mother probably meant to show me how familiar she was with the Grunwald family, and she twisted the knife with an innocent air while gossiping knowingly about them.

"How has he been doing? Because they haven't a penny left, poor things, since they lost that manufacturing license, what was it for again?"

"A monopoly on photographic gelatin."

"Oh, yes, that was it."

"Actually, *young* Grunwald happens to be in his forties and he's a lot more wealthy than his family!"

"Really! And how did he manage that?"

"Because he made a fortune!"

"Ah, he's the one who married a model, or something like that?"

"Yes. Although I'm afraid he might turn out to be a bit of a show-off," I confessed prudently to my mother, hoping that with her love of argument, she would immediately defend him if I went on the attack.

"Oh! That's only natural if he's earned a lot of money . . ."

"You're right, of course, but I mean, is that any reason to arrive by helicopter—"

"What, he's coming by helicopter? But that's grotesque! Where will it land?"

"On a copter pad in Cannes, I believe."

"That's ridiculous. Besides, he'll get caught in traffic. And it will be his own fault, too."

"Whose own fault?" asked Marie, joining us in the bathroom.

"Darling!" exclaimed our mother delightedly. "When did you get here?"

"What's wrong?" I asked Marie as soon as we were alone.

"Nothing, why?"

"Come off it, I know you. What's going on?"

"Nothing, at least, not much, really . . . It's stupid . . ."

"What is?"

"It's a dog . . . in Rio . . . that I can't get out of my mind. I found him on the lawn outside my room the evening I arrived. A little black dog with a white spot around his right eye. He sat down in front of the bay window. And he kept looking at me, without moving. Imagine! I tried to ignore him, then I closed the curtains, hoping to forget about him. That was impossible, obviously. I couldn't stand it, I let him into my room. He was full of fleas, thin, and *famished*. So I ordered him a steak and I gave him a bath. He didn't struggle, was so relaxed, trusting. . . . No, but I mean, are you getting what I'm saying? I've lost my mind! I'm worried about a stray dog, in Rio, the city of favelas! Isn't that pathetic?"

"Yes, particularly since you seem to be ignoring world hunger and global warming . . ."

"Meaning?"

"That you have every right to get emotional without having to fix all the problems of the world."

"You don't think I'm being silly?"

"No, I really don't. Go on."

"Afterward he fell asleep. I left him on the floor although I wanted to bring him up on the bed. In the morning I gave him the slip in the hotel garden before going off to work. I thought about him, though, all day long, and I came back early to the hotel that evening, hoping to find him outside my bay window."

"And was he there?"

"Yes. He was wild with joy, and I ordered him another filet mignon."

Her voice suddenly broke. "He was there every evening. And I gave him the slip as usual, the morning I left, except that . . . And now I can't stop thinking about him."

"Poor dear, I'm so sorry. But I'd have been worried if you hadn't reacted just like that."

"Really?"

"Yes, it simply means that you're human, that you're very sensitive. Which doesn't keep you from being strong, doing everything well, and seeming absolutely perfect. You know, we always use something outside ourselves to open the door to our emotions. And since wars, famines, and earthquakes are tragedies too vast for us to feel directly concerned about them, we find something closer to us to cry over, or something more specific, like a doll with a shattered eye, an episode of *Little House on the Prairie*, or a dog."

"But in this case, he was the one who chose me, and . . . I abandoned him."

"Yes, and in fact that's what's at stake here."

"What is?"

"Abandonment."

"But what are you talking about?"

"I'm saying that this dog embodied all the moments when you felt abandoned, as lonely as he was, with no one to give you a bath or order you a steak. But don't worry, you'll get over it."

"You think so?"

"Sure, but I also think you have love to give and no-where to give it. Me, I'm lucky, I have Félix. Perhaps it's time for you to deal with this. Maybe that's what your dog is telling you."

I was uneasy about imposing Mathias Cavoye on my parents, but my success in managing to bring Béno Grunwald to the house made up for that, because before suggesting Béno to my sister as a "blind date," I'd done all the requisite research into his background. And he was so divine, according to *Who's Who*, Google, and *Fortune*, that he seemed almost like a jackpot just waiting to be won.

Béno Grunwald was a self-made man from a family of means. Perfect, I'd thought, catching myself starting to hope that he would have both the good manners and sex appeal of a self-made man. No one had helped him in any way, neither his father, who had never wanted to see him, nor his mother, a worldly and uncaring woman.

Dyslexia had made studying difficult, so Béno started out by enjoying himself, but since he was charismatic, trusted his instincts, and had good business sense, he opted to make his fortune instead of self-destructing in trendy night clubs. He began by selling bonds and soon did fabulously well. Sniffing out good deals, he never stopped speculating, investing, even when on vacation. Quick off the mark, he would visit a house for sale in the Bahamas, then buy it and snap up all the surrounding properties as well, selling them off later, one by one, for huge profits. He knew how to plan far ahead, too, and in anticipation of the death of Castro, he had gone to Cuba to buy up all the photos of the Cuban revolution he could find, just as he had explored Panama in the expectation of an imminent economic boom, acquiring a forest there as big as a French *département*.

He lived large in London, with pieds-à-terre in Paris and New York, yet he also understood the real value of money, because he had already found out what it was like to go bankrupt. Down practically to the change in his pockets, he'd bought a Basquiat just before the graffiti artist took off, which allowed him to bounce back so high that he now managed a hedge fund worth more than twenty billion dollars.

At forty-five, twice divorced (first from an Anglo-Iranian beauty, then from one of the five highest-paid models in the world), he was single again. He was filthy

rich, generous, ran an enormous charity he'd put to-
gether from scratch to support girls' education in Africa,
and he knew how to have fun. Plus he knew everyone,
from Mick Jagger to Bill Clinton to Nelson Mandela.
The *New York Post*'s Page Six even claimed that the letter
*B* in his address book listed, among others, Brad (Pitt),
Richard Branson (the fifth-richest person in the United
Kingdom), Bono, Bongo (Omar), Lord Balfour, War-
ren Buffett, while the letter *K* included Kaddafi, Kravis
(Henry), Kravitz (Lenny) . . .

In fact, *that* might actually prove to be the sticking
point—the fact that he frequented only the rich and famous, with a weakness for people whose family names
are those of countries, like the Greeces, the Yugoslavias,
Rania of Jordan, or Felipe of Spain.

He never stayed long in one place, and went only
where it was in his interest to go, so why then was he
coming to L'Agapanthe when the world was full of lumi-
naries who were only too eager to welcome him?

Had he heard about the view, the cuisine, his hosts,
or their guests? Was he expecting to find old friends
or make new ones here? In that case, he risked being
let down, because we were too low-key for him, and he
wasn't going to find anyone of transcendent interest
among my parents' Old Faithfuls. Unless he was coming

to check out Marie and me . . . which might also prove a disappointment, because lovely and rich though we might be (as Frédéric never tired of telling us), we surely weren't lovely and rich enough for Béno Grunwald, who deigned to look only at spectacular women.

So upon reflection, I'd decided that I should give up any idea of seduction where he was concerned. One, simply because I was no raving beauty, and two, such a competition depressed me from the get-go, leaving me without any desire to enter the lists. So I was counting on Marie—more gorgeous, feisty, and attracted to the glamour of her conquests—to meet the challenge and try her chances with him.

Instead of being insufferable, as I had feared, Béno turned out to be truly charming. Indeed, he became our hero as soon as he arrived, thanks to the grace and good humor with which he reacted to the incredible cock-up that greeted him at L'Agapanthe.

No doubt eager to downplay the bad impression produced by his arrival via helicopter, Béno countermanded the driver my mother had arranged for him in Cannes and drove up casually in a Mini Moke at 7:00 p.m. He had to ring several times at the front gate before gaining entrance to the property, because the servants were at dinner and the bell rarely managed to make itself heard on the first ring over their animated table talk. But to his surprise, greeted at last by Marcel, he was asked to park his car at the service entrance before being taken on a tour of the house!

Nevertheless, Béno complied, thinking that perhaps this was some peculiar family custom. He began to suspect a mix-up when Marcel, beginning with the garages, explained that we had originally had our own gas pump but now fueled our vehicles like everyone else at the local gas station, where we did not even maintain an account because the attendants there no longer knew what such a thing was and required payment via Carte Bleue with each transaction. Old Marcel's indignation seemed genuine, but Béno could not understand why this man— the chauffeur? the butler?—had decided to engage him in a conversation that was doubtless urbane but singularly unusual.

As his guide led him off toward the servants' quarters, Béno decided it was a case of mistaken identity, but he was enjoying the mishap too much to clear matters up just yet. Besides, before introducing himself as a house-guest, he was curious to discover for whom he'd been mistaken!

"There are ten bedrooms along this hall," Marcel informed him, "but they are all essentially alike and I think you will have a good idea of them all if I show you just one."

Was he supposed to be an architect? Were the Ettinguers contemplating some remodeling? But the other shoe didn't drop until Marcel added, "I'll show you the beaches; Madame advised me explicitly to take you along the service path so as not to attract the notice of the guests or the rest of the family, because not everyone in the house is happy with this idea, you understand." A real estate agent! The Ettinguers were putting their house on the market, and trying to do it discreetly.

What kind of a hornets' nest had he gotten himself into? Thinking quickly, Béno felt it was time to wrap up the joke before the butler said something more explicit he might later deeply regret. Since it was better to seem like a simpleton than to humiliate this man and upset the Ettinguers, Béno came up with something to save face all around.

"Ah, now I understand why you showed me the garages and servants' quarters! But I must tell you, I'm not the architect you were clearly expecting. My name is Béno Grunwald, and Monsieur and Madame Ettinguer have very kindly invited me here for the weekend."

When Marcel went pale at the thought of the gaffe he'd just committed, Béno gently reassured him.

"I'll tell Madame Ettinguer how much I envy her, having someone like you in her employ, trustworthy enough to handle things as demanding as important renovation projects. And allow me to thank you, because I must be the only guest ever invited to such a house tour!"

Meanwhile, I was having a mirror-image misadventure, since my sister was still suffering from jet lag and had assigned me to welcome Béno. Up in my bedroom, it was impossible for me to distinguish among the different bells ringing through the house, so I'd been waiting with a book in the loggia to be certain of hearing his car arrive.

The pantry was in fact the only place where one could hear all the sounds of L'Agapanthe, a kind of acoustic pilot's cabin allowing the staff to interpret such signals and respond accordingly. Hanging on the wall over the house telephone exchange was a bell board, an old-fashioned apparatus we used more frequently than the household phones that rang in jangling anarchy here and there and, for the most part, in vain.

In every bedroom were a pear-shaped wooden bell-pull by the bed and a push button near the bathtub, so that the occupant could summon help in case of need or ask for breakfast to be sent up. Each call bell had its distinctive tone; my mother's sonic signature, for example, comprised two *re* notes in succession, whereas a short *do* and a long *re* meant Flora's Room, where I was.

If there were the slightest doubt about two call bells with similar notes, the servants could consult an auxiliary panel on which the name of the room in question would light up.

The pantry was also equipped with the most modern technology, to wit: monitors for the security cameras around the house and grounds, in particular the one at the entrance gate, where the electronic chime had a hard time cutting through the summons of our good old bell rung at mealtime for the staff, a ringing that echoed easily all over the property.

I'd barely had time to watch a few lizards stroll out onto the veranda when Gérard appeared to announce Béno's arrival.

"Monsieur Grunwald has just driven up, Madame. In a Bentley Continental GT coupé." Probably taking my astonishment for curiosity, he added, "a model halfway between the Ferrari 612 Scaglietti and the Aston Martin DB9. I mention this simply for Madame's information."

I was just struggling to keep a straight face while thanking Gérard when a nattily dressed man strode into the loggia. Although I'd never met Béno, I had seen several photographs of him (half hidden behind his supermodel wife, to whom he was wisely ceding the spotlight), but I had the strange feeling that I'd never seen this dapper man before. Given the circumstances, I proceeded with caution.

Instead of introducing himself, he announced, "I'm so thrilled to find myself here. You cannot imagine how impressed I am!"

"Well, good, how nice," I replied, playing for time in the hope he would soon say something easier to interpret.

The man's age and corpulence seemed to match my image of Béno, but something still wasn't right. He was too *rich* looking, too flashy to be the real thing, I finally decided, remembering the lesson I'd learned the first time I'd seen Laszlo Schwartz. He and I had landed in Nice at the same time and my mother had asked me to bring him in the car she'd sent to pick us up at the airport. The only description she'd given me, however, was, "I'm sure you'll manage to find him somehow. He'll be accompanied by a graphic artist whom you'll drop off in Antibes on your way here." Which I had done, except that I had mistaken that artist for Laszlo, and all because he'd seemed the spit and image of a painter, with his longish hair and a shirt with a ruffle at the neck, whereas the real Laszlo, having nothing to prove in the creativity department, had been dressed like a banker in a three-piece pin-striped suit. And it wasn't until I saw the graphic artist leave the car in Antibes that I'd realized my mistake.

Well, this guy in the loggia was gleaming, impeccable. And his watch was too showy, his city shoes too polished for him to be Béno Grunwald, who was certainly going to show up in linen slacks and espadrilles with a plastic watch on his wrist.

"And what," I ventured to ask, "may I do for you?"

After explaining who he was and what real estate company he represented, the fellow recapitulated the phone conversations he'd had with my parents prior to this visit and finally assured me he was quite aware of the discretion he should show regarding the houseguests and other family members, who had not been informed of this appointment. Obviously taking me for the secretary, he asked me a touch nervously if we shouldn't leave this rather exposed veranda to begin viewing the house more "behind the scenes," as it were.

"You're absolutely right," I agreed, ushering him into the pantry, where I asked him to await a colleague who would conduct him around the premises.

Then I summoned up enough courage to barge in on the staff in their dining room, causing a pall of silence to fall around the table. When I interrupted the secretary at her meal, she was so taken aback to discover that I'd found out about the hush-hush visit from the realtor that she seemed relieved to take charge of it, in return for my silence about this unfortunate incident.

Hardly had I placed the real estate agent in her hands, however, than I had to dash to my room for a good cry, because at their first mention of habitable square footage and exceptional luxury property, I'd thought I was going to throw up.

I realized that I had not for an instant believed my parents would actually put L'Agapanthe up for sale. I'd found it perfectly understandable that they might feel the need to play around with the idea, but I'd never doubted that they'd reject it. And *that* had left me feeling carefree enough to launch into husband hunting—an undertaking made appealing doubtless because it had little actual connection to its supposed raison d'être.

Now that a real estate agent had turned up, however, my parents' idea had become a project they might just carry out. Even so, I still had trouble considering all its implications, as if the entire business were frankly unreal, like a sudden death. As if I could no longer feel what

I knew and know what I felt. Which was why I kept telling myself, "They did it, I don't believe it."

I was in shock, chain smoking as I wondered if I should awaken Marie to break the news to her, when I noticed that Félix had tried several times to reach me on my cell phone. The message he'd left said nothing about why he'd been so eager to reach me, which left me high and dry, especially since he did say specifically that I would have no way of getting in touch with him before the next day. My throat tightened with anxiety.

So I was understandably light-years away from Béno Grunwald when my mother rang me in my room.

"I'm told your guests are wandering around the house. Really, you might pay some attention to them!"

Béno, Mathias, and Lou were indeed drifting on their own in the front hall of a house left to its own devices while the secretary and butlers were busy confessing their blunders to my mother, but it didn't take me long to show the guests to their rooms, tell them when dinner would be served, and notice that Béno bore a slight resemblance to Steve McQueen. A dreamboat, this guy, I mused, and tried to stop worrying about my son, who kept interfering with my thoughts.

News of Béno's misadventure had made the rounds of the house before cocktail time, but that didn't stop him from stealing the limelight from Mathias and Lou Léva, who paled in comparison when he gave a hilarious account of the fiasco.

Béno may have been a dazzler, but he still set out to win over everyone in sight, as if he'd had a handicap or something to make up for. He began with my mother, whom he captivated in record time. To begin with, he had the good taste not to mention his helicopter trip, plus he brought her the ideal gift: a hundred matchbooks engraved with the name of L'Agapanthe. He then deployed in her direction a panoply of attentions between flirting and deference, by rising to his feet the moment she seemed about to move elsewhere in the room, by praising her voice ("You've never thought about a career in radio?"), and by flashing her a radiant smile whenever she spoke to him. Next he tackled my father, to whom he pledged allegiance with a few words over an apéritif: a modest and convincing spiel about his hedge fund, followed by a request for a five minute tête-à-tête sometime that weekend for a few words of advice—and that was that.

For his finale, Béno sent us all into stitches by making fun of his family's embarrassment over the original recipe for that photographic gelatin, which turned out to be made with bones from India. "Okay, fine, sometimes there were a few femurs," admitted his mother. And he didn't spare himself, allowing that his expensive habits were such that he'd really had no choice but to make a fortune. He'd studied up on his Cap d'Antibes history, too, and was abreast of all the latest juicy inside scoops.

Béno commanded so much attention that Mathias attracted very little in spite of his glaring blunders, which were legion. With striking linguistic ineptitude, he proudly claimed to have been the "investigator" of my encounter with Béno, and he introduced Lou to my parents as an actress "destinated" for a great future. With a flourish, he then produced his gift, a particularly garish scarf, which he presented to my mother who, although she had an absolute horror of designer logos, nevertheless went into ecstasies with professional aplomb over the entwined pink and blue initials that formed the sole decorative pattern of her gift.

Nothing, as it happened, was more vulgar in my parents' eyes than *luxury brands*, two words they considered a perfect oxymoron. The offspring of marketing and manufacturing, *brands*—Walmart, H&M, Monoprix, Zara—were used to put objects within the reach of everyone, whereas luxury implied the made-to-measure expertise of craftsmen skilled at rendering material goods worthy of interest. Which ruled out any desire to possess the latest accessory *de chez* Dior, Vuitton, or Prada, an ambition my parents found as pointlessly petit bourgeois as going into raptures over the purchase of an ice-cream maker or a fondue set.

When Lou Léva made her appearance at cocktail time, I felt a ripple of disappointment pass through every man present. The gentlemen had doubtless envisioned some sexy creature, bold as brass, and had hoped to find the actress dripping with sensuality à la Marilyn Monroe, a girl whose heart would belong to daddy. Instead of which, in walked a thin, pale young woman who rather disappointingly resembled an orchid: exotic, true, but somewhat off-putting. With short black hair, a hank of which fell across one side of her face (when it wasn't held back by a girlish barrette), she was pretty, but in an ethereal way. She might even have been touching, if she hadn't affected a fragile and sorrowful air she hoped might lend her some gravitas, for she thought that sadness was chic.

Lou seemed to have stopped short of achieving the desired level of soigné manners, however, for she approached my mother with an utterly unchic, "Come on, let's kiss-kiss-kiss."

A greeting devoid of elegance, from the appallingly informal "Come on" to the grotesque "kiss-kiss-kiss," not to mention the excessive familiarity toward my mother, whose customary welcome was a genteel nod or, at most, a handshake. As for triple cheek kisses, nothing was more provincial.

For everyone in France should know by now that Parisians give only two pecks on the cheeks, unlike the rest of the country, where regional differences gave rise to all sorts of variations with three or even four kisses, to which the average Parisian good-naturedly adapts by attempting to imitate an embrace of unknown rhythm and duration, like a beginning dancer following the lead of an experienced partner.

Then, when the butler announced that dinner was served, Lou exclaimed with a shriek, "I'm starving! I haven't had a bite since noon!"

This was another botch, since she should not have used the slangy "a bite" so baldly.

In short, Lou was not one of us, because she was unable to grasp the subtleties of our particular jargon, a fact that we initiates—who recognize one another, like freemasons of refinement—noticed immediately, without comment, but did not dismiss. And we had every right to hold it against her, strange though that might appear, for fewer and fewer people still understood what we were talking about when we talked about such things.

# *Dinner, Friday, July 21*

**FIFTEEN PERSONS**

| MEN | WOMEN |
|-----|-------|
| Edmond Ettinguer | Flokie Ettinguer |
| Frédéric Hottin | Laure Ettinguer |
| Odon Viel | Marie Ettinguer |
| Henri Démazure | Polyséna Démazure |
| Laszlo Schwartz | Gay Wallingford |
| Charles Ramsbotham | Georgina de Marien |
| Mathias Cavoye | Lou Léva |
| Béno Grunwald | |

**SEATING:**          **SEATING:**
**EDMOND'S TABLE**          **FLOKIE'S TABLE**

| | | | | |
|---|---|---|---|---|
| Charles | | Odon | | Henri |
| Lou | Polyséna | Gay | | Marie |
| Mathias | Frédéric | Laszlo | | Béno |
| Laure | Georgina | | Flokie | |
| Edmond | | | | |

## MENU

*Oeufs à la Chartres*
*Dorade Royale*
*Potato Purée*
*Salad and Cheeses*
*Green Apple and Cinnamon Ice Cream*

Seated next to Charles Ramsbotham, Lou quickly struck up a conversation.

"I believe I heard that you were English. How come you speak French so well?"

"My mother was Swiss and silent," intoned Charles in a sinister voice that did not discourage Lou in the least.

"Are you married?"

"Yes."

"Why didn't you bring your wife with you?"

"Because she is boring."

Charles's reply happened to fall loudly into one of those unexpected moments of silence that occur during conversations, and so, after a moment of astonishment, our table collapsed into hilarity in spite of my father's attempts to restore order. After all, none of us had seen

Lady Sally for years because, like an exotic fruit, she did not travel well, given that she cared only—in order of importance—for white wine, gardens, dogs, and horses.

Georgina came nimbly to the rescue. "Edmond, these oeufs à la Chartres are heavenly, perfectly poached and with *just* enough tarragon. I'm tempted to have more, but that depends on the main course. What will come next?"

"I was wondering the same thing," added Frédéric. "This sauce is to die for. What is it? Madeira? Veal stock?"

"Help me out, Marcel," said my father, turning toward the butler. "I've no idea what to tell them . . ."

"Veal stock, Monsieur. And the next course will be dorade, and for dessert, ice cream, I'll have to inquire about the flavor."

The episode with the real estate agent had so shaken me that I didn't feel up to helping my father with his duties as host, and I left the handling of table conversation completely to him. Art was often the chief topic of our dining discussions, and it cropped up all the sooner in this case since Mathias spoke right up in his capacity as a dealer, thus proving he was keeping his eye on the prize.

"Do you buy much?" he asked my father.

While I was guessing whether Mathias would have the nerve to try selling him something before dinner was over, Polyséna began deploring the contamination of the art market by money.

"Money as pollutant, or money as patronage, it's a classic debate," my father told her.

In his eyes, Polyséna's besetting and inconvenient sin was to be both intoxicated by her own learning and stuffed with opinions so conventional that she became the very caricature of a pedant, so my father couldn't help condescending to her slightly when he focused the argument on money as the sole common denominator of our fragmented societies, and the trendsetter henceforth of an artistic taste forged in the past by European courtly life. Vexed at being caught *en flagrant délit de cliché*, Polyséna played her trump card, making a daring rapprochement between a Renaissance painter and Damien Hirst in a bold attempt to leave my father speechless.

Frédéric, who had no particular desire to take part again in another discussion on art, turned quietly to Georgina. "So, it seems you live like a deluxe nomad . . ."

Georgina countered by observing that travel gave her the impression of making some progress. At first, lost in a new city and sometimes even unable to speak the language there, she would feel alone and disoriented, but since she thus had every reason to feel bad, this dispensed with the need to ask herself existential questions and brood over the latent depression that plagued her. Besides, the challenge of establishing herself in a strange place made her feel brave, adventurous, even heroic. And that persuaded her to accept the austerity of her life while awaiting the blossoming of her adjustment to her new home.

I was overhearing Georgina while listening to Polyséna as she developed her theory.

"It was largely for his contacts that Cosimo I de' Medici, Grand Duke of Tuscany, hired Vasari in 1555 to decorate the interior of the Palazzo Vecchio in Florence, which displayed works by Michelangelo, Leonardo, Pontormo, and Il Rosso. Why Vasari? Because, like Damien Hirst, he was professionally and socially ambitious. He lacked originality but displayed sound judgment formed by the cultivation of his peers and the demands of his patrons, as well as the genius of the zeitgeist, the mood of the times, which he caught like no one else."

Uncommitted, I couldn't manage to become engrossed in either of these conversations, so I decided to amuse myself by both following the story of Georgina's peregrinations *and* keeping an expression of rapt enchantment turned toward Vasari, thus learning how hard it was to listen to a conversation without watching the person speaking!

Georgina was describing to Frédéric the marvelous moment when a city became familiar to her, when the mystery of its language was resolved and expressions, turns of phrase, grammatical rules and correct intonations would appear in her mind like revelations: the "far or near corner" indispensable for getting around New York in a taxi, as were *lado montaña* and *lado mar* in Barcelona (the mountain side, the sea side), or *"Gung hay fat choy!"* so essential in China for the New Year.

In spite of my efforts to follow Georgina, however, staring intently at Polyséna led me to pay attention to what she was saying.

"I mean, Vasari was a marketing genius. He gathers a team to renovate the site with what we would now describe as installation art. Hirst does the same thing today with his 160 employees. And Vasari thus became the artist of the decision makers of his day . . ."

Getting a grip on myself, I then strained to hear Georgina's voice without taking my eyes off Polyséna.

"So now I gain confidence, I try out the local specialties, the foul-smelling durians of Asia, American cupcakes, crumpets, British Marmite, Spanish 5J ham. And soon the streets are filled not with strangers but with neighbors and acquaintances . . ."

The discussion of art now shifted without warning from a guarded tone of civil conversation and took on a more vehement turn that caught my attention.

"But it's sheer nonsense!" my father exclaimed abruptly. "The way those people who dabble shadily in contemporary art say, 'One must live with one's times, risk the adventure of discovering artists, open oneself to what is new, dare to leave the beaten paths,' when contemporary art is the rendezvous of every cliché in the book!"

"Meaning what?" replied Mathias, who was clearly responsible for this angry outburst.

"Well, retorted my father, it really takes some nerve to drape oneself in virtue, courage, and intellectual audacity—only to do exactly what the rest of the herd does! Because collecting today's art is in reality the surest way of broadcasting the fact that one has money. *And* it's a way to pose as a person of taste without having to possess the slightest artistic education, simply getting by on only the thinnest veneer of culture. Which is a lot easier than studying the history of art! In any case, there are very few people in the field—as in any field, by the way— who know what they're talking about. Which explains the supercilious and pedantic airs of the others who tackle the subject, meaning the ninety-five percent of people who are simply afraid of betraying their ignorance."

"You're not being fair," Mathias protested. "For these collectors, it's often a real commitment."

"A commitment!" sputtered my father, whom I'd never seen so agitated. "When the calendar of events in contemporary art, with its fairs, salons, openings, biennales, and atelier visits, provides them with a social whirl in an international playground to which they would never have access on their own!"

Unruffled, Georgina continued the tale of her adventures. ". . . And then one day, I have the feeling I've gained the advantage over the unknown, as if I'd managed to outrace the wind. I take the plunge, give a dinner party, because I feel familiar enough with the customs of the country to avoid making any gaffes. For example, in China I never dress in white, or invite four people to a bistro (since four's the number of death), and I don't open the gifts I'm offered in front of others, so as not to make any of my friends lose face."

"But then, explain to me," asked Frédéric, "why you don't stay in the city where you've done so much to feel at home!"

"Because as soon as I begin to feel comfortable, the anguish returns. So I give myself a few months until I move again. I'm well aware that I'm in headlong flight, but I console myself with the thought that the need to have some kind of project is part of human nature, and that by moving from city to city, I'm behaving no differently from a film director or a playwright. . . ."

". . . It's not that complicated, after all! Everyone loves contemporary art, they all find it fascinating!" my father exclaimed. "That's suspicious right there! Do you know of any other subject as popular? No, and here's why. Simply because all these idiots who want to pass for what they are not—discerning, cultivated, intellectually curious, wise, and (of course) original—are drawn to contemporary art, which makes for quite a crowd!"

"You can't say a thing like that!" Mathias interjected.

"I'm going to lose my temper!" said my father. "But hold on a minute, don't have me saying what I haven't said: I'm not claiming that *everyone* who takes an interest in today's art is an imbecile . . ."

Like a brief gust of wind, the conversation about art suddenly subsided, and Mathias kept a low profile for the rest of the dinner. Unlike Lou, who had only just realized who Frédéric was and the profit she might find in the company of this celebrated playwright. She seized the chance to sell herself with a certain aplomb and a flurry of mannerisms, confiding that she'd recently spent a week workshopping with Andréas Voutsinas at the Bouffes du Nord in Paris in the company of Nathalie Baye and Fanny Ardant, just to get back up to speed before a casting call for an important American director who'd bought the rights to the latest Dan Brown best seller.

"But who is Andréas Voutsinas?" Charles asked Frédéric.

"An Actors Studio guru who makes you return to the 'essentials' with improvs like 'Dig down into yourself to find your first cry at birth,'" Frédéric whispered back with a straight face, before sidling up to me as we left the table to say, "She is one tough cookie, that girl!"

*Friday, 11:00 p.m.*

I hadn't had time to see Marie before dinner, still less to tell her about the arrival of the real estate agent, and I was counting on talking with her privately after dinner. Had she finally forgotten her dog in Rio? She seemed so entranced by Béno, who was questioning her eagerly about her profession, that I left her alone and took up a post in a corner of the loggia where I hoped to pass unnoticed until bedtime.

"So tell me, how does it work when the Élysée Palace or the Quai d'Orsay needs your services?"

"Well, the first thing I do is find out if it's a 'little chair' job, in which case I always decline the offer."

"A little chair? What do you mean?"

"It means the interpreter sits slightly in the background between two guests at a banquet to translate their conversation. I've been at this too long to be treated casually by my employers. Luckily, I can afford to be choosy, because I'm rather in demand."

Never one to pass up an opportunity, our mother spoke right up. "Béno, you cannot imagine how sought after she is! For example, the president asks for her for all his official trips. It's no secret, after all, and if you look at the pictures of his travels, you'll see Marie constantly at his side. Naturally! She's both lovely *and* discreet, and she has mastered the art of wearing an evening gown!"

"Mummy, please stop the sales pitch, it's embarrassing! And besides, you know quite well that I can be dismissed at any moment, at the slightest ministerial reshuffling . . ."

Turning toward Béno, Marie added, "Anyway, long story short, I mostly do consecutive and whispered translation. Although I am sometimes called upon for simultaneous work, as at the G8 or Davos summits."

"I haven't a clue what you're talking about, but I'd love you to do some whispered work for me. That said, I wouldn't say no to some of the consecutive or simultaneous kind, either."

When Marie let out a throaty laugh, I sprang to attention, as it were: it was a signal that those two weren't making small talk anymore but playing with seduction.

"No, no—here, I'll explain it to you. Consecutive means that when a CEO is speaking at a podium, he will periodically pause while I translate what he has just said. I therefore take notes while he speaks, but I'm lucky, I have a good memory, and I can hold on for up to thirty minutes if he doesn't trot out too many numbers. For the whispered work, I sit next to my client, who doesn't speak the language being used by whoever's at the podium, and I whisper my translation in his or her ear. This whispered kind is often followed by the consecutive one, because usually the person to whom I'm translating sotto voce will then step back to the podium in turn."

"Then that's the kind I like the best, the one where you press up against me to whisper in my ear!"

Marie was done for. I could see that from the way she ran one hand through her hair in a sweeping theatrical gesture that always meant she was attracted to a man, a mannerism that had one day suddenly replaced her childhood habit of twisting a lock of hair around her index finger to give herself a silky mustache, which comforted her when she was sad and helped her to fall asleep.

And Marie had good reason to be done for. Béno wasn't one of those antiheros tossed at us by today's romantic comedies, those Don Juans in their fifties with their erectile troubles and their fears of growing old, the balding Jack Nicholsons, grumpy and swathed in bling, or the bitter, egotistical university professors whom women half their age—beautiful, sensitive, accomplished, independent, generous women—had endless trouble turning into acceptable suitors. In short, emotional cripples, with whom such women had to content themselves (if Hollywood was to be believed) after agonies of self-persuasion. Were men therefore in such bad shape that they had to be repaired like old cars before they could be used?

Well, Béno was not only handsome, young, ambitious, dazzling, and openly courting Marie, he also knew a few moves to set even the most sophisticated women dreaming. He began evoking the unusual places where he would have liked to take her: the pine-and-maple bowling alley (circa 1914) in the basement of the Frick mansion in New York; the Rocca di Papa slope near the pope's summer residence at the Castel Gandolfo, where through an optical illusion, gravity seems to reverse itself and objects slowly roll uphill; the underground railroad station at the Waldorf-Astoria where an armored car concealed the special vehicle that allowed President Roosevelt to be driven around without revealing that he was in a wheelchair.

Then, like an entertainer warming up a room, Béno gradually lightened the mood of our little gathering. And he had his work cut out for him, because he had not only to elude Henri Démazure's deadly questions about international finance but also to put the brakes on Odon, who was in full swing.

". . . The French have *always* detested free-trade policies! I mean, they're devoted fans of Louis XIV—and Napoleon, whose life makes for best sellers at bookstores, whereas Napoleon III and Louis Philippe don't earn diddly. Anyway, the French take themselves for the aristocrats they decapitated! They think they're living in a society of rights untrammeled by responsibilities, a leisure-oriented civilization of thirty-five-hour workweeks, the safety of which inspires them to travel around as boldly as if they were the titled adventurers of yore, off to discover Turkey! No, it's true! You'll notice

that it's always the French who set out on the most ab-
surdly daunting challenges, walking across Guyana or
the Frozen North, sailing around the Atlantic in a nut-
shell. Now in *that* department, they're the champs."

As Odon paused to take a deep breath, Béno turned
to Frédéric.

"I hear you've composed a song about the Giraults,
and you know, I'd be willing to grovel to hear it . . ."

"Aha!" exclaimed Frédéric who, like all good writers, preferred to play hard to get, to heighten the dramatic tension, even though he knew exactly what Béno
was up to—namely, having some fun, and Frédéric was
delighted to help him out.

"A song about what?" asked Lou.

"The Giraults, some friends of our parents who'll be
coming next weekend," explained Marie.

"So, well, the song?" insisted Béno.

Then, as Frédéric vacillated, Gay, Laszlo, Charles,
Marie, and I all shouted in concert, "The song! The
song!"

"You're very kind," said Frédéric, "but just because I
write songs in my idle moments doesn't mean I want to
sing them around a campfire in the evening."

"What if I sang first to put you at ease?" asked Béno,
who then launched immediately into a bit of opera,

arousing our enthusiasm with a nerve and dash that we
applauded vigorously, leaving Frédéric with no choice.

*Foie de veau with the Giraults*
*What could be more* rigolo
*Than to sip sublime porto*
*In the evening chez Girault?*
*Jean-Claude and his fine bon mots*
*Fresh from that day's* Figaro
*It was oh so comme il faut*
*This evening spent with the Giraults* . . .

Riotous applause, stamping, the works.

"Once more, all together now!" cried Béno, playing to perfection the choirmaster revving up the parish
faithful.

Once we had complied, and he had pulled off the feat
of uniting us all in that surprising moment of good fel-
lowship, we found ourselves happy but already unsure,
hoping for a new suggestion from our emcee, which he
in fact provided by proposing that we play some party
games, thus relieving my mother from the onerous duty
of entertaining us.

As I watched Béno emceeing, though, it occurred to
me that my parents must have gotten older without my

noticing, for it had been some time since L'Agapanthe had welcomed guests mischievous enough to think of playing games and even practical jokes, like short sheeting beds, and having a good time that way.

On the lawn sloping down toward the water, the automatic sprinkler came on, drawing our attention to the navigation lights of the boats and their reflections in the inky black sea.

Béno suggested a hidden words game, in which a guest would be sent out of the room while the rest of us chose a three-syllable word; we would then slip this word into all our answers when questioned by the designated word detective. Frédéric was asked to leave for a moment, and we chose the word "favorite." When he returned, Frédéric sat in the center of the circle we formed around him and reviewed the rules.

"So, if I understand correctly, I ask you questions about anything I want, you'll all slip the same word into your answers, and it's up to me to discover what the word is."

The scent of jasmine was heavenly. And there was a feeling of innocent excitement in the air, the kind that draws *ohs* and *ahs* from children when the lights dim for a movie or the curtain goes up onstage. Not all of us were ready with our lines, though, and we were nervous, the way we used to be in school when we had to solve a problem up at the blackboard. No one wanted to be chosen first by Frédéric, who took a wicked pleasure in dragging out the suspense by pointing at some of us as if hesitating whom to pick.

"Me, I'm not up to this, I don't think I really understand how to play," announced my father.

"Now don't be silly," my mother scolded him, fearing her husband's candor would make him look like an idiot.

Showing his sense of fair play, Frédéric pounced on Béno.

"Since you are the master of ceremonies, my dear Béno, I'll start with you. What did you hope to find by coming to this house?" he asked, flicking a sly look my way.

"What did I hope for?" replied Béno, looking over at Marie with an enigmatic smile. "Well, I hoped that my stories and sprightly conversation would meet with *favor; it* is always nice, isn't it, to be appreciated."

"Oh no," exclaimed Lou. "That's like what I was going to say. He stole my answer!"

"Would you just be quiet!" Mathias hissed at her.

"Ah! Mathias, thank you for catching my attention," said Frédéric archly. "Let's see, what would you say if I asked you what you do in your spare time?"

"I don't rightly know, actually, because you see, I don't really have any *favorite* pastime."

"Hey, don't work too hard!" sneered Lou.

Noticing that my mother was twitching with impatience to be questioned, Frédéric turned amiably to her.

"You're next, Flokie. Tell me, when do you plan to stop stuffing us like geese with your diabolical menus of goodies?"

"Oh, but you know, in my mother-in-law's day, her menus went on forever, people ate much more and never thought a thing about it, so in comparison, I'm actually doing you a *favor, it* seems!"

My mother had trotted out her reply so quickly and with such girlish glee that I was frankly astonished.

"Well, that's twice someone has said *favor*," mused Frédéric, "but not Mathias, so I'm not . . . wait a minute, he did say *favorite*, so that's it, right?"

Caught up in the game now, we sent Georgina out of the room and picked *Handi Wipe* as our next word, which inspired Béno to come up with, "When you've already got something *handy, why* putz around with anything else?" and Lou to trot out, "Because I'm always equipped with tissues before*hand, I wipe* my nose the second I've sneezed!" It was Charles who'd already gotten the biggest laugh, though, back when we'd settled on our chosen word.

"A *Handi Wipe*, what in heaven's name is that?"

"Really, Charles, you're such a snob!" exclaimed my mother.

"Ex*cuse* me?" he'd huffed. "*Just look who's talking!*"

The evening came to an end when Béno—still going strong—asked Flokie for permission to invite Cheryla to lunch the next day.

"But of course," replied my mother, completely under his spell, without really having any idea whom he meant.

For she pretended to adore music in general and the opera in particular, even though the only opinion I ever heard her utter on the subject was that Bach's cantata BWV 51 as sung by Suzanne Danco—famous for her silvery, aristocratic tone—was the most sublime thing in the world. As for my mother's knowledge of lighter fare, it stopped with Barbra Streisand and Liza Minnelli.

Trust my father to put his foot in his mouth. "Who's she? You all seem to recognize her name . . ."

Odon and Gay were equally at sea, however, and relieved that he'd asked.

"I can't believe this—she's only America's greatest star!" exclaimed Georgina, clearly a fan. "And what a stunning career: she's been reinventing herself for twenty years now, changing her look every few years and setting fashions, like the recent flurry of interest in the kabbalah, which Cheryla studies quite seriously. She's an icon who fills the Stade de France when she gives a concert in Paris, and that's the fifth-largest stadium in Europe! I mean, next to her, Céline Dion just fades away!"

"Céline who?" asked my father.

"Oh, don't make it worse," Marie said with a sigh.

After bowing practically in half when he said good night to his hostess, Béno left the room, leaving us orphaned and adrift in a space he had claimed for his own. We felt as if we had somehow been drained of all energy. Especially Marie, now apparently completely enthralled by Béno, who had singled her out for a particularly meaningful glance before vanishing like a magician.

So enthralled, in fact, that I'd given up all thought of having any private conversation with Marie and was about to go off to my room when she informed me that Béno was planning on joining her later in her bed!

"What should I do?" she asked.

"As if you were really wondering! Go on, what do you expect me to say?"

"You think it's a dumb idea?"

"Yes, but I get the impression that you're too far gone to listen to reason."

"You're right. Isn't he sublime, though?"

"Maybe even a little *too* much so."

"Perhaps, but so what? I'm going to go for it. May I remind you that all this was your idea?"

"Don't I know it! Well, here's your chance, take it, and have a wonderful night."

*Saturday, 9:30 a.m.*

Early the next morning I phoned Félix, who'd forgotten what it was he'd wanted to tell me the day before. Relieved to find him so cheerful, I asked him to describe what he was wearing so that I could picture him, all tanned since the last time I'd seen him, and then I closed my eyes, the better to hear his voice and the bright ring of his laughter.

After I hung up, I waited impatiently for Marie to come down to breakfast, only to see Frédéric and Mathias appear and discreetly get into a new tiff while pretending to review the day's obituaries in *Le Figaro*. Because there was truly no love lost between the old guard and the beau past his prime, a pair as incompatible as clashing colors. With his out-of-date vocabulary, Frédéric persisted in using words like "automobile," "bathing costume," "icebox," "big bum," and "lady." He always referred to Juan-les-Pins as a "village," for example, when that seaside resort no longer bore much resemblance to the shady town square, church steeple, neighborhood bakery, and café-tabac evoked by such a bucolic term.

"I'm not going into the village this morning because it's too full of idiots on Saturdays."

Mathias, on the other hand, who was on the wrong side of fifty but wore jeans, T-shirts, and running shoes, still clung to a more youthful way of speaking full of slang he punctuated with expressions such as "that's cool," "too much," and "it's the pits" to camouflage his lack of linguistic sophistication. Probably a good idea, insofar as he was largely unaware of his faux pas in that department.

Lou made her entrance wearing a black bustier and matching sarong, an ensemble meant to evoke an elegant evening gown. Amused, I asked Frédéric, "You think it has something to do with the arrival of Cheryla?"

"And how."

Enough time passed for Mathias and Lou to run a mysterious errand in Juan-les-Pins—to get the papers, they explained evasively, citing their desperate need to see that day's edition of the *Corriere della Sera*—and for me to watch the entire household parade by before Marie and Béno materialized as if by magic toward noon, five minutes before Cheryla arrived.

In spite of what Béno had announced the previous evening, the Fondation Maeght had clearly not been part of his morning's activities. Marie had dark circles under her eyes and, if I was not mistaken, telltale marks on her neck. Unwilling to risk betraying her secret idyll by publicly observing her too closely, I simply watched her reaction when I asked her, "Isn't Cheryla arriving here a little early? I thought she wasn't expected for lunch until two."

"True," replied Marie without even a glance in my direction, "but she was trapped in her room at the Eden-Roc, besieged by the paparazzi who've set up camp among the rocks, en masse. So Béno suggested she come for a swim here at the house."

Marie's attention was completely fixed on her lover, at whom she gazed unabashedly, leaving me to feel terribly sad and abandoned. Carried away by her playboy, Marie had forgotten me. Well, so what? There was nothing so unusual about that. And I, like her, had outgrown the need to demand my sister's exclusive love and devotion. So why then could I not rejoice in Marie's happiness, when only the day before I had advised her to find someone to love? Was it jealousy? Egotism? Was it my suspicion that Béno seemed only distractedly charmed by my sister? Unless I was simply finding it hard to accept that this whole "blind date" project, which I had launched with the expectation of reinforcing our sisterly complicity, might turn sour by eliminating me from subsequent developments, like that horrible game of musical chairs from my childhood, which always terrified me with the idea that I could be left high and dry.

A sudden surge of anguish and dismay left me breathless. That's all I need, I thought: to burst into tears in front of everyone.

I announced casually that I was going to fetch some cigarettes from my room.

Strolling around to get some air, I couldn't help noticing that the news of Cheryla's imminent appearance had spread through the house like wildfire. L'Agapanthe was in a real ferment, even to the point of luring out into the open its most discreet and rarely seen inhabitants: the cooks, who were having a smoke at the bottom of the service stairs, just around the corner from the front courtyard; the gardeners, suddenly intent on raking the gravel in front of the house; and the chambermaids, all gathered in the linen room overlooking the front door. Not to mention the new head butler, who was pacing up and down the salon with a preoccupied air, no doubt instructed by the rest of the personnel to bring back an exhaustive report on the star's arrival. As for Gay and Georgina, firm believers in mornings spent lounging lazily on the beach, they just happened to be in the loggia, which had drawn us all in for the occasion, like a watering hole in the desert.

Only Lou, immune to the light euphoria permeating the house, seemed out of sorts. Was she worried about the limelight our famous guest would surely steal from her, or was she simply refusing to appear impressed?

The crunching of Cheryla's car out on the courtyard gravel threw into stark relief such a revealing silence that my mother felt compelled to speak up.

"She must be very *me, myself, and I*, no?" she asked Béno.

Béno, always Béno! I groused to myself in sudden indignation. Was the entire house now in orbit exclusively around him, his guests, and his opinions?

"By that you mean . . . ?" I interjected, just to get my oar in.

"Well, an egotist!" replied my mother.

"As a matter of fact, no, she's a doll. She's shy and cultured, quite unlike her public image," observed Béno so soothingly that my mother was instantly reassured.

Judging from the clatter of her heels on the travertine floor of the vestibule, Cheryla was descending the stairs. And we all pretended not to watch her do it. She appeared at last: slim and yet incredibly muscular, she looked quite sophisticated with her red lips and platinum blond hair. There was a look of intelligence in her eyes, and her chocolate-colored linen dress of striking sobriety—clearly haute couture—corrected any first impression of vulgarity. In short, she was a bombshell. What presence! What charisma! None of which prevented us from keeping up appearances by affecting an air of placid indifference, as befitted our status, while we greeted her and suggested that she might like something to drink—an offer Cheryla unpretentiously declined, however, eager for the refreshment of her promised swim.

"She made quite a good impression on me," announced my mother as soon as Béno and Marie had escorted Cheryla off to the changing room down by the beach.

Firmly in Béno's corner, my mother was clearly determined not to be offended by anything his friends might do, no matter how outlandish their behavior. Not even by the fact that Cheryla had thanked her with grateful effusions way too extravagant for a simple luncheon invitation, gushing "You've saved my life!" as if we had just granted her political asylum. She'd overdone it. And in so doing behaved exactly like the star she was. For I'd had occasion to notice that although wannabes of all kinds display an arrogance they imagine to be indispensable to the prerogatives of a star, the real ones usually seek to be forgiven for their cumbersome notoriety by trying to behave in what they feel is the proper fashion—even though they haven't the slightest idea of what normal propriety is anymore.

And how could they? They're used to stepping out onstage before tens of thousands of people, some of whom go into raptures or faint dead away; they're obliged to sneak out of their homes in the trunk of a car and leave restaurants through the kitchen, and their slightest action is dissected by the press, which often buys information from certain members of their entourage incapable of saying no to easy money. In sum, there is nothing normal about their lives, so their ability to correctly determine how to behave in the most ordinary situations is often impaired, and they may find it hard—as it was for Cheryla with us—to behave naturally in all things, even when simplicity is all that's needed.

"I loved her orange Croc leather shoes," I said perversely.

My mother went on the defense: "Yes, a bit gaudy, I grant you, but very cheerful."

"Yes, very . . . like her yellow hair . . ."

Frédéric burst out laughing, followed by Gay and Laszlo, while Lou, eager to rejoin Cheryla, let us know it was time to set out for the beach by pulling Mathias along by the sleeve. My mother never went down in the morning, so none of us expected her to accompany us, but I knew she was dying to go along, even though she was too much a prisoner of her own snobbery to admit to herself that she was as curious as any ordinary mortal about the star in our midst. And I knew that she would allow herself to come only if she could follow us as if this were nothing at all unusual, without anyone drawing her attention to the fact that her presence among us was truly exceptional. What did I want to punish her for? Putting L'Agapanthe up for sale, or her flirtatious enthusiasm for Béno's attentions? Whatever it was, I turned toward her with a smile.

"Are you coming with us? I think it would be fun to get a closer look at her, don't you?"

My cruelty was so wrapped in solicitude that it was almost the perfect crime, but I was filled with shame when I saw that spark of childish excitement die out in my mother's eyes as she changed her mind with regret, turning away from us now to return to her room, where nothing and no one awaited her. Not even my father, who was going with us to the beach for a scuba-diving expedition he'd been looking forward to for a long time.

I tried to minimize the importance of what I'd done: at least this way, my mother would not have to witness the grand tour performed by Charles, who set out sputtering around the bay on the brand-new Jet Ski as soon as we reached the beach, thus driving into hiding all the fish my father was longing to see. Nor would she have to endure the fresh blunders of Mathias as he kept tripping up over his own native tongue.

"Everyone talks about mankind's role in global warming, totally forgetting the role of the sun, which they completely denigrate—"

"I think you mean 'deny,'" observed Frédéric, who positively enjoyed correcting him.

But humor and lightheartedness could not dispel the bitter taste of my unkind action, and I could not manage to take pleasure in anything. Not the foaming edge of the waves embracing the rocks of the bay. Not the sight of Cheryla, whose ravishing body strapped into a suit made entirely of laces had utterly dismayed Lou, who hadn't anticipated having to go up against a woman twenty years older than she was. Not the conversation, which, hampered at first by the silent presence of the singer, grew more fluid once Charles rejoined us. He was so cheery and naturally at ease that he immediately enlivened the atmosphere by talking about London, where he lived, as did Cheryla, Béno, and Georgina.

While I pretended to take part in the conversation, I was looking at the sea, hypnotized by the mosaic of its shifting shapes and nuances. I felt down at heart. With good reason: watching Béno coddle Cheryla instead of my sister wasn't going to buck up my morale. Especially since I had only to look away from that distressing spectacle for my mother to emerge from the dark corner of my thoughts, where she'd been biding her time, and reclaim the spotlight in wrenching scenes of her wandering the house like a soul in torment.

It was Lou who dispelled my morose mood. Passably entertaining when she was trying to vamp Frédéric and perhaps further her career, or when she tried to attract Cheryla's attention by joining Mathias in a show of indifference, or when she boldly moved in to pepper the singer with questions, she now grabbed my attention for real when she kicked up a serious fuss by claiming to have lost a golden comb from her hair. She managed to mobilize the guests—one after another and including Cheryla—to help her search for it over by the diving board, where she'd supposedly lost it.

That's when I spoke up, somewhat bemused. "Really, I know Lou is upset, but no matter how valuable this comb is, perhaps we needn't all be busily . . ."

It was too late, as I soon saw. Because Cheryla was standing right next to Lou at the foot of the diving board when a yellow boat hiding behind some rocks on the Saudi property next door suddenly shot out to the bottom of our ladder. It was loaded with apparently well-informed paparazzi, who snapped a barrage of photos from all angles, shouting "Cheryla, how 'bout a little smile!" and "Lou, get closer to Cheryla!"

The attack—because that's what it was—came so abruptly that I needed a moment to gather my wits, and even then, I really understood what had happened only when the boat scooted off toward the Russians' place, which it skirted respectfully. Béno was the only one with the presence of mind to shield Cheryla from the photo lenses still keeping up a steady fire, and he was the first as well to suspect Lou of having set up this ambush. The rest of us, inexperienced in the pitfalls of celebrity, began to catch on only when we noticed how furiously he glared at Lou while apologizing awkwardly to Cheryla, to whom he'd promised privacy in a house well known for its discretion.

That's when I remembered the errand Lou and Mathias had run earlier that morning in Juan-les-Pins, and their embarrassment about it. Silly me, I'd wondered if they were trying to score some drugs, but although I was bold enough to imagine that, I was too naïve to believe it, and finally concluded that having arrived empty-handed, like so many guests before them, they were now trying to find a nice little inexpensive gift for my mother, who clearly didn't want anything. I would never have imagined, however, that our two guests might be negotiating a deal with paparazzi to sell stolen faked pictures for cold cash—and the promise that Lou would be photographed next to the star, to give a boost to her sagging career.

Horribly embarrassed, Marie and I apologized as well to Cheryla, who was obviously used to this kind of misadventure and who could not have been more courteous as she kindly assured us that she knew we'd had nothing to do with the affair. Turning my back on the other guests gathered, still a little stunned, around the singer, I spoke to Lou and Mathias.

"I'm going back up to the house. Are you coming with me?"

Was it something in my voice, or their certainty that they would have to pay the price of their treachery? They followed me in silence to the top of the lawn and said not a word in protest when I ordered them to pack their bags and leave the premises before lunchtime.

I was proud of my reaction. Because in kicking out those two boors I now deeply regretted inviting, I felt as if I'd avenged all those who, like me, had been afflicted with an old-fashioned upbringing and were thus condemned to be preyed on by shameless spongers and other obnoxious leeches, who take cruel advantage of our innate inability to fight dirty the way they do, forcing us to put up with all sorts of aggravation.

I still remember a story my father told me once to prove it.

A man approaches a Rothschild sitting at a table in the restaurant L'Ami Louis.

"Forgive me for disturbing you, Monsieur le Baron, but I have a favor to ask of you."

"Yes?"

"Here's the thing: I'm dining with a man to whom I owe a considerable sum, of which I possess not one penny. Once he realizes this, he'll seek to get rid of me, but I'm sure that if he thought that we knew one another,

I would rise in his esteem and he would treat me gently instead of skinning me alive. So I would like to ask you to pretend to know me when I wave to you."

Too polite to send the importunate man packing, Rothschild agrees. And so, after finishing his meal without having seen the other man wave to him, he feels duty bound to speak to him while leaving the restaurant.

"How've you been since I last saw you?" he says affably.

"Listen, my fine fellow, just because you're a Rothschild doesn't mean you can take liberties. And this is not the first time I've had to ask you to stop bothering me!"


*Saturday, 1:30 p.m.*


So, having dealt with the problem of Lou and Mathias, I realized that I should inform my mother of the incident, for she certainly had a right to know the details of the adventure I'd robbed her of through sheer meanness. After taking a deep breath, I headed for the bathroom where she was doubtless getting ready for our usual luncheon party. I knocked on the door. No answer. Except for a kind of muffled, indeterminate noise I found rather scary, so I entered the bathroom, where I was stunned to find my mother crouching in a corner with her head down and blood on her fingers, trying to stop up her nose.

"Mummy!" I cried. "What happened? Did you hurt yourself?"

I grasped her chin firmly, as if to remonstrate with a child, and raised her head, which she had kept stubbornly down until that moment. It's only a nosebleed, I thought with relief, until I saw the lost look in her eyes brimming with tears.

"Mummy, please, get up, these things happen, we'll take care of this," I told her, in the midst of a silence that felt even more alarming than weeping would have been.

I put cotton compresses in her nostrils and ordered her to stretch out on the daybed that sat in the middle of the room.

"Lie down. I have news that will perk you right up."

To settle her nerves and make sure she remained calm, I told her all about the episode of the paparazzi but made no attempt to find out why she'd been crying and what had brought on the nosebleed. I kept her company like that until lunchtime when, after redoing her chignon, she returned to her role as mistress of the

house as if nothing had happened, welcoming Diane
von Furstenberg and Barry Diller, Christian Louboutin,
the landscape architect Louis Benech, Larry Gagosian,
Ty Warner, the contemporary art collector Patrizia Sandretto Re Rebaudengo, and other members of the "cafeteria club."

# *Luncheon, Saturday, July 22*

## MENU

*Salade Niçoise*

*Deviled Eggs*

*Chicken Croquettes*

*Tomato Rice*

*Skate Salad with Lemon and Capers*

*Endive Salad with Roquefort*

*Poached Peaches with a Coulis of Crushed
Raspberries*

*Salted Caramel Macarons*

The events on the beach and the news of Lou and Mathias
being sent packing made a great impression on our luncheon guests, who pressed us with questions, thoroughly
regretting having just missed out on an adventure right
up their alley. My mother gathered Barry Diller, Rebaudengo, and Ty Warner at her table, while Marie and
I had Béno, Frédéric, Charles, Gagosian, Louboutin,
and Cheryla at ours. Cheryla's embarrassment at having
been the cause of the morning's disturbances seemed to
have broken through her reserve, because she began to
tell us about her brother's role as her stage manager and
how her sister was in charge of her dressing room.

"How many pairs of shoes do you have, for example?"
I asked her.

"Seventeen hundred."

"Oh, my goodness, I see! And how many are Christian's?" I continued, gesturing toward Louboutin, who was just tackling a deviled egg.

"Come on, enough!" said Béno with theatrical impatience. "Leave Cheryla alone!"

"And what happens when you buy clothes, how does that work?" inquired Marie, but Béno cut right in.

"She only shops at boutiques after hours, of course, or there'd be a mob scene!"

Why was Béno intervening between us and Cheryla? Did he find our questions out of order, indiscreet? Or was he trying to remain her exclusive spokesman? Given the number of rich and famous people in his circle, she was really only one celebrity among others, but then I realized that perhaps wealth does not prevent stinginess, so it was entirely possible that Béno wanted to keep his glittering friends for himself.

". . . Do you know that her career sales over twenty-eight years add up to more than two hundred million albums? That she's just begun a tour that will take her to 85 countries for 101 concerts? Which means that if she catches a cold, eighty people in her management team hold their breath, because if she cancels a tour date, millions of euros go up in smoke."

And there we were, exclaiming in the usual astonishment expressed at such revelations. I still found it
strange, though, that Béno kept insisting on talking up
Cheryla instead of letting her chat with her table companions the way she seemed to want to do. Was I the only
one who thought so? There was no point in turning to
Marie, who was gazing at Béno like a moonstruck calf.

". . . Her jet, the equivalent of a Gulfstream V, is a
Global Express, made by Bombadier. Jay, her pilot, is a
Vietnam veteran, a brilliant guy and supernice. . . . You
know, she's just back from South Africa where—she's too
modest to say so—she donated the profits from her first
concert to Nelson Mandela for his foundation. And she
visited two orphanages for children with AIDS and dis-
tributed food to the needy in Soweto. . . ."

But Frédéric had had enough and pleaded, "Cheryla,
have pity—hire him as your press agent, enough already!
Or we're going to feel obliged to kiss your feet and won't
dare speak a single word to you anymore."

And thank goodness for Frédéric's outburst, because
it shut Béno up and allowed Cheryla to get Charles talking about his gorillas.

"He's racking up points, ol' Goat's Butt," murmured
Frédéric to me.

"'Goat's Butt'? Oh, yes, Ramsbotham, silly me!"

Our respite didn't last long, however, because my sister's lover suddenly asked Larry Gagosian, "Do you BI?"

"BI?" I repeated, utterly at sea.

"Sure! *Better invitation*, you've never heard that? It's when you accept an invitation but intend to beg off if something more glamorous or fun comes up."

Seeing that Gagosian hadn't taken his bait, Béno smoothly went on, "When you think about it, actually, there are only two expensive tastes: philanthropy and modern art . . ."

Like many eminent specialists who'd rather avoid talking about what they know best once they feel relaxed, Gagosian didn't pick up the allusion about contemporary art. Therefore, Béno had no other choice than to come up with something else.

"You know what folks say about people like your next-door neighbors? That they know so little about how to live that they're *not* rich, just poor people with a lot of money. *And that's exactly my point!*"

The laughter that greeted this last sally must have persuaded Béno that he had us in the palm of his hand. I saw him finally relax, like a migraine sufferer calmed by an analgesic. And I felt relieved as well, so oppressive was the tension I sensed behind his need to seduce every audience. And I must not have been the only one to feel that way, because taking advantage of this respite, we had a lively discussion right through to the coffee about satellite phones, a subject on which Charles was in his element. His comparative study of the different models currently on the market allowed Cheryla to measure the failings of her own phone, which presented the inconvenience of functioning only outdoors and unsheltered, meaning in full sunlight. In short, lunch was winding down. I slipped away just as Marie was assuring Cheryla that she would always be welcome at our house (including that very evening for dinner, if she would like to come) while at the same time casting a glance at Béno that left no doubt about the kind of nap she intended to take with him.

I thought about Béno while resting in my room. Why did I have such a feeling of having lost my sister forever? This certainly wasn't the first time that I'd been witness to one of her affairs. And far from languishing, our sisterly bond had always formed my only real family, a family my son had joined, unlike my husband and the lovers Marie and I had had, who'd never really belonged. I had to admit that until then, men could count themselves lucky if they landed a small speaking role instead of simply a walk-on part. Béno, however, had grabbed himself a starring role from the first moment, throwing me off balance. Was this a sign that Marie and I had outgrown the age when we could settle for the family founded by our parents?

Yet the idea of loosening my bond with Marie made me feel ill. What if this affair were to last? I tried to peer into the uncertain future that seemed to lie ahead. What would the house be like under their care? Béno was a successful and ambitious man; he would doubtless modernize the place and give it a tastefully fashionable veneer. I had the feeling the beach, like an open-air nightclub, would acquire sleek furniture, canopied beds, and fresh style remixes of old standards selected by a sound designer for a lounge ambience. *How awful!* I thought, solely for the pleasure of falling back on a snobbism as comforting as a lighthouse in the fog. Crisscrossed by golf carts, as in the TV series *The Prisoner*, the property would also have its heliport, its home movie theater, and a workout center with a treadmill, a Power Plate, gleaming dumbbells, and mirrors everywhere. Oof, we'd be a long way from my grandparents' gymnastics room with its abandoned trapeze, rings, vaulting horse, and grand piano.

This detour through our childhood brought me back to Marie. I imagined her, with Béno, as the proprietors of L'Agapanthe, where they would receive their friends, a crowd of handsome, rich, and famous stuffed shirts, whereas I would be only . . . their guest. An idea that would have made me shudder—if I hadn't pulled myself up short. Really, I just didn't know what I wanted! Béno was an ideal suitor, if we meant to keep the house. Thanks to him, L'Agapanthe would retain all its luster. In which case, he might well transform it into a show-business showcase, if he felt like it. Especially since, if I'd read him correctly, he would make it over into a highlight of the Cannes Film Festival, a venue touted on the Promenade de la Croisette like a password among the happy few invited to parties worthy of Fitzgerald's *Gatsby*. What more could I ask?

# The shortcut

*August 3, 1990*

*I'm thirteen. Instead of the grown-ups' usual route to the beach, I prefer the one that leads me from the heart of the house to the path running past the lawn down to the sea. I am as proud of this shortcut as if it were my own creation. It begins, like the universe of a fairy tale, in a ground-floor junk room next to the guest powder room, where the elevator, behind a forgotten folding screen, gives off a strange and delightful scent of forest undergrowth. The basement, I've been told, was laid out by some Russians before the Great War and was meant to house a casino. A wide corridor leads down with a series of landings to the foundations of the house, giving onto areas planned as game rooms along the way. Papered with bamboo matting and feebly lit by jaunty little sconces, the corridor aspires to the* rakish atmosphere of a nightclub from the Roaring Twenties, but the game rooms, frozen in midcompletion by the Russian Revolution and the First World War, now seem like dungeons with their rough stone walls, gravel floors, and those iron doors with their little barred windows.

Is it the cool air of the corridor, the semi-obscurity, the insouciant casino atmosphere of going on a spree? I breathe deeply, inhaling the ambience of adult pleasures, dreaming of leaving boredom behind. But the shadows of the cells now storing a jumble of lawn mowers and old armchairs soon encroach on the subdued light in the corridor. Suddenly, I think I hear rats. I freak out . . . so I avoid looking too closely around me as I move through this underground passage that both scares and excites me. And I settle for regretting the peace I might enjoy if only I had the courage to stay there, because this basement would make an ideal hiding place. One just like the tiny space concealed behind the fake books in the library where a man hid during the Second World War when some Italian officers decided to set up their headquarters in the house—a disaster narrowly avoided by a stroke of genius from the caretaker at the time, who took advantage of the pocket windows, an American innovation as yet unknown in Europe, by sliding them back into the walls, thus persuading the Italians (in mid-December) that the unfinished house had no windows yet.

*Simply emerging into the daylight on the path along the lawn persuades me that I have just been through a great adventure and triumphed over hostile underground terrain. And now I'm ready to spy on my parents' guests behind the sparse hedge that separates me from the lawn, the way a curtain walls off the wings from a stage.*

A mosquito roused me from my torpor; impossible to
fall back asleep. In any case, it was teatime. Leaving my
room, I noticed my mother in the entrance hall, consulting with Roland, the chauffeur. Wishing neither to
interrupt nor disturb her, I slowed my approach, intending to wait so that we could go down to the loggia
together. She had her back to me, and half hidden by the
open front door, Roland couldn't see me either. I would
not have tried to overhear them, though, if they hadn't
been whispering.

"My dear Roland, I find I'm running a little low . . ."

"Very good, Madam. Shall I proceed as usual?"

"Yes."

At first their remarks seemed as harmless as they
were incomprehensible, and I would have thought no

more of the whole business if I hadn't seen my mother quickly press some bills into the chauffeur's hand. Something was wrong here. Her gesture was too practiced for someone who insisted that all tips should be handed to the servants in envelopes. I retreated and huddled in dismay behind a pillar while my mother rejoined her guests. Then, knowing that my father would be swimming with Georgina at that hour, I shut myself inside the master bedroom to review my evidence: the overfamiliar "My dear Roland," the mysterious "running a little low," the chauffeur's "as usual," not to mention the money . . .

What hidden vice could she have? It wasn't sexual, obviously, since there was nothing louche between my mother and her chauffeur. Alcohol? There were rivers of it in the house, she wouldn't need Roland to get her some. So I came face-to-face with the conclusion I'd already reached. Because although I'd been wrong to think of it that very morning to explain why Lou and Mathias had dashed into Juan-les-Pins, it fit too well with my mother's nosebleed before lunch. No doubt about it: my mother was a drug addict.

This was so appalling, so hard to accept, that I tried to imagine her with a dealer in some shady neighborhood— which was silly, since Roland was her go-between. I was definitely mired in clichéd scenarios about the problem: drugs were no longer the privileged playthings of rock stars, flower children, or fashionable hipsters. Hadn't my grandmother once told me that her women friends from before the war used to "arrange things" with hotel concierges? And I'd been floored when she'd made such remarks as, "No one would ever *think* of leaving for Saint-Moritz without her morphine!" And of course, there'd been Baudelaire, and later on Malraux and the others . . . Yes, but my *mother*! Of course, she did already take Temesta for her nerves, Rohypnol to help her sleep, as well as the sedative Mogadon. But to go from that to cocaine . . .

Why hadn't I noticed? Naturally, since she didn't work, no one expected her to be superefficient or even a paragon of lucidity, which made the state she was in all the more difficult to discern. But that was no excuse. The proof? I'd paid no attention to her increasingly frequent bouts of ill humor. How could I have been so uncaring! And yet, why should I have worried? Wealthy, still beautiful, loved by my father, my mother had an easy life. As if that were enough to give her a sense of fulfillment! Especially if she felt almost useless, good for nothing but making conversation and worrying about who sat where at meals, I thought, rummaging through her vanity table drawer . . . where I soon found a crystal snuffbox with a bit of caked white powder at the bottom. *I'm running a little low . . .*

"Oh, God," I moaned.

What should I do? I had no idea, none, and was too devastated to think. I couldn't help recalling a misadventure I'd had a few years earlier, however: eager young psychoanalyst that I was, I'd confronted the cleaning lady I'd recently hired about her alcoholism, which I had diagnosed from the falling level of my liquor bottles. I'd been soft-spoken, supportive. And she'd been so touched that to my surprise she had given up drinking. So I was rather pleased with the help I'd given her—until she decompensated into schizophrenia, which until then had been anesthetized by alcohol. And that had taught me once and for all about the limits of therapeutic discourse.

My mother must have found a form of equilibrium between tranquilizers and cocaine. And aside from the fright she'd had over her nosebleed, there was no indication that she wanted to stop. Why not simply give her the name of a psychiatrist? Because I did *not* see myself having a word with her about the situation. All the more so in that she was probably less than eager to talk things over with me or any other member of the family. And then I wondered: was her addiction an open secret, a problem I was the last to discover? For in spite of my illusions of shrewdness in psychological matters, I was doubtless, like all children, in a particularly poor position to see my parents with clarity and understanding. Did my father know what was going on? I had to sound him out as soon as possible.

*Saturday, 7:00 p.m.*

I found my mother having tea in the loggia with Laszlo, Gay, Frédéric, and the Démazures. In good spirits? Overexcited? I tried to look at her in a normal way in spite of my suspicions, which I sensed would be difficult to shrug off.

"But . . . where is Odon?" I exclaimed, with a gaiety intended to mask my concern. "If he were here, the Little Band would be at full strength!"

"Not back from Vallauris yet. Listen, I've entrusted Charles with a mission. He was at such loose ends . . . and as it would never occur to him to open a book, I had to keep him occupied."

"You know your mother," added Laszlo. "A heart of gold. She had the bright idea of asking Charles to do her the favor of organizing the wine cellar. So don't be surprised if you see him emerge in triumph from the lower depths, because he surfaces from time to time to give us bulletins on his progress."

"He's phenomenal!" confirmed Frédéric. "Speaking of which, after the wine cellar, you ought to sic him on the library so he can arrange all the books in alphabetical order."

I suddenly felt completely alone. Which was only natural, since I hadn't talked to Marie all weekend, and given that nothing was likely to change on that front until Béno's departure, I decided to go down to the beach in hopes of running into my father.

"Oh! Just the person I wanted to speak to," he said, coming out of the water. "Georgina went on up already. You didn't see her? She's not well, and I'm worried about her, she seemed both wild and depressed. In fact, she scared me a little."

"Yes, because you didn't know what to do, but maybe she is just sad and that proves she's alive."

"You want to know something? It's lucky your mother isn't that way!"

"You think so? I'm not sure about that . . ."

"No, believe me, beneath that fragile exterior, she's a rock! In fact, I've always preferred women like Flokie to those who seem like tough gals when they're really spun glass, like Georgina. Because me, I need someone solid to lean on."

# Dinner, Saturday, July 22

## THIRTEEN PERSONS

| MEN | WOMEN |
|---|---|
| Edmond Ettinguer | Flokie Ettinguer |
| Frédéric Hottin | Laure Ettinguer |
| Odon Viel | Marie Ettinguer |
| Henri Démazure | Polyséna Démazure |
| Laszlo Schwartz | Gay Wallingford |
| Charles Ramsbotham | Georgina de Marien |
| Béno Grunwald | |

## SEATING: EDMOND'S TABLE

Laure  Béno

Frédéric  Henri

Marie  Gay

Edmond

## SEATING: FLOKIE'S TABLE

Laszlo

Polyséna  Georgina

Charles  Odon

Flokie

## MENU

*Asparagus Vinaigrette*
*Poularde Mancini*
*Salad and Cheeses*
*Apple Soufflé*

Entering the summer dining room, I saw that my mother had seated everyone very nicely: she had kept Odon and Laszlo to help her with Charles (whom she hadn't brought herself to seat on her right), while sending Frédéric and me to liven things up at my father's table, where we'd been placed the previous evening.

Slipping a knife under his plate to tilt it and so pool the vinaigrette from the asparagus, Frédéric began teasing Béno.

"You're a financier, a collector, a jet-setter, a man of property, and who knows what all else. And I heartily approve, as I myself am a night owl, a playwright, and a pillar of this house. But some would say that you're spreading yourself too thin. Don't you ever, as I do, worry that you're doing everything the wrong way?"

"Oh, you're right, I probably do everything wrong. What do I do well? Let's see . . . Oh, yes: I sleep well!"

Yes, Béno certainly had the gift of charm. But he was still driven to vamp his audience, because he now undertook to explain to us his family's crazy lexicon based on favorite anecdotes, such as the "Your Uncle Syndrome."

"It all started with the fact that my great-uncle was as puffed up as a marshmallow with his own importance. He was a bureaucrat of the utmost obscurity, yet he thought himself so closely engaged with momentous events that he felt he was on an almost equal footing with the great men of his day. Convinced of this herself, his wife used to tell us, for example, in accents of deep concern, that 'your uncle is angry with de Gaulle' whenever the president (whom my uncle had never met) had taken a decision that displeased him. As if de Gaulle always took my uncle's opinions into account when he decided on a course of action, and chose to ignore his opinion only to exasperate him. Ever since, whenever someone takes himself for God's gift to creation and puts on airs, we say he's *your uncle*."

"Well," observed Henri Démazure, "then it seems certain French writers suffer from the same syndrome, because I know some people who write biographies of great men simply to compare themselves with them."

"Just whom did you have in mind?" inquired Gay.

But my father, fearing a tedious detour into Left Bank gossip, made a preemptive strike: "Have you got any more like that, other family expressions?"

"Oh, yes, for example, *the little wild strawberries*."

"The what?"

"It's a term we invented for people who imagine that there's nothing like a dollop of criticism to properly season a compliment. For example, saying 'Your dress is ravishing,' then adding, to be more convincing, 'I can't say the same for your coat.' It seems idiotic, but you wouldn't believe how many people do that."

"But what does that have to do with wild strawberries?"

"Nothing. The name comes solely from the time a guest at my grandparents' house in the country, wishing to be gracious about the strawberries served for desert— a luxury at the time—along with some wild strawberries picked by the children, had exclaimed, 'These strawberries are delicious! Not like the little wild strawberries, which are awful!'"

"Wonderful!" my father said, laughing. "Sorry, dear," he told me, "but after all, it is a more poetic way of describing people than the psychologizing jargon of today!"

"Yes, I see what you mean," observed Gay. "It's the triumph of Proust's maladroit Aunt Léonie over Flaubert's cataloging obsessives, Bouvard and Pécuchet!"

"Precisely!"

Seeing a chance to take over the conversation with a nod to me, Henri Démazure began to defend my profession.

"Psychiatrists are fascinating, though! I'm reading a book now by one of them, Patrick Lemoine, in praise of . . . boredom! In fact it's called *Being Bored, How Wonderful*, published in 2007 by Éditions Colin . . ."

"Oh, really!" said Gay, scratching her dog's ears under the table.

"Anyway, Lemoine talks about two sorts: pathological boredom, a symptom of psychiatric illness, and the normal kind, which he considers indispensible for the construction of the self."

After a swallow of Gruaud Larose, Henri pressed on: "He claims that when children are bored, they develop their imaginations and become more independent in a natural way, and that without boredom, their healthy individuality and creativity would be compromised. But these days, parents are growing less and less tolerant of boredom in their children's lives. Just consider how they drag them from the soccer field to the swimming pool or a tutoring session . . ."

That was when I noticed that Marie had hardly touched her poularde Mancini, even though it was her favorite dish. Had love taken away her appetite? And my father was growing impatient because Henri, carried away by his thoughts, hadn't realized that the butler was waiting stoically to his left, presenting him with a dish as hot as it was heavy.

"... and he says it's rooted in the proscription against masturbation."

"Fancy that!" exclaimed my father, whose relief at seeing Henri serve himself at last probably sounded like sincere interest in the conversation. Henri, in any case, was warming to his theme.

"Aristotle affirms that melancholy is the affliction of the superior man. And to be melancholy, in those days, meant being inactive, meditative, sad, humble, and therefore of superior intelligence, since hyperactive people were rarely geniuses."

Failing to pick up my father's desperate glances around the table in a mute appeal for help, Henri charged ahead.

"Moreover, when you take a look at history, boredom has always been on the winning side, from tedious old Louis XI, called the Prudent, who triumphed over the warrior Charles the Bold, to the Catholic faith, which had a troubled relationship to boredom and idleness, so conducive to impure thoughts and actions—although this didn't prevent the church from inventing the convent, a whole universe of boredom!"

Gay was probably thinking up a way to stop Henri in midflight as she sat delicately cutting her mimolette and Gouda with cumin into tiny cubes, as she did every evening, before popping them in her mouth . . .

"Of course, everything changed when the Anglo-Saxon—and therefore Protestant—model took over the world, and the notion of leisure (etymologically, that means *licit*, in other words, permitted) replaced that of vacation (derived from the concept of vacancy) . . ."

. . . because with a definite wink at my father, she abruptly broke in: "Speaking of vacations, my dear Henri, have you any plans for the rest of the summer?"

Turning back to Marie, I saw that she seemed strained, so closely was she watching Béno in hopes of catching a glimmer of interest in his eyes, but like everyone else, he was probably more captivated by the soufflé, and the way the piping-hot apples, like lava from a volcano, overflowed from the core of ice cream perfumed with flecks of vanilla that crunched between our teeth.

"I adore desserts that combine hot and cold things, don't you?" asked Marie.

"Yes, absolutely," agreed Frédéric. "Let's see, what others are there? Ah! There's the Norwegian omelet, *crêpes* royale . . ."

Then I understood that something clearly wasn't right. Because Béno, who should have smiled at Marie when she spoke up, had kept his nose in his dessert, as if avoiding meeting her eyes. I didn't have time to get any further with this, however, because we were all leaving the table.

I was going over to Marie to make her tell me what was going on when Béno stepped in front of our mother.

"My dear Flokie, may I ask you to excuse me. I promised Cheryla to be her escort for the rest of the evening, so I will discreetly slip away," he announced, then turned on his heels and left without even looking at my sister, who was visibly dumbfounded.

"Shall I be 'mother' and pour the tea?" asked Odon, sensing a tension in the air that he didn't fully grasp and pleased to be acquitting himself so easily of the playful duty he knew he must perform in this house, which demanded from its guests a lightness of being often at odds with the seriousness associated with their professional success.

In short, busy with their herbal tea ceremony, my parents and their guests picked up the conversation as if nothing had happened, never noticing my sister's distress. "Let's go for a walk!" I said brightly, leading her off to the library, where she instantly dissolved in tears.

"My poor lamb!" I murmured, taking her in my arms.

"But the way he behaved—what can it mean?" she gasped between sobs.

"But what do *you* mean? You didn't have an argument, some sort of fight? He hasn't said anything to give you a clue why he's acting like this?"

"No, nothing! He made love to me the whole afternoon with all sorts of sweet talk and promises. . . . It was only at cocktails that he began to seem distant. Then at the table, that was the giveaway, when he turned really weird. But to go from that to . . . to . . . It's insane!"

"Nothing happened? No phone calls, no nothing?"

"Well, yes, Cheryla called him just before dinner, and he went off to talk to her. But what are you telling me? That he dropped me for her? All it took was one phone call to stand me up like that?"

"I'm afraid so."

"But that's not possible! If you knew what things he said to me . . . he was so touching . . . Oh, he was just *using* me!"

"No, I'm certain he wasn't lying to you, I bet he believed everything he said when he was with you. That's even why you believed him, because he was sincere."

"But then . . ."

"He's a seducer, and like all seducers, he's always sincere in sequence. He says different things to different people at different moments."

"But *why*?"

"Because he loves only the *conquest*. And once he's seduced a woman, he needs to move on to the next one."

"But that's vile!"

"Yes, but it has nothing to do with you! So, since that's the way things stand, you're a whole lot better off without him, because it's his vocation to make women unhappy."

"Even those more beautiful and glamorous than I am?"

"Yes, even those, since that's just simply how he functions. And I'm telling you, he'll do the same thing to Cheryla."

"You think so?" Marie murmured hopefully.

"I'm sure of it. So, that consoles you, the idea that she'll go through the same hell as you?"

"Oh, well, yes! Listen, can I sleep in your room tonight? I don't want to be in mine in case he might try to visit me, because I wouldn't be able to resist him. And I don't want to be there in case he *doesn't* try, either, because that would make me just as miserable. You understand?"

Everyone had gone to bed by the time we left the library, so after taking off our shoes so the heels wouldn't clatter across the travertine hall floor, we turned out all the lights, one after the other.

It had been a long while since Marie and I had shared a bedroom, and I couldn't help enjoying, in spite of her sorrow, how we talked in the dark the way we had as children. And now we were doing it again, except that it was our inventory of all possible ways to get even with Béno that kept us awake until the wee hours of that night.

*Sunday, 9:30 a.m.*

But we never got the chance to test our findings the next day, because Béno cut and ran at breakfast.

"My dear Flokie, I've come to thank you and to take my leave because Cheryla has very kindly offered to drop me off in London this morning. And so, unfortunately, I cannot stay for breakfast. Please believe me, I'm truly sorry, but you know how it is, hitchhiking by plane . . ."

Then, without even a semblance of bidding good-bye to Marie in particular, he merely said, "Laure, Marie, thanks for this weekend, and I hope we'll see one another one of these days . . . in London or Paris, who knows?"

His behavior was so monstrous that Marie simply froze, appalled into numbness. But I knew it wouldn't last, that her unhappiness of the day before would flood through her afresh, so I tried to get her off on her own.

"Hey, come on, let's take our usual swim in the bay—we haven't done that yet this year!"

"And if you're lucky, girls," piped up our father, "you'll bump into the whale calf that's wandering lost along the coast. I just read about it in *Nice-Matin*."

"Wait—I'd be scared stiff to wind up nose to nose with a whale!" exclaimed Marie. "Why are you trying to drag me into a major sporting exploit *right at this moment*?"

"Ah . . . because it's one of our rituals, like doing the fridge or swimming at midnight," I stammered, before whispering, "At least we'd be off on our own, and it would help clear your mind, which would be no small thing, given the circumstances. Plus I've got some serious developments to tell you about . . ."

"Oh, well, why didn't you say so in the first place! See you later, everyone! We're off for a swim!" she caroled in a jolly voice I didn't trust at all.

And I was right, because that burst of euphoric indifference sank into a wave of sadness that swept over her just as we began our swim. In an effort to distract her,

I pointed out some flying fish in front of us and started babbling off the top of my head.

"You remember the Polish exhibitionist who used to swim over from the Hôtel du Cap to enjoy being admired half naked in the loggia among the guests? It's been years since I've seen her. I wonder whatever happened to her—we'll have to ask Mummy and Papa . . ."

Then I just kept quiet and let her cry. Anguish and sorrow, I know them. And although I'm no genius at it, all day long I calibrate my silence to give free rein to my patients' emotions, or stanch the pain of some torment with a word—attentions much easier to manage in my office than swimming in the sea with my dear sister! So I had to keep reminding myself that Marie needed to feel her grief in order to rise above it. And as I swam, I saw again, as I did every year, how the bay that seemed quite modest from our beach was so vast that we would need a good hour and a half to swim along its shore.

Judging my moment, I asked Marie, "Don't you find it hard to swim and cry at the same time?"

"Yes, it's exhausting, and I'm fed up!" she confessed ruefully, and we both slowed down. Luckily, the water was calm, as it often was in the morning, and since we were both strong swimmers, we adjusted to a more leisurely stroke so we could talk without running out of breath.

"So, are you ready for my update? You'll see, it's some heavy stuff."

"Fine, I'm ready for a change of pace."

I began at the beginning: the mix-ups over the visit of the real estate agent, my distress at the possible sale of the house, then my panic at the idea that she and Béno might become the owners of a jet-set L'Agapanthe, and finally, our mother's addiction to cocaine.

"Oh, that I already knew—"

"You're not serious!"

"Yes, really; I caught her one day sticking it up her nose. I never told you?"

"Are you kidding? Of course not—I would never have forgotten that!"

"That's strange, I could have sworn I told you. I must have thought about it so many times that I wound up thinking that I had."

"Never mind, but tell me what happened."

"Well that's just it, nothing, that's what was so bewildering about the whole thing. All she said to me was, 'So? It's simply the best way to stay thin,' and then she shrugged: 'What do you want me to say?'"

"I don't believe it!"

"It's the truth! And then she started talking about something else as if it were no big deal. So if you're worried about her possible inner suffering, I think you're on the wrong track, because she takes that stuff as if it were cod liver oil."

"But what about Papa, who I thought was so clueless when he told me she was as solid as a rock?"

"But he's right! She's a bulldozer!"

"So you're not going to do anything?"

"No! I mean, what would you want to do? Just forget about it!"

"But it's not good for her; she's having nosebleeds!"

"And so what? When that starts bothering her, she'll go to a doctor and she'll stop. Just drop it, really!"

"I can't get my head around this . . . I'm speechless!"

I must have looked so flabbergasted that she stopped swimming to laugh.

"Ah! I'm so happy to be with you!" she crowed. "You know, I never feel good like this except with you."

"Me, too."

# *Luncheon, Sunday, July 23*

## MENU

*Tomato and Mozzarella Salad*

*Miniquiches, Minipizzas*

*Eggplant Caviar*

*Grilled Shrimp and Sardines*

*Polenta*

*Spinach Salad*

*Figs à la Crème*

Famished, Marie and I headed for the buffet table, and when our mother cautioned us as usual in a low voice to "wait until the guests have been served," Marie and I chimed in spontaneously to complete her sentence: ". . . I'm afraid there won't be enough!"

"Too bad," I added, "because we're dying of hunger!"

Then we laughed like crazy. I was actually shaking and wondered if it was with relief to see my sister happy again or with joy at renewing our old complicity. I brushed away tears while our mother placed Marie in charge of one table and assigned me to my father's, where he was so openly glad to see me arrive that it probably meant boredom was in sight. I soon understood why, sitting next to a Swiss banker who began to inform me all about Belgium and the fractious relationship between the Flemish and the Walloons.

"I've often wondered why no one takes an interest in the Swiss as a model for democracy. We are nevertheless quite good at concocting a federation out of people who have nothing in common . . ."

I pretended to be vaguely interested and turned to my father in the hope that something better was in the works.

"Can anyone explain to me," he asked, "this mania people now have for always walking around with a bottle of water? This is quite a recent development, you know. It's as if, out in the fresh air, they had the limited autonomy of fish . . ."

It was the kind of reflection that amused me. But my father's originality seemed lost on our tablemates; pearls before swine, I thought, while the woman next to him attempted to reorient the conversation toward more familiar terrain.

"Who is your favorite painter?"

"What do you mean by that?" he replied. "It depends. Of which century and country do you wish to speak?"

I almost smiled with pride. The woman, who wore a tank top barely covering huge veined breasts that spread out over her big belly like a pair of goatskin-covered gourds, was definitely not in my father's league and seemed unable to discern the degree of knowledge implied in such a response. How, therefore, could she have understood that even beyond his culture and education, my father was above all civilized? Nor could she ever appreciate the refined modesty with which he refused to show off anything at all, save incidentally, as when he might say, "Yes, that's pretty, isn't it; that vase belonged to Marie Antoinette. It was one of a pair, but the other is at the Petit Trianon . . ."

In short, there was no joy to be had from the gang of nitwits on our hands, and indeed I wondered who had saddled us with them. Opting to limit the damage, I decided to please my father: "Oh, Papa, I saw a documentary the other evening about bears . . ."

"Ah! I adore bears! You know, they don't lose any muscle mass or proteins during the winter, because their fat reserves recycle wastes into energy. Discovering the secrets of their hibernation could therefore have phenomenal applications, such as speeding up the healing of wounds for athletes, or prolonging the viability of organs for transplants, by putting them into a state of clinical hibernation. Just imagine!"

"We'll talk later?" asked Marie before she left for the airport.

"Of course, but will you be all right?"

"Yes, don't worry. You know, what you said is true: I had a close call with Béno, he's the sort to be avoided at all costs, even if it's rather flattering to have slept with him. But I've thought things over and what really puzzles me is what we can possibly think we're doing with our flop of a plan to find a husband. Anyway, in that department I feel I've done my bit. Share and share alike! So it's your turn next weekend, don't you agree?"

*Four*

# WEEKEND OF
# JULY 28

# *Weekend of July 28*

## THE FAMILY

Marie Ettinguer          Laure Ettinguer

Flokie Ettinguer         Edmond Ettinguer

## THE PILLARS

Gay Wallingford          Frédéric Hottin

## THE REMAINDER OF THE LITTLE BAND

Odon Viel                Laszlo Schwartz

## THE ODDBALLS

Georgina de Marien       Charles Ramsbotham

## THE END-OF-JULY REGULARS

Jean-Claude Girault      Astrid Girault

## THE NEWCOMERS

Alvin Fishbein           Vanessa Courtry

Nicolas Courtry          Barry Sullivan, aka Anagan

# SECRETARY'S NAME BOARD

| | |
|---|---|
| M. and Mme. Edmond Ettinguer | Master Bedroom |
| Mme. Laure Ettinguer | Flora's Room |
| (*Arrival from Paris Air France Friday 5:00 p.m.*) | |
| Mlle. Marie Ettinguer | Ada's Room |
| (*Arrival from Paris Air France Friday 5:00 p.m.*) | |
| Lady Gay Wallingford | Peony Room |
| M. Frédéric Hottin | Chinese Room |
| M. Odon Viel | Turquoise Room |
| M. Laszlo Schwartz | Lilac Room |
| Count and Countess Henri Démazure | |
| (*Departure 5:00 p.m. for the flight to Florence*) | |
| Viscountess de Marien | Annex: Peach Room |
| Earl of Stafford (Charles Ramsbotham) | Annex: Lime Room |
| M. and Mme. Jean-Claude Girault | Annex: Coral Room |
| (*Arrival via rental car approx. 5:00 p.m.*) | |
| M. Alvin Fishbein | Yellow Room |
| (*Arrival 6:00 p.m. by their own means with M. and Mme. Courtry*) | |
| M. and Mme. Courtry | Sasha's Room |

On Fridays the house hummed with a kind of industri-
ous tension like the buzzing of a beehive. It was flower
day. And if our head butler hadn't been chafing in a rest
home, he would have been as busy as a bee. Roberto,
a florist by training, customarily returned from the
market with a van full of flowers of different scents and
sizes intended for the various rooms in the house. He
usually selected dahlias, thistles, lavender, cosmos, or
amaranths for the loggia; branches of mulberry, wild
angelica, or hawthorn for the entrance hall; and a selection of sweet peas and heirloom roses mixed with
lady's mantle, snowball bush, or astrantia for the table
centerpieces. As for the room bouquets, they tended to
include hydrangeas, dahlias, poppies, or phalaenop-
sis orchids. After unloading the van, Roberto would

swiftly closet himself in a room equipped with copper sinks, next to the pantry, where he spent a good part of the morning creating bouquets he then placed throughout the house.

Fridays were also filled with the comings and goings of departing guests and new arrivals, so that day saw the Démazures leave for Italy as the Giraults arrived for a stay at L'Agapanthe, as they always did toward the end of July. Well-bred without being pedants or socialites, the Giraults were considered dream guests by their friends, who invited them for visits the length and breadth of France all summer long. Jean-Claude was known as a man of "exquisite" taste—a vague but pertinent term for his many qualities of refinement. To begin with, he was soigné, elegant in the English style but without ostentation, a personable man who always made a good impression. Judiciously modest and discreet with regard to his success in the field of furnishing fabrics, he was a good sport and a man of fair play in hunting, tennis, golf, and cards who appealed to men as well as to women, whom he charmed with seductive but lighthearted compliments. Astrid, on the other hand, was usually described as "a good sort," for she was a touch provincial and completely maladroit, quite capable of saying to me, for example, "You see, Laure, you and me, we're alike: frumpy in our youth, we get better as we get older."

But she liked to be of service, was very practical, knew the addresses of such places as a good lampshade shop, and had pull at the most sought after schools in Paris. None of us would ever have held her gaffes against her, since it warmed our hearts to forgive her so benevolently.

*Friday, 6:00 p.m.*

Hearing the enthusiastic level of decibels resounding from the loggia as we rang the front doorbell at L'Agapanthe, Marie and I knew right away that the Giraults had arrived. Every year, the opening of their present was a welcome ritual: "Is it what I hope, what I think it is?" my father would cry, gazing at a wicker tray wrapped in opaque cellophane, which he would feverishly tear open to make sure that he really would find candied fruit. Then, after asking a butler to bring him a dessert knife and fork, he would make their silver gilt gleam against the flesh of the fruit as he sliced it in delight, while comparing its colors to the ochers of the Nabis and the vermilions of still lifes painted by Chardin or Zurbarán.

"Right, shall we go on in?" I asked Marie, in a voice tinged with stage fright, like an acrobat about to go before an audience.

It was clear that this weekend would be decisive for our future and that it was my turn to play the lead part. I owed it to Marie, who hadn't completely recovered from her heartrending disappointment of the previous week. And I'd have only myself to blame if I got nowhere, because I was the one who'd chosen our last guests—well, Nicolas Courtry, in any case, who'd been my first love. I still spoke to him regularly on the phone, even though I hadn't seen him since three years earlier, when he'd moved to New York. And when I asked him for help, he had suggested Alvin Fishbein, a professional acquaintance.

"But I'm not sure if he's your type."

"Doesn't matter!"

"Even if I don't know him well enough to guarantee that he likes women?"

"Why do you say that?"

"His plane . . . is pink."

"Aha! That *is* interesting!"

"Listen, you want a rich guy, single, and available for the last weekend of July, you can't be picky, come on!

Anyway, the pink plane might well be explained by the fact that he's a toy manufacturer . . ."

"You're right, he'll be just perfect," I'd said that day.

For I'd expected that the sale of L'Aganpanthe would no longer be a problem by the time I met Alvin, about whom I'd completely forgotten in the meantime.

"Well, don't get your knickers in a twist!" said Marie, slipping her arm through mine as she warbled "Frédéric's song," which we hummed together as we headed for the loggia.

*Foie de veau with the Giraults*
*What could be more rigolo*
*Than to sip sublime porto*
*In the evening chez Girault?*
*Jean-Claude and his fine bon mots*
*Fresh from that day's Figaro*
*It was oh so comme il faut*
*This evening spent with the Giraults . . .*

Flanked by Gay, Frédéric, Odon, Laszlo, and the Giraults, my parents formed a picture that I recognized as soon as I entered the room, because it hung permanently in the museum of my memory, with landscapes and scenes of domestic life at L'Agapanthe.

It was a group portrait.

And yet, like all the tableaux in that imaginary gallery, the portrait was composed by the superposition of my memories, in this case those of my parents and their guests, seated year after year in the same room, on the same sofas, around the same tea service. Until that moment, I had thought that L'Agapanthe was the frame and sometimes the subject of these images, but I suddenly understood that the house was closer to a material base (like a painting under glass) on which the images were made and without which they would not exist. Would they vanish with the sale of L'Agapanthe? I wondered, and I felt a cold wave of anguish, because I could not imagine myself without such moments, such touchstones, such landmarks, for they gave my life a permanence and continuity on which my equilibrium depended. I was thus particularly attached to the immutable character of the house and quite attentive to every detail susceptible to change.

# Trop bien élevé
# [Too well brought up], 2007,
# by Jean-Denis Bredin

. . . *Bourgeoisie, wretched bourgeoisie, dear bourgeoisie! On my mother's side, good taste reigned supreme. One loved fine furniture, rare books, great writers, music, pretty women: not from pleasure, but to satisfy the requirement for refinement. Virtue, intelligence, and social success were prized, of course, but these were secondary values when compared to good manners. Only distinguished people with "elegant" occupations mattered. Neither things nor animals escaped this rigorous selection. As a child, I didn't dare bring home my little comrades for fear they would be judged inferior. Money revealed many things: this family claimed to use it with distinction and to good ends, while others, with stinginess or ostentation, put their money to mediocre use. And it was in order to behave*

---

* Jean-Denis Bredin is a prominent French attorney and a member of the Académie française.

*"with distinction" under all circumstances that the adults in my mother's family always smiled and, even at funerals, concealed the slightest sign of emotion. It was vulgar to cry, plebeian to complain, banal to laugh out loud. And so I have kept the memory of impassive faces, barely touched by chilly smiles, that all look alike. Few gestures. An almost uniform tone of voice. Neither imagination nor disorder ever disturbed that harmony. Everything was sacrificed to appearances. I knew this. And suffered, envisioning what might happen when they closed the doors of their bedrooms, removed their masks and, in the darkness, took off their clothes.*

*. . . On my father's side, it was only virtue that counted: work, loyalty, seriousness. Refinement was suspect, a sign of frivolousness, a pretext for expense and licentiousness. This bourgeoisie wanted to ignore the fact that it was wealthy, spent only what was strictly necessary, loathed luxury, stayed mostly at home, and knew no other distractions besides family and friends. "Respectable people" were those who worked a lot, led regular lives, fulfilled all their duties. Doubtless they were bored. But boredom was like the furniture or the servants: unnoticed. The reasons for living and dying were obvious and eternal. Amusements were undertaken only in moderation. Any suffering was borne with discretion. Even death provoked no revolt, as long as one died with dignity.*

*. . . These two bourgeoisies ignored each other, and probably despised each other. The one claimed to be virtue incarnate, and the other, the embodiment of elegance. Each accused the other of being narrow-minded and annoying, or flighty and perverted. They never saw how similar they were, attentive only to appearances, so distrustful of life!*

"What are those dreadful things?" I exclaimed, pointing to two tall glass cylinders of cloudy water, placed at either side of the couch on the veranda, in which bundles of lilies stood leaning like brooms in a closet.

My mother sighed. "Oh, spare me. It's the new head butler. He finds this more elegant than our bouquets . . ."

"Ha! Well, he's done quite a job on us!" Marie said sarcastically, noticing that our coffee tables now held plates of gravel bearing square vases filled with cacti and sticks of dark wood.

"You did say something to him, I hope?" I asked.

"Yes, but . . . the time it takes to fill a new order . . . He won't be able to change the vases until Monday."

"My poor Flokie," Gay said cheerily, feeding a morsel

of cake to Popsicle, "at least it's a change from Roberto, who sprays all your bouquets with Visine!"

"With eyewash?" marveled Astrid Girault. "Whatever for?"

"Really, dear: to make them look dewy fresh!" Gay laughed.

"Gracious, I never would have thought of it!"

"And on top of that," added my mother, "speaking of domestic problems, just imagine: the chef is marrying off his daughter tomorrow and has found us a replacement for the day."

The Giraults then launched into the story of how they'd just bought a house in the hinterlands of Nice, but I was listening only distractedly to their tale, musing nervously about the imminent arrival of my guests as I watched squirrels clambering through the parasol pines, when my father startled me with a sudden question.

"So, girls, who are your clients?"

"Well, Nicolas Courtry is the only one I actually know," I replied. "There will also be his wife Vanessa, and a friend of his, Alvin Fishbein, whom I've never met."

"And speak of the devil!" announced Frédéric, who had detected the crunch of gravel out in the courtyard.

I soon heard a faint exchange between my guests and the butler who directed them to their rooms, so I thought I still had a little time before the new arrivals would join us in the loggia. And then a sublime creature materialized in the doorway! Hypnotized by her beauty, Laszlo missed his cup and poured tea into his saucer, while Frédéric cried gaily, "My gosh, Penelope Cruz! What a good idea to invite her!"

And it was true that the young woman standing before us and looking faintly embarrassed closely resembled that Spanish actress. But she was even more beautiful.

"I'm . . . Nicolas's wife. I'm looking for Laure," she said softly, batting her eyelashes.

"I'm Laure, and welcome, Vanessa!" I replied.

"Nicolas would like to see you. He's upstairs."

"Ah? Fine, I'll go see what he wants. I'll leave you to introduce yourself."

I went up the stairs four at a time to the main entrance hall, where I found two men I had no time to acknowledge and Nicolas, who, far from greeting me with his customary effusiveness, cut right to the chase.

"Here's the situation: your suitor (don't worry, he can't speak a single word of French) doesn't go anywhere without his yoga teacher. But what I've just learned is that he wants to have him stay in a room next to his."

"Which is, naturally, out of the question."

Nicolas seemed so worried that I added, "But we can find him a hotel room nearby."

"We could always try . . ."

"I mean, with advance notice, that would have been another story, but as it is, he's got some nerve!"

"Yes but, put yourself in his place! He was so astonished to be invited that I told him you weren't people who stood on ceremony, that you'd really welcome him. So now, to have to explain that the house rules are so strict . . ."

"Oh, I see . . ."

"Well, listen, I did my best to get him here and it worked! That's why I'm telling you, I'm not going to be the one to break the news. You'll have to deal with it, however you want."

"Which one is he?" I asked, glancing at the other two men just long enough to make me hope my guest was the tall one, rather handsome in a smoldering way, and not the one with the pasty complexion and a ponytail.

"The tall one," replied Nicolas to my great relief, before introducing me in English: "Laure, here are Alvin and Barry, also known as Anagan. Alvin, Anagan, let me introduce you to Laure, who is our hostess, and the dear friend I have told you about."

I gave them a big smile before describing to Alvin the situation with the house, unfortunately (and most unusually!) completely full, and the charming little hotel that would certainly have room for Anagan, whom I placed in the capable hands of Roland, the chauffeur. But although I blithely ignored my suitor's extreme irritation, I had by no means dealt completely with the problem of his guru, I gathered, when Nicolas informed me that Anagan was not only Alvin's yoga teacher and spiritual guide, but also his cook.

"His cook!?"

"Yes, didn't I mention that? Your suitor is a vegetarian or vegan, whatever, because I don't really see the difference."

"This gets better and better," I groused, escorting the American to his room, and when Nicolas seemed about ready to start in again, I spoke up first: "Yes, I know: I asked for it, I got it, but still . . ."

The second we entered the Yellow Room, Alvin interrupted me to ask if he was allowed to move the head of his bed to point north, because otherwise he would be unable to sleep, and seeing my amazement, he added that this was one of the golden rules of feng shui.

"Of course," I replied.

"I have the feeling we're going to have some fun," Nicolas told me as we watched Alvin drag his bed around.

"We can only hope." I sighed, leaving Alvin in his care until dinnertime.

I still had to ask my mother to put up the guru and speak to the chef so that he would allow him into the kitchen.

"It seems your guest is rather eccentric, so we can certainly allow him the same leeway we give Charles, with the excuse that he's an English lord!" she said before busying herself with finding a room for the yogi and asking Roland to get him settled there.

In short, she was so pleasant about the whole business that I was at first disconcerted. Then I realized that she was critical only of people with whom she was familiar, and Alvin's lifestyle was so different from her own that she had no point of comparison from which to judge him. And I couldn't help noting, watching her adopt this benevolent and open ethnological approach to him, that she seemed content to be relieved of her role as the supreme arbiter of gracious living by this case of force majeure.

"In your opinion, this yogi, do we invite him to sit with us?" she asked.

"I think not, since he'll be in the kitchen!"

"How silly of me, of course. Anyway, luckily for your vegetarian, this evening there is a soufflé."

The sea was still glittering like sparkling amethysts when Alvin arrived for cocktails, wearing a *shalwar kameez* ensemble, a collarless Indian shirt of tunic length worn over loose pajamalike pants gathered at the ankle— a sartorial choice that seemed like a manifesto it was up to me to interpret. Stalling for time, I wondered whether the subtle exoticism of this beige and off-white palette was intended to evoke the Eastern subcontinent . . . or perhaps Western beatniks, or hippies? I didn't want to succumb too quickly, as a psychologist, to the reflex already prompting me to examine Alvin's possible relationship with his parents. One of the pitfalls of my profession!

Still, I couldn't help thinking that his choice of clothing betrayed a desire to step outside the family circle.

Then I brought myself to heel: Alvin was not one of my patients but a suitor, so I would do better to consider him strictly from that angle. And noticing once more that he was handsome in a dark, Jeremy Irons sort of way, I imagined him dressed differently to see if I liked him: tall, graceful, aristocratic, he would no doubt be stunning in a dark suit. When Alvin spoke to my mother, however, my retouched vision of him went up in smoke.

"L'Agapanthe faces the northwest, does it not? Did you know that with an earth element between the building and the sea, whose energy circulates toward the house—while firmly anchored by the Lérins Islands near Cannes—L'Agapanthe has the ideal site of 'the earth dragon's lair,' like Hong Kong, where the energy entering the bay is safeguarded by Victoria Peak?"

Convoluted as it was, Alvin's compliment struck me less than did his gestures, because he punctuated his delivery by holding out his right hand, palm up, and systematically ticking off his points by bending each finger back in succession with his left index finger, as if seeking to give structure to his little speech. Well, I thought, so much for trying to set himself apart from the average American with his clothes and his yoga and meditation! Alvin still exhibited American behavior patterns, like that mania for counting anything and everything on his fingers. Next he'd be raising his arms and twitching two sets of fingers to sketch imaginary quotation marks, those clichéd precautions demanded by political correctness whenever a controversial subject crops up.

The truth was that I was particularly annoyed by all the American gestures that have spread throughout the world via that country's many TV series. As disastrous as their fast food, American behavior has insinuated itself into the smallest corners of our rituals, changing even the way we pass around the holy-water sprinkler at funerals! I'd observed that instead of crowding around the coffin the way we used to do, we all now stood a few yards away with the patient docility of model citizens, a routine we felt obliged to adopt when waiting everywhere from now on, from the post office to customs clearance to restaurant lines, stepping one by one over imaginary boundaries on the ground. And at funerals, as it happens, this is truly inconvenient, since the single person up at the coffin has to go back to the other mourners to hand over the aspergillum to someone else, making everyone wait that much longer.

But, given the flippancy with which I'd recruited my suitor, I reflected, I might have had worse luck, because he did seem intent on being courteous to my mother.

"Laure tells me that you live in New York?"

"Yes, for part of the year, since I also live in California."

My mother hesitated to go on, for her familiarity with the genteel neighborhoods of Manhattan risked proving useless in conversation with this bohemian, and she refused to make a fool of herself trying to find out if they knew anyone in common, under the pretext of knowing lots of people there. Still, she did venture to ask, "And where in New York do you live?"

"Fifth Avenue, at 998."

"No!" exclaimed my mother, who couldn't believe it.

Because she knew all the prestigious buildings on the Upper East Side by heart and by name, considering only those built before the Second World War, such as 720, 740, and 778 Park Avenue, or 810, 820, 830, 834, and 960 on Fifth, to mention a few. Not forgetting 998, which occupied an entire block and still had apartments with columned ballrooms and extensive servants' quarters. All those buildings were co-ops run by powerful owners' committees, which made buying an apartment there more difficult than joining the Jockey Club.

But Alvin went on to tell her about his mansion in Rhinebeck, on the Hudson, a gigantic main house with an annex containing an indoor tennis court and a white marble swimming pool.

"Was that the house of the So-and-so family?" asked my mother.

"Yes, it's where they used to organize 'white weekends' in the 1910s."

"What are those?" I asked, to join the conversation.

"Cocaine weekends," replied my mother with disarming casualness.

With a pang, I realized that my mother's cocaine dependence had completely slipped my mind since the previous weekend, when Marie had convinced me that her addiction bothered my mother even less than if she'd suddenly developed a sweet tooth. And there she was, indeed, as lovely and serene as always.

"Do you know the Lachmans?" she asked, encouraged by the tokens of upper-echelon tribalism Alvin had just given her.

"No, I can't say that I do . . ."

"Oh, you must, that's the *l* in Revlon: there was Charles Revson and Charlie Lachman . . ."

I thought I saw Alvin wince in distaste at the bowl of shelled peanuts into which we were all happily plunging our hands for a nibble, which suggested that hygiene was clearly one of his pet peeves, but before I could ponder his reaction any further, Nicolas and Vanessa made their entrance onto the terrace.

Since Nicolas had come often to L'Agapanthe when we were together, Vanessa had been informed of our house rituals regarding dressing for dinner, and she had gone all out. What's more, this was a woman who, living in Manhattan, habitually dressed to the nines for a little dinner in a corner bistro.

She was wearing a very short baby-doll dress in red organza and bronze shoes like a web of laces that added another six inches to her already endless legs. And the combination of her slyly "innocent" dress and her bewildering shoes startled our gathering into an eloquent silence. Unless we were, quite simply, stunned by her beauty. Because beauty is a strange thing, exciting stupor and fascination more often than desire. And Vanessa seemed used to seeing her beauty freeze timid men and neurotic women—when it didn't provoke such bedazzlement that those around her just stared, deaf and dumb.

I imagined how frustrated she must feel by thinking of my son, who was often both pleased and angry that I loved him too much to love him properly whenever I found myself distracted while listening to him, overcome by the joy of seeing him, there in front of me, so healthy and so handsome.

Vanessa must have had real personality to want so much to cut through the screen of blinding beauty that obscured her, I thought, as I watched her make an effort to get us to talk to her and return to our conversations, but the poor thing could not keep us from gazing at her. Even worse, Odon started talking about beauty itself.

"Do you agree with Allison Lurie's idea that beauty, far from provoking desire, more commonly inspires love?"

That was too much for Vanessa, who blushed and began to stammer, but Nicolas came to her rescue.

"I agree wholeheartedly, my dear Odon, because I'm head over heels in love with my wife. Now, has Alvin told you that he's the champion of air rights?"

"Madame, dinner is served!" bellowed the head butler.

"*Air rights?* What are they? You must tell us all about them over dinner," said my mother, rising to lead the way.

# *Dinner, Friday, July 28*

## FIFTEEN PERSONS

| MEN | WOMEN |
|---|---|
| Edmond Ettinguer | Flokie Ettinguer |
| Frédéric Hottin | Laure Ettinguer |
| Odon Viel | Marie Ettinguer |
| Jean-Claude Girault | Astrid Girault |
| Laszlo Schwartz | Gay Wallingford |
| Charles Ramsbotham | Georgina de Marien |
| Nicolas Courtry | Vanessa Courtry |
| Alvin Fishbein | |

| SEATING: | SEATING: |
| EDMOND'S TABLE | FLOKIE'S TABLE |

|  | Gay |  |  | Laszlo | Frédéric |
|---|---|---|---|---|---|
| Odon |  | Marie | Laure |  | Georgina |
| Charles |  | Nicolas | Alvin |  | Jean-Claude |
| Vanessa |  | Astrid |  | Flokie |  |
|  | Edmond |  |  |  |  |

## MENU

*Soufflé Mornay*
*Sole Murat*
*Salad and Cheeses*
*Mille-feuille with Raspberries*

Dinner began in general confusion. Alvin thought we were crazy when he saw our reaction to the tables in the dining room, which the new head butler had decorated with his disastrous floral arrangements. He had also seen fit to set out plastic bottles of mineral water in order to avoid having to serve us from our silver carafes! Although our American guest definitely disapproved of the plastic bottles, which offended him more from the ecological than the aesthetic point of view, he found the vases of cacti and weathered wood very New Age, in a Sedona, Arizona, sort of way, and he rather liked them. What he really didn't understand, however, was why our animated conversation took place mostly after the butlers had left the room, like those secret confabs in children's camps and boarding schools after lights-out, when the volume of noise varies according to the proximity of adult supervision.

As for my mother, she made an effort not to take offense over Alvin's worries about the menu, because although he had obviously decided to eat what was put in front of him without making a fuss, he was finally compelled to ask, "Are the eggs organic?"

Finding his question absurd, since—organic or not—the chef always bought the best products at the market, my mother bluffed without blinking an eye: "Absolutely."

She almost lost patience, however, when Alvin asked her if he might have an egg-white omelet instead of the delicate marvel of eggs, butter, béchamel, and Gruyère on a base of impeccably soft-boiled eggs soon to be placed before us and which never failed to elicit cries of admiration from the most hard to please of our guests, such was the skill required to bring a soufflé Mornay to perfection. Then, rallying to her initial open-mindedness toward this new guest, my mother rose to the occasion: "Why not!"

"So, these air rights?" asked Laszlo brightly, to lighten the atmosphere.

Alvin explained that after making his fortune in toys, he had moved on to real estate and dealt a great deal in the rights to use and develop the empty space over buildings in New York.

"I don't understand. Who would be interested in them?"

"Well, developers intending to put up buildings taller than the limit anticipated by the local zoning map. Because all a developer needs to do is buy the air rights over adjacent buildings and turn their space into extra stories for the building he wishes to construct."

"You mean that the lower the neighboring buildings are, if they're small houses, for example, then the more air they have to sell, and the higher the developer can build?"

"Exactly."

"Unbelievable . . . and how much does the open airspace cost?" asked Laszlo.

"Between 213 and 430 dollars a square foot, let's say 50 to 60 percent of the sale price of a plot."

Frédéric was electrified. "But that's a gold mine, your angle! Because I figure that, if they have the choice among several adjacent properties whose airspace they can buy, the developers must set all the neighbors against one another and force them to accept an offer that is nonnegotiable."

"Yes," continued Alvin, "unless on the contrary the potential seller finds himself in a solid position as the key to the developer's entire project, which requires that he purchase not only his air rights but those of all his neighbors."

"Ah! Because that can go on ad infinitum?"

"No, only within the framework of one city block."

"Fascinating . . ."

"Oh, wonderful, filet of sole Murat, I love that!" exclaimed Jean-Claude, taking a generous helping of fish, potatoes, and artichokes from the proffered serving dish.

"Do you eat like this every day?" asked Alvin, in the mixture of surprise and indignation adopted by an American citizen who sees someone throwing something on the ground or cutting in line.

"Yes, why?" replied my mother, honestly surprised.

"But it's such a rich diet, I don't see how you can stand it . . ."

Alvin then delivered a minutely detailed rundown of the calorie counts in our dinner, followed by a dietetic sermon on one's ideal weight, a screed that entailed deep discussion of proteins, lipids, carbohydrates, vegetarian diets, omega-3 benefits, oils from fish, argan, and borage, flaxseed oil supplements, and iron pills—or better yet, iron in liquid form, to avoid constipation—and that brought us to the salad and cheese course.

My mother leaned toward Jean-Claude to tell him just what she thought of this nonsensical chemical babbling. "Rich! Rich! In the first place, we eat chicken, fish, or pasta, not proteins or hydrates of carbon, whatever that means!"

My mother was about to explode, while the rest of us were succumbing to boredom like a congregation benumbed by a Sunday sermon. And since it was easier and more courteous to change the subject instead of trying to shut him up . . .

"Alvin, I fear you are talking to a brick wall. Why don't you talk to us about your interest in yoga?" I asked.

Alas, we realized that we were in for another dose of pontification when he announced that "diet and yoga are linked, because digestion requires a level of energy incompatible with . . ."

So we were treated to a course on Jivamukti yoga while Marcel served us the mille-feuille with raspberries.

"Five thousand years ago, India gave birth to yoga, which means 'union' in Sanskrit. Its goal is to attain an understanding of the interdependence of all forms of life . . ."

Too beaten down even to consider reacting, we simply relaunched him now and then so we could eat our dessert in peace.

"Yes, but what about Jivamukti?"

"It was created in 1984 in the United States. And it shifted the practice of yoga in America from an esoteric ritual observed by a few initiates to a discipline followed by sixteen million Americans."

Suiting the action to the word, Alvin began fiddling with the fingers of his right hand again, but this time with confident ease, as if he'd delivered this particular litany many times before.

"The definition of Jivamukti yoga is 'liberation through life,' meaning a way of being in the world. Reserved for those who seek to expend intense physical effort, it has won over such adepts as Sting, Christy Turlington, Donna Karan, and Gwyneth Paltrow."

"But what *is* it exactly?" I asked gamely.

"There are five pillars of Jivamukti instruction . . ."

But instead of listening to Alvin, I was waiting for the moment when he would start ticking things off on his fingers, which he then proceeded to do.

"The first pillar, nonviolence or ahimsa, might be described as: recognize yourself in others, in humans as well as animals. The second pillar, devotion or bhakti, stipulates that we must offer all that we experience to a higher entity than ourselves. The third pillar, meditation or Dhyana . . ."

"Well, now, that's certainly *much* clearer," exclaimed Frédéric sweetly at the end of Alvin's lecture, while the rest of us sat speechless.

Floored by Alvin's virtue and gibberish, we were about to leave the table when the butler came to tell me that my son was on the telephone.

Wondering if he'd timed his call to reach me just after dinner, I went to the "phone booth" (it looked rather like a confessional) just outside the living room, in which you had to sit down on the banquette to activate the ceiling light.

"I can't go to sleep, Mummy! Do you think it's serious?"

At first I dealt with this lightly, but I soon realized that Félix was really worried. My idiot ex-husband had managed to terrorize him by predicting disaster if he didn't get "a good eight hours of sleep."

"But what will happen if I sleep less? Or more?"

Although I tried to soothe him, his anxiety kept him focused on that quota of hours.

"You see, it's eleven now, Mummy, and the au pair's going to come wake me up at eight, so if I don't fall asleep in an hour, I won't get enough . . ."

It was hard to stop his looping. And my growing ill temper wasn't helping my attempts to calm Félix down. What infuriated me wasn't that his father would want some time to himself in the evening to be with his new companion, which was only reasonable, but that he would as usual formulate his needs and desires in the guise of an educational principle. Why would he upset a child on vacation like that? He should have told our son, 'I need to be on my own now, so why don't you hang out in your room, do some reading or play until you get tired.' Félix would already be asleep instead of phoning me—and developing a sleep problem it would probably take me at least six months to get rid of! In the end, I comforted him as best I could, at least I hoped so, since I couldn't do more over the phone.

When I returned to the living room, I sat down next to my father in the vague expectation that he might comfort *me*, but before I could open my mouth he began telling me how entertaining it had been to sit next to Vanessa at dinner.

"She's a living doll!" He beamed. "She told me that until Nicolas came along, she'd only been interested in stuffy, affected guys who were always droning on about something. Who could have imagined she would ever find pomposity attractive!"

Was it the ecstatic twinkle in my father's eyes? The attention he was paying to the American beauty instead of to his daughters? Whatever it was, I found myself blowing up at him.

"Fine, then I can assure you that Alvin takes himself seriously enough to be her kind of guy! But luckily Nicolas won't have to worry—first, because Vanessa seems crazy about him, and second, because I've decided to put the moves on Alvin to get him to marry me so that he can buy L'Agapanthe, since you've put it up for sale without even consulting us . . ."

Taken aback, my father looked at me in puzzlement for a moment but then acted as if he'd misunderstood me or just hadn't heard correctly. And instead of asking me to repeat what I'd said or replying in his usual way, he turned without a word to my mother, who was freshly appalled by the butler's latest blunder: setting out tea bag packets of every color on a coffee table, like magazines in a waiting room.

"Tea bags, how awful!"

"And fanned out, like a shop-window display!" added Astrid, to show that she, too, found the sight distasteful.

Alvin asked around if anyone could give him the house telephone number, since his BlackBerry seemed unable to get any reception and he was expecting some phone calls.

"My poor fellow," replied Charles, "the technology at L'Agapanthe is still stuck in the 1920s! It would be no help at all to you if I provided the phone number here, because when the ancient switchboard rings, no one hears it, and if you answer when it rings in the booth next to the living room, picking up the receiver while sitting in front of a skirted vanity table and a tarnished mirror is positively a trip backward in time!"

"But then what does everyone else do? Am I the only one not to get any reception?"

"Some of us have resigned ourselves to our fate and even learned to appreciate this peaceful atmosphere of a spiritual retreat, while the others—and I am one—haunt the driveway like poor damned souls just outside the entrance gate, where the reception's a little better. But it can depend on the rooms: which one are you in?"

"The yellow one."

"Lucky you! If you go stand by the window, you should get some reception."

"And the Internet?"

"Here again you're in luck, because this is quite a recent development: Edmond and Flokie have just had a bathroom remodeled into an office equipped with an Internet connection. But I'm warning you," added Charles with a sly smile, "there's stiff competition for access to this lifeline!"

The sudden swoop of a dragonfly over the sofa drew my attention away from Charles and Alvin, whom I was only pretending to listen to, since I felt I deserved a breather, so I let Alvin shift his interest to the Giraults, who were busily chatting with Georgina, Marie, Frédéric, and Odon. Determined to remain mopey and ill humored, I contemplated my father, flushed with love, talking to Vanessa and Nicolas who, against all expectation, wound up saving my dinner party.

In fact, they were a huge hit when they told us about the role-playing game they liked to get up to at winter resorts. Nicolas enjoyed pretending to be a domestic tyrant in front of skiers lined up at lifts, who make the ideal public for his kind of performance. He would hand his skis off to Vanessa to carry and swat her on the butt, saying in a loud, grumpy voice, "Get going, you dope! I'm paying, you're lugging, that's how it is!"

And Vanessa would meekly comply, as the onlookers stared in appalled astonishment.

Then Vanessa explained to us that the reason their little number (which made them laugh until they cried) was so convincing was . . . that she actually *was* a submissive woman and her husband a bully.

"Oh, really?" cried Laszlo, Charles, and my father with one voice.

"Decide for yourselves," she said and began a story about the university studies she'd undertaken (rather on the late side), all because she felt stupid and uneducated after skipping them when she was younger while trying to make her way as a model.

After pausing for sympathetic expressions of commiseration from the misty-eyed gentlemen in the audience, Vanessa continued.

"The only problem was Nicolas, who was dead set against my plan and insisted that my passion for studying was unseemly and even perverse."

"Surely *not!*" I exclaimed, commenting ironically on the idiocy of men with an up-front bitterness not unrelated to my father's earlier attitude.

"Oh, yes, but the worst thing was, you see, that Nicolas was right! It was perverse. In his place, I would have been jealous, because I went off to my classes as happy as a lark, even though I did feel sorry for him, dying of boredom in his office. So one day, to buck up his morale, I went to Madison Avenue and spent a fortune. I came home completely bushed, naturally, after such a marathon of shopping. Then when Nicolas counted the number of bags and saw that I was too exhausted to give him the slightest little caress . . ."

And here Vanessa heaved a huge sigh.

". . . well, he begged me to go back to school!"

Dazzled by Vanessa's cheek, the gentlemen turned toward Nicolas in wonderment at how he'd managed to win such a prize, only to find him already deep in conversation with my mother.

Nicolas is short and rather ugly, but he has charm, confidence, and never feels obliged to make a show of his success.

"What does he do in life, anyway?" my father asked me.

"He made a fortune on the Internet, but don't ask me how, I have no idea."

At that point Alvin, repressing a yawn, got up. "I'm sorry to run out on you like this, but I'm the early-to-bed type, and I meditate at sunrise. Good night, all!"

Alvin's departure prompted others to follow suit, and Marie and I soon found ourselves with Nicolas and Vanessa, who seemed unwilling to call it a night.

"Some Trivial Pursuit?" I suggested halfheartedly, then did my best to take an interest in a game won handily by Nicolas, a history buff.

"Who crowned Clovis, the first king of the Franks, at Reims?"

"Archbishop St. Rémi."

"Who discovered Greenland in 982?"

"Eric the Red."

Since the jet lag was in their favor, our guests appeared eager to keep going all night, and Marie seemed ready to stay up with them.

"I'm about to drop," I announced. "Would it destroy you utterly if I toddled off to bed?"

And I did.

*Saturday, 8:oo a.m.*

I awoke with a start the next morning and waited until eight o'clock to call Félix. When I asked him if he'd slept well, I learned that his father, who had a hard time accepting that his son was afraid of the dark, had come into his room several times to turn out the light, which Félix had turned right back on. My ex found this fear ridiculous. And he probably thought his method of dealing with it was educational! The sadism of his behavior left me fuming, however, and I realized that it wouldn't take much more for me to begin hating my former husband, a man from whom I had parted without the slightest resentment.

"Don't worry," I told my son. "In two days we'll be together!"

As I hung up, I felt that I'd been reassuring myself as well as Félix. And I knew it was time for July to be over so that I could have him back—because the present state of affairs could not continue. Really, his father . . . But when I thought about seeing my son again, my anger melted away.

And only then did I think about what had happened at dinner the night before. Fascinated by Vanessa, my father had paid no attention to what I'd blurted out, and clearly I couldn't expect him to speak frankly with me about the situation, so I had no time to lose if I wanted to highjack its outcome with a love affair. True, Alvin Fishbein wasn't about to fall into my arms, given my less-than-charming attitude toward him so far, and yes, he'd struck me as something of a prig, but would I ever be satisfied with anyone? I was critical, narrow-minded, and on the defensive. No matter *what* goal I had in mind, it was time for me to change my attitude. I went down to the beach.

From the top of the steps leading to the sea, I could see Alvin and his guru sitting facing one another in the lotus position. There was something strange about witnessing this oriental ritual, so spiritual and austere, on a beach that was so French and so perfectly designed for pleasure, yet the stillness, the silent concentration of that solemn prayer commanded such respect that one instinctively kept one's distance. And in any case, I could hardly see myself barging in on their communion like a thoughtless fool. Then I had a bright idea, one that made my pulse quicken: I could spy on Alvin and Ana-gan from the servants' beach! It's not every day that one may play the voyeur with a clear conscience under the pretext of not bothering someone, and besides, wasn't it my duty to take a more serious interest in Alvin?

"We'll perform a pranayama, the Nadi Shodhana," said the yogi.

Hidden behind a bush, I saw Anagan lead a breathing exercise that involved closing first the right nostril with a thumb, then switching to the left nostril with the ring finger.

"Let's move on to Sat Yam, or the purification of the heart. Imagine a light in the heart chakra," the yogi said softly. "You will feel it grow with each intake of breath, and draw back toward the heart as the breath leaves. Now, for eighteen minutes, you will think of nothing. If a thought occurs to you, push it away and return to nothing."

Unwilling to admit my disappointment with what I was witnessing, I reflected that meditation was by its very nature hardly a spectacular sight. I would have abandoned my spying on the spot had I not been such a voyeur!

Placing his hands over his eyes, the yogi concluded the séance, intoning, Om Namah Shivaya. Om shanti shanti shanti, namaste."

"Namaste," replied Alvin.

Since I couldn't very well pop out of my thicket to say hello, pretending that I'd neither admired nor seen them, which would have been a lie in both cases, I retraced my steps to the loggia, where all the men in the house had found different excuses to be courting Vanessa. As soon as I showed up (were they hoping to head off any caustic comments I might make?), they bombarded me with questions, inquiring after the state of the bay at the bottom of the lawn as if it were a dear relative bedridden in a distant clinic: was it cold, turbid, sandy, infested with jellyfish?

As the butler brought me my breakfast, Gay looked up from her *Financial Times*. "Can someone explain to me what these subprimes are?"

"No. Listen to this article in the *Nice-Matin* instead," interrupted Frédéric.

"In the what?" asked Astrid.

"The *Nice-Morning*, the *Nice-Matin*, you know. Here it is: 'For a week now, a lost whale calf has been roving off the Côte d'Azur. The orphaned finback whale had suddenly appeared in the middle of the harbor at Antibes, but rescuers had not had time enough to put their floating stretcher in place before the calf headed on to Salis Beach. Sightings have been reported since then in the bay of Cannes, at Théoule, and even at Saint-Tropez, according to the coordinator of the rescue effort, who seemed exhausted by a search that has so far been in vain. A plane had been chartered to locate the baby finback, but the keen eyes of the pilot, an experienced leader of whale-watching excursions, failed to find his quarry. He did, however, spot a pod of adult finbacks just to the south of Cannes, and there is speculation that the calf might have joined them. That would be the calf's only chance of survival, according to the pilot, who speculated that although there has never been a confirmed case of adoption among cetaceans, by copying their behavior, the calf could learn from the adults how to dive to hunt for food. Since the calf is almost old enough to be weaned, it might thus be saved, because its intestinal flora are sufficiently developed to cope with the change in diet.'"

Like a divine apparition, her lips still puffy with sleep, Vanessa passed briefly through on her way to the beach.

"Why don't we try to catch sight of this whale calf?" suggested Laszlo, who set off with all the other men in tow.

When I got back to the beach with Laszlo, my father, Charles, and Jean-Claude, however, I saw that the yogi had gone off to the kitchen, Nicolas was swimming in the bay, and Vanessa and Alvin were deep in conversation.

Which didn't prevent us from noticing that they were both superb physical specimens. Alvin was slender but finely muscled, and his sculpted ribs made him look like Mantegna's Saint Sebastian, yet this body, disciplined like a dancer's through effort and privations, still left me cold. The men, however, could not resist casually lowering their newspapers or books now and then to sneak glances at the golden, silky, svelte but nicely rounded figure of Vanessa. A student of yoga herself, she had engaged Alvin on the subject, and I went over to hear what they were discussing.

"Your yogi, has he achieved samadhi?" asked Vanessa.

"Yes."

"What's that?" I asked quickly, positioning myself near Alvin, the necessary first step toward any future relationship between us.

"That means he has achieved enlightenment."

"And *that* means?"

"Practically speaking, that he can enter a state that may be studied by scientists: the yogi is awake, but he allows his brain to rest, producing the same brain waves that occur in deep sleep."

"And where does that get him?"

"He manages through meditation to enter into communion with the cosmos, to be at one with the universe. Because we are part of the universe, but the universe is within us," explained Vanessa.

"It opens his third eye, which is called ajna, and that brings him clairvoyance," added Alvin.

"Which is . . . ?" I prompted, with the unpleasant feeling that the more I asked, the less I'd understand.

"It means he can know certain things in advance or learn things during meditation sessions, during flashes when he can instantly master the techniques of painting or photography, for example."

"And is he a Sohami?" continued Vanessa.

"And what's *that*?" I asked faintly.

"An honorary title for yogis."

It was a foreign language they were speaking, Alvin and Vanessa, for I had the uncomfortable and humiliating impression that I did not understand them, as when I was a child who couldn't make any sense of the adult world, unable to fathom their words or how they used them.

I was in hostile territory, reduced to interpreting the most diverse signals, smiles, frowns, postures, all in an effort to deduce if we were speaking almost in jest, or quite seriously, or condescendingly, or frankly—and this feeling of exclusion was so painful that I understood only too well how someone confronted with a sect and its enigmatic vocabulary might join the sect simply through a desire to penetrate its mystery and to rise in the ranks of an esoteric ideology conceived precisely as a come-on. Then Alvin and

Vanessa—kindly, gently, exactly as if they had been members of a sect—tried to rescue me from my confusion.

"Your body is made of the five elements of the universe: earth, fire, water, air, space. In ayurvedic medicine, there are three doshas, or body types: vata, pitta, kapha. Each of us has all three, but to varying degrees, with one dominant . . ."

Alvin was attentive enough to take my pulse, which allowed me to confirm that I felt not the slightest thrill at his touch. And I was thoughtful enough to ask him a few more questions, in an effort to make my interest in his beloved yoga seem a little more than just cordial.

The truth was, however, that although I respected Alvin's spiritual aspirations, his thirst for purity and the absolute, I was not impressed by his intelligence. Seeking reassurance and structure, he displayed a great need to impose rules for living on himself, and I felt that he was not free but imprisoned by restrictive protocols that I found frankly off-putting, as was the smug and self-satisfied way he preached about them, going on like a broken record.

I have always tried to be a decent person, with a code of ethics that drives me to improve and even perfect myself in every way, and I feel it is essential that everyone should have this same aspiration. At the same time, I feel equally strongly that religion, which I believe demands no creativity from its passive, obedient followers, appeals chiefly to imbeciles. In general as stultifying as television, religion can nevertheless provide matter for reflection, on an equal footing with philosophy and the other human sciences. Thanks to Jung, though, I still remained convinced that God—or fate—was nothing more than our unconscious.

What should I do? Where Alvin was concerned, I felt no attraction, physical or any other kind. Should I abandon the idea of seducing him and resign myself to seeing L'Agapanthe put up for sale? To tell the truth, since the very beginning of our plan I'd found it hard to imagine what lay in store for the house because I felt so anxious and uncomfortable thinking about that, although I hadn't liked to admit it. And suddenly, I knew why: imagining the future of L'Agapanthe meant envisioning life without my parents, which meant envisioning their death. And I was not ready for that.

In any case, if I had to take stock of our campaign, the least I could say was that it had been inconclusive. Even worse, it seemed that Marie and I were unable to maintain our close sisterly bond if one of us took an amorous interest in some attractive man, because although we took pleasure in our unanimous rejection of an unsuitable suitor, like the unfortunate Jean-Michel Destret, any flicker of interest in a possible lover disrupted our complicity completely. Hadn't Marie wounded my feelings, back when I'd met Rajiv, without even realizing that we'd both been attracted to each other? As for me, feeling desperately alone when she'd been bowled over by Béno, hadn't I recovered my joie de vivre only when I could console her over her broken heart? Oh, we'd been quite a tight team, all right!

I went back up to the house only to run into my mother, who asked me to go see how our substitute chef was doing—without letting on that I was on a mission, of course.

I walked into the kitchen just before the bell was due to ring announcing the staff mealtime break.

"I've come to see if things are going well," I told the cook, who had a swarthy complexion and startling blue-green eyes.

"They are, thank you."

"And what's the menu?" I asked, nodding to Anagan, whom I'd just noticed in an adjacent room.

The cook seemed so pleased with himself, as he handed me a handwritten sheet of paper, that I was careful to let nothing show on my face as I read it.

Scramble of Eggs on a Bed of Tomato Concassée
Symphony of Vegetables en Demi-Deuil

Farandole of Salads

Melon Soup

Salmon Carpaccio

Cheeses

Apricot, Mango, and Passion Fruit Sorbet

Good Lord! I thought, he's certainly gussied things up.
I could just see the face my mother would make at this
grandiloquent menu.

"And what menu were you asked to prepare?" I asked
sweetly, and was handed the house menu book open to
that day's page.

Scrambled Eggs with Truffles

Artichoke Salad

Beef Salad with Cornichons

Melon with Parma Ham and Figs

Cold Salmon with Green Sauce

Tomato and Green Bean Salad

Cheeses

Apricot, Mango, and Passion Fruit Sorbet

Nothing like, of course! I noticed, for example, that the
cook had promoted the artichoke salad to a "symphony
of vegetables en demi-deuil."

"And what is that, exactly?" I asked him with feigned enthusiasm.

I then discovered that the cook had a thing for the same square vases that the new butler had used for his flower arrangements. Had they pooled their orders to buy them in bulk? Did I dare ask him about that? Chickening out, I studied the alternating layers of artichoke purée and tapenade that filled the vessels.

"So what do you think?" asked the cook.

"They remind me of Daniel Buren's striped columns at the Palais Royal," I replied, instead of remarking that the culinary use of the term *en demi-deuil*, "in partial mourning," implied—as I understood it—the use of truffles, not black olives.

But luckily I did not run short of diplomatically thoughtful metaphors, for I next compared his scrambled eggs to the ice cores geologists punched out of Arctic glaciers, because the cook had presented his egg dish as a *verrine*—layered ingredients in a small glass, in this case about the size of a vodka glass—on a bed of coarsely chopped tomatoes, instead of in tartlets of puff pastry, the way our chef usually did. Then I reviewed the entire menu in its "reconceptualized" form. And the cook seemed so proud of having transformed the salmon into carpaccio, and the melon into soup, and of having presented the salads in fancy individual bowls of different sizes and shapes, that I congratulated him before leaving the kitchen.

In the name of what, after all, would I have criticized this young man's efforts to put his personal touch on a menu that seemed too simple to him? But then I asked myself what made his menu seem so silly to me. Was it the emphasis on presentation (a successful effort, moreover) affected by this Adonis? Or his love of innovation, which betrayed a kind of contempt for, or ignorance of, the past and its traditions? Or was it that in cuisine as in couture, less is more? And just as it was vulgar to overplay elegance by being overdressed, or outfitted from head to toe in some ostentatious "total look," thus betraying a desire to *appear* and a social angst synonymous with an absence of natural elegance, food should never be either pretentious or overelaborate. It should be simple in its presentation, as in its menu description, and look as if it has only just come out of the oven. It should be unostentatious, like my grandmother's shaved sable.

I thought about Alvin's clothing, all in earth tones,

and about Vanessa's simple, confident sense of style, that chic baby-doll dress she'd worn the previous evening without any jewelry, with her hair hanging loose, even tousled, and I decided that appearances notwithstanding, their wardrobes made compatible and even related statements. Because if Alvin's clothing announced his ecological sympathies, his preference of the essential over the accessory, the East over the West, of being exotic, his garments succeeded all the better since they distinguished themselves from the ordinary garb of the average American who seeks comfort above all else in shorts or jeans.

In the same way, Vanessa's elegance, to which we all aspire, showed a sense of refinement that was the visible sign of an *art de vivre* implying a constant choice of spiritual over material concerns, of art and culture over materialism, and discretion over crass display. Her elegance was also, however, a reflection of a desire to distinguish herself from the middle classes, who are constantly engaged in a restless search for style in a consumerist orgy of accessorized and designer-labeled fashion.

I saw confirmation of that demand for sobriety and detachment in my mother's reaction when I reported the changes our young cook had wrought in the menu, most particularly with the variety of bowls and dishes he had used to "modernize" our meal, because she simply said, "It's the fable of the Fox and the Stork,[4] what you're telling me. But what can we do about it?"

---

4 Old Father Fox, who was known to be mean,
Invited Dame Stork in to dinner.
There was nothing but soup that could scarcely be seen:
Soup never was served any thinner.
And the worst of it was, as I'm bound to relate,
Father Fox dished it up on a flat china plate.
Dame Stork, as you know, has a very long beak:
Not a crumb or drop could she gather
Had she pecked at the plate every day in the week.
But as for the Fox—sly old Father:
With his tongue lapping soup at a scandalous rate,
He licked up the last bit and polished the plate.
Pretty soon Mistress Stork spread a feast of her own;
Father Fox was invited to share it.
He came, and he saw, and he gave a great groan:
The stork had known how to prepare it.
She had meant to get even, and now was her turn:
Father Fox was invited to eat from an urn.
The urn's mouth was small, and it had a long neck;
The food in it smelled most delightful.
Dame Stork, with her beak in, proceeded to peck;
But the Fox found that fasting is frightful.
Home he sneaked. On his way there he felt his ears burn
When he thought of the Stork and her tall, tricky urn.
—Jean de La Fontaine, "The Fox and the Stork"

# *Luncheon, Saturday, July 29*

## MENU

*Scramble of Eggs on a Bed of Tomato Concassée*

*Symphony of Vegetables en Demi-Deuil*

*Farandole of Salads*

*Melon Soup*

*Salmon Carpaccio*

*Cheeses*

*Apricot, Mango, and Passion Fruit Sorbet*

# ALVIN'S MENU

*Kale with Gomashio*

*Gluten-free Sesame Noodles*

*Stuffed Tomatoes*

*Swiss Chard with Sliced Grilled Tofu*

*Romanesco Cabbage Pie*

*Miroir aux fraises*

More than the menu had changed at L'Agapanthe, I thought. glancing around at our luncheon guests, I spotted a current government minister and an anchor on the eight o'clock news among them.

"Now we've seen everything!" I murmured to Marie, who patted my arm in commiseration.

Although my mother did try to avoid the journalist, he seemed to win her over by promising to mention the word "agapanthus" on the evening news that very day.

"Especially since there are still as many suck-ups where he comes from," Marie whispered back.

That's what my sister and I called sycophants. Their sort had never had a problem, when we were children, with pushing us aside to get close to people whom they considered important. Nothing surprising about that, since we were of no use to them. Still, we did find it strange that they were also less than considerate with the partners and collaborators of those whom they besieged, so Marie and I felt it our duty to keep those neglected guests company in the far corners of the living room where they invariably wound up.

Shouldn't the flatterers have been buttering *them* up as well? Unless they thought that powerful people never spoke to those close to them and that their employees would never be promoted to more important positions.

In the end we realized that they didn't give a hoot about making a bad impression, as long as they got what they wanted: to be seen in the company of people in the limelight, be able to get their phone numbers or extort a favor from them, or greet them familiarly if they ever crossed paths again. These toadies knew that their status as sycophants was in fact their trump card, since they advertised the importance of those they flattered, like a motorcycle escort in an official procession. Even better, their experience added to their luster, for they had entrapped a flicker of the brilliance of all those for whom they had served as foils and whose prestige enhanced their own. That was why I'd never seen anyone resist them, not even people who still resented them from leaner times, now too happy at seeing their own success applauded at last to bother making an issue of their flatterers' former rude manners and tactics.

When I told Alvin what I'd been thinking, he said I was cruel. I was "judgmental," he told me. And in his mouth, this was not a compliment. As a good American respectful of the current conformist norms, he was confusing the critical spirit, which is the essence of judgment, with sheer criticism, so he felt that expressing the slightest negative opinion was arrogant and inappropriate. It seemed to me, however, that this was precisely what *he* was busy doing with me, and had been doing ever since he arrived, oscillating as he had between blame and reserve. Which I found quite a bit more cowardly, disagreeable, and stuck-up than simply expressing an opinion.

Alvin's silent disapproval, in any case, gave free rein to conjecture, and it lodged in my mind like a thorn. I felt it at the table with Marie, Nicolas, and Vanessa when I had a laughing fit over Vanessa's little joke: she'd been recycling the answers from their Trivial Pursuit game of the previous evening to answer her neighbor, who'd asked her "what good book she was reading at the moment."

"A biography of Eric the Red."

"Who's he?"

"The man who discovered Greenland."

"Must be fascinating. Who's the publisher?"

"A private company, Editions Saint-Rémy in Reims."

Then I caught the shocked look on Alvin's face when Astrid asked Frédéric, "What does Perla de Cambray really *do* in life, anyway?"

And Frédéric replied, "Dumb things! Gobs of 'em! What do you expect her to do, when she sounds like the sister of that candy, *bêtises de Cambray*? 'Would you like some *sillies of Cambray*'?"

So even though Alvin had said nothing unpleasant about L'Agapanthe, I was suddenly certain that he hated this place cluttered with people and furniture and paintings, where everyone dressed to the nines to eat indigestible posh meals during which they all chattered like jackdaws.

Probably to avoid admitting that the whole business had been a sheer waste, I forced myself to talk to him anyway, even though I was deathly bored when he discussed the percentage of soy proteins in his stuffed tomatoes and felt deeply guilty when he pointed out that when I ate meat, I was eating the dead body of an animal raised in captivity. In fact I was listening to him so assiduously that I began to see the familiar faces of our house through his eyes and abruptly saw them in their ugly, frightening light: dry lips clinging to teeth like the grimacing muzzles of wild animals; lips slick with saliva, drawn back over obscene gums; or even more repulsive, lips at the corners of which clung whitish crusts . . . No doubt about it: Alvin was a killjoy, whose presence changed L'Agapanthe—a place that had for me the lightness and sophistication of a racetrack scene by Dufy and the gaiety of a Matisse collage—into a stark nude by Lucian Freud or a scream by Munch. Horrible!

Then I recalled the revulsion I'd felt as a child at the sight of certain perspiring guests as they left the luncheon table, their cheeks aflame from the rosé wine, while I was dreaming of running down to dive into the water and splash about instead of taking a nap, as Nanny insisted I do for the sake of my digestion. Was it a way of taking revenge on that past obligation, or the need to draw a line under my pitiful amorous projects? Barely had the last bite been swallowed when I vanished to plunge headfirst into the sea, where a few swift strokes were all I needed to conclude that this whole thing with Alvin was impossible. I didn't even need to consult Marie on this: he was disqualified.

My thoughts were interrupted when two good-sized hunting dogs, white, short haired, and strong enough to seem dangerous, appeared abruptly at the foot of the diving board, where I'd left my clothes. They'd come from the Russians' property next door and ran on up toward our garden. Paralyzed by surprise, I was at first relieved to have been in the water and not on the beach, but then I realized that they might attack the guests still lingering in the loggia. It was a good thing Marie, Nicolas, and Vanessa had gone to visit the Villa Ephrussi, I thought, as I rushed up to the house, where I arrived dripping and out of breath.

There I found Gay, gray with fear, kneeling near Alvin, who had his ear to Popsicle's heaving little chest and soon delivered his verdict: "He's more frightened than hurt."

This incident created such a rapid swirl of emotions that I wasn't sure at first what had struck me the most, the shocking invasion by the dogs, Gay's anguish over her Maltese bichon, or the relief that led her inadvertently to allow me a glimpse of the number tattooed at Auschwitz on the inside of her left forearm. Then, alerted by her earlier cries, a constant stream of friends, guests, and servants appeared in the loggia, and just as a lithograph may require successive printings of different colors, reality left its mark on my mind only after I had explained what had happened to the new arrivals, one after the other. And even then . . . Because it was only after interpreting their reactions to my news that I perceived the danger we had run.

"Okay, so, everything's fine," announced Georgina. "All's well that ends well. Everyone's okay. Fine! Now I can go back to my nap."

"And I must get back to my duties," said the new butler, who left without further ado.

On the off chance that those two announcements hadn't tipped me off, Astrid put her foot in it nicely.

"You mean to say that those mastiffs are still roaming around, and they could attack us at any moment? Well, you do as you like, but me, I'm going to go shut myself up in my room!"

"Now there's some good old-fashioned common sense!" remarked Jean-Claude, by way of apology for his wife's bluntness.

"Yes, women and children first!" exclaimed Frédéric, to relieve the tension.

Visibly pleased that something exciting was happening at last, Charles tried to persuade Laszlo to join him in the search party he intended organizing, while Odon and my mother drew themselves up heroically, putting on a good face, instead of taking refuge inside as they would have liked to. As for me, I was deeply shaken, having suddenly understood how fragile our charmed existence at L'Agapanthe really was.

Our fight-or-flight dilemma did not last long, however, for my father now returned from the Russians' place, where he'd gone as soon as he'd heard about the dogs.

"They're Argentinean mastiffs. They trotted quietly on home after terrorizing all of Cap d'Antibes!"

"Did you see the owner?" asked my mother.

"No, and the caretaker doesn't even know his name. He deals only with an intermediary, whom he'd already phoned, and who agreed that the dogs could be shut up until a fence can be installed around the property."

Everyone was relieved. Indeed, the tea service was soon replaced by a few glasses of cognac to settle our nerves, which meant that we were a couple of sheets to the wind when Marie, Nicolas, and Vanessa returned from Cap Ferrat—especially Gay, who tried to describe how Alvin had saved Popsicle's life, driving off the Argentinean mastiffs by hitting them with cushions.

"Cushions?" marveled Marie.

"Yes," insisted Gay, producing a ripped-up cushion as prime evidence before praising Alvin's courage, and our guest was the hero of the hour until we all gathered to watch the evening news.

"Well, you know what Noël Coward said: 'Television is for appearing on, not looking at!'" exclaimed Frédéric, as we took our places in the library to see if the announcer on the evening news would follow through by using the word "agapanthus" as he'd promised to do at lunch.

"Yes, but since Coward was a model of distinction only for English grocers' wives in the 1950s, who cares?" shot back Gay, just when the opening credits appeared for the newscast.

"I bet you five to one he'll stick 'agapanthe' in the beginning to get it out of the way!" said Charles.

"Well, I'd be surprised if he managed to find a spot for it in the social policy or foreign slots," drawled Laszlo.

"Oh, you," Gay said teasingly to Laszlo, "I think you weren't too pleased with the impression he made on Flokie!"

Had we ever all watched television together? I wondered, enjoying the silly informality of a moment that nobody would have imagined possible among such a serious and accomplished crowd, having decided already to ignore Alvin who was scandalized that a so-called journalist would play games like this with his broadcast.

"Our bees—are they the victims of disease or poison? That is the question preoccupying certain scientists, who are studying a phenomenon that is troubling apiculturists and numerous ecologists, economists, and other experts because of the economical and ecological importance of the bee as a pollinating agent. Indeed, if there were no more bees to buzz around our agapanthus . . ."

"Hooray!" we shouted.

After which my mother, gauging the extent of Gay's inebriation, sent Marie to the kitchen to say that we would be happy to sit down early to dinner.

# *Dinner, Saturday, July 29*

**FIFTEEN PERSONS**

| MEN | WOMEN |
|-----|-------|
| Edmond Ettinguer | Flokie Ettinguer |
| Frédéric Hottin | Laure Ettinguer |
| Odon Viel | Marie Ettinguer |
| Jean-Claude Girault | Astrid Girault |
| Laszlo Schwartz | Gay Wallingford |
| Charles Ramsbotham | Georgina de Marien |
| Nicolas Courtry | Vanessa Courtry |
| Alvin Fishbein | |

| SEATING: EDMOND'S TABLE | SEATING: FLOKIE'S TABLE |
|-------------------------|-------------------------|

| | | | |
|---|---|---|---|
| Alvin | Laure | Gay | |
| Jean-Claude | Odon | Laszlo | Frédéric |
| Georgina | Vanessa | Marie | Astrid |
| Edmond | | Nicolas | Charles |
| | | Flokie | |

## ORIGINAL MENU

*Coquilles Saint-Jacques*
*with Onions on a Bed of Mâche*

*Veal Cutlets Pojarski*

*Salad and Cheeses*

*Chocolate Profiteroles*

## REVISED MENU

*Blood Orange and Olive Oil Soup with Green Olives*
*Sheets of Pressed Fish Skin*
*Melon Caviar*
*Quinoa Glazed with Duck Foie Gras*
*Shrimp au Naturel*
*Iberian Ham Confit with Spider Crab Cantonese Style*
*Oyster Foam with Smoked Bacon*
*White Asparagus Eggs*
*Potato Gnocchi in Consommé*
*Cheese Popcorn*
*Parmesan Marshmallow*
*Fried Lime Thai Ice Cream*

## VEGETARIAN MENU

*Sesame Tofu Tidbits*
*Avocado Terrine*
*Creamed Cauliflower Soup*
*Asparagus Tagliatelle*
*Chocolate Floating Island*

My mother was in such good humor that she had finally decided to seat Charles on her right, and she had indulged my father by placing him between Vanessa and Georgina. As it happened, she needed her good humor, because our dinner had nothing to do with the menu she'd ordered. The chef, an adept of Spanish molecular gastronomy, had decided to dazzle us by serving a few samples of his signature dishes in porcelain spoons, delicacies that were solemnly announced and explained to us by the butler as if we'd been in a gastro restaurant. This made conversation impossible, so none of us managed a peep beyond the occasional vague "how interesting!"—until Georgina burst out with, "Oh, for a nice roast chicken with oven-browned potatoes!"

Her exclamation triggered an avalanche of passionate culinary desires.

"A piping-hot, crusty gratin dauphinois! Or how about a meltingly tender leg of lamb? . . . Me, I just love boeuf Bourguignon and frogs' legs . . . Well, *my* favorite is a savory pot-au-feu . . . Oh, no, I prefer a blanquette de veau . . . And a good old chicken stew? . . . Don't all shout, please; I vote for a spicy *andouillette* sausage! . . . For me, duck confit, and coq au vin . . . My personal weakness? Spring lamb casserole . . . What about poached eggs in red wine sauce? You're forgetting oeufs en meurette! . . . Yes, but in that case, why not include a juicy boudin aux pommes? The apples are *so* perfect in the pork sausage . . ."

Jean-Claude tried to reconcile us all. "The paradox is that one cannot find such dishes anywhere nowadays, except in restaurants patronized by rich Americans, places like L'Ami Louis or Le Voltaire, which luckily have never changed their décor."

"Speaking of rich Americans," added Alvin, "you know they are often patrons of the arts, philanthropists . . ."

"Yes, and so generous, I find that impressive," said my father.

Odon could not help favoring us with some of his encyclopedic knowledge gleaned, in this case, he informed us, from a book by Bill Clinton: "Did you know that in the Jewish tradition, *tzedakah*, charity, is an obligation that should entail the donation of at least ten percent of one's income? Islam as well requires *zakat*, which corresponds to two and a half percent of one's income, and *sadaqah*, a voluntary donation from well-to-do Muslims, who are morally obliged to give generously. As for Christians, they are supposed to give ten percent of their income to the church and to love their neighbors as themselves."

"Without forgetting the Buddhists," added Alvin. "They believe that giving to others is an essential step on the path to illumination."

"I find it surprising," continued Odon, "that no one has thought to write a history of philanthropy in the United States since the Civil War. These donors are, in their way, very Greek, because in ancient Greece, the wealthy citizens would meet to divide up cultural expenses and thus relieve some pressure on their city-states."

Then he went on to describe the Clark Library in Los Angeles, where William Andrews Clark had commissioned ceilings crowded with naked ephebes without anyone batting an eye. Thus inspired, my father evoked the Sapphic ceilings of the Fondation Singer-Polignac, and the dining room of the French Senate, where diners break bread under some truly imposing asses. He then voiced his amazement that no one ever shows much reaction to the insane eroticism of artworks, as if time or the artistic setting had desensitized any sensual effect.

Alvin returned to the charge, however, emphasizing the Buddhist tenet that the practice of charity is essential, "because whether we're religious or not, we all live in an interdependent world. And our survival is linked to an understanding that our collective humanity is more important than our differences."

I wasn't sure where he was going with this, but I soon found out.

"I'm involved with a foundation that finances marine expeditions to study the deep ocean and evaluate the condition of the planet. The foundation also builds solar housing and educational programs to make schoolchildren aware of ecological problems . . ."

I then realized that Alvin had come to L'Agapanthe only for that, to put the bite on us. Which wasn't surprising. Because everywhere in the world, foundations and organizations draw up lists of potential donors for museums, opera houses, botanic gardens, châteaux, schools, universities, hospitals, or to provide assistance to disadvantaged children, the dying, the victims of war, of AIDS, hunger, sexual crimes, genetic diseases . . . And they ask all their donors to spread the word, to proselytize creatively to recruit new benefactors. In that way, hunting the rich had become an activity that expands exponentially. And it was only to be expected that any encounter among wealthy individuals might turn into an ambush. In short, the charity business was a reality we had learned to deal with. Which did not mean that my parents, discreet and generous donors, were not occasionally taken by surprise, as when I would see them returning somewhat disappointed from a dinner they had looked forward to with pleasure only to report, "Actually, they just wanted to put the touch on us."

And was I disappointed as well to see Alvin make such use of an invitation to visit some wealthy strangers? Mind you, *I* hadn't invited *him* just for the hell of it. And the least one could say was that saving the planet was a lot more legitimate cause than my husband hunting. But beyond that, I was not happy at having inadvertently allowed my father to be hit up in his own house, and by one of my guests, for a cause in which he was not particularly interested. So I tried to get him out of this awkward position.

"I don't believe in humanitarianism," I announced loudly.

"What?" gasped my father. "That's preposterous! Whatever do you mean by that?"

"Well, I don't believe in altruism, in the idea of generosity . . ."

"How can you say such a thing! So we're supposed to just throw up our hands?"

"Unless we consider the idea from the angle of egoism . . ."

"Meaning?"

"Look at it this way: looking after other people, supporting any aid organization at all, is a good way to help oneself, to give meaning to one's life, or to lick one's own wounds. It's a form of egoism, but a more constructive one than shopping or drugs."

"Then by your reckoning, Bill Gates is a titan of egoism! Because with a fortune estimated at fifty billion dollars, he has become the biggest benefactor in the world, endowing his foundation with almost thirty billion dollars of his own money. But I'm not sure that a fellow who has decided to give away in his lifetime ninety-five percent of his fortune to help the needy should be called an egoist."

"You're right," I admitted.

Not only had I lost the argument, but my provocative remarks produced exactly the opposite effect from what

I had intended! For my father then invited Alvin to discuss his cause in private.

"Let's talk about this in the living room, shall we?" said my father, as we all left the table.

The evening dragged on, and I was feeling morose, because that ill-advised exchange with my father had upset me just as much as had my discovery of Alvin's hidden agenda. I was watching Georgina recruit Marie for a game of cards when it occurred to me that I hadn't really seen my sister all weekend. Had she made herself scarce to leave me a free hand with Alvin? Or had she been avoiding me so as not to confess how stupid she thought my plan was? Unless . . . our connection was fading. It was the first time that I had seriously doubted not only our relationship but the power of L'Agapanthe, too, which until then had so fostered our togetherness that I'd come to believe it was the very source of our bond.

"Come see me in my room before you go to bed," I told Marie before heading upstairs myself.

I did not want to draw any conclusions about the failure of our husband hunting unless Marie was with me, because I felt that thinking about the future alone in my room would mean risking a future lived without her. Hardly had I climbed into bed, though, when I fell into a sleep so deep that I barely heard Marie gently peek into my room later that night.

～

I awoke at dawn and found my parents in conference in the loggia.

"We've found a buyer for the house," my father told me straight out.

Was it the effect of his news, or my surprise at hearing it that way? I felt like a sailor on the high seas, hit out of nowhere by a rogue wave.

"Who is it?" I asked, trying to master my reeling emotions.

"A sort of club for the rich."

"What?"

"A real estate company, organized as a private club, that buys properties it maintains and staffs for its clients, people of means who are no longer content, it seems, to have a house on the seashore, for example. They also want a castle in England, an apartment in New York, a pied-à-terre in Paris, a chalet in Gstaad, an island in the Seychelles, as well as yachts and private planes and—"

I didn't let him finish. "But *why* are you selling the house if you're not in any financial trouble?"

"Because it's becoming impossible to keep it. It no longer makes sense! It's terribly expensive to run, and the taxes are horrific. And then, you can see for yourself, everything has changed. We don't even know who our neighbors are anymore. Their dogs attack us! It's getting harder to find decent personnel—just look at the new chef. Try to understand: it has become so complicated to manage a monster of a house like this that from now on, the proud owner is likely to be a company!"

He was right. The way we lived there, L'Agapanthe was a memory of times gone by, a dream we were trying to keep alive against all reason, protecting it from time like a dike holding back the ocean, but our house was doomed to disappear.

"But what will you do during the summer holidays?"

"We'll go on cruises, and I'm looking forward to them."

The guests were slowly drifting into the loggia. On the horizon, the sea was flecked with whitecaps.

"Oh, no! It's awful! Did you see what happened?" exclaimed Frédéric, who then read us an article in the *Nice-Matin*: "'While emergency personnel were preparing to approach the baby fin whale that had wound up just off a beach in Fréjus, the misguided attempts of a crowd of sunbathers prevented the dying animal from being rescued . . .'"

"People are so desperately dumb," Georgina said, sighing.

"'. . . Toward the end of a trying day, the marine mammal ended up in the cove of La Galiote, at Saint-Aygulf, where it had been trailed by two inflatable dinghies carrying firemen, Mike Ridell (coordinator of the rescue effort), and Véronique Vienet, the veterinarian of the Alpes-Maritime Fire Brigade. The site had seemed ideal, allowing the rescuers to keep the stricken animal afloat in the shallow water while the veterinarian examined, fed, and cared for the whale until the floating sling arrived. Human stupidity, however, then intervened. A woman suddenly shouted, "We have to push it back out," and dozens of people approached the young fin whale to move it out to deeper water. The creature fled in a panic toward a breakwater, colliding with it, and mass hysteria ensued. Someone shouted, "I have a bit of its skin," and others threw a policeman into the water when he tried to keep them from going out on the breakwater. "We're still in shock," said a disgusted and discouraged Mike Ridell.'"

"Really, that's unbelievable! I've never liked crowds, they scare me," observed Jean-Claude.

Frédéric continued reading.

"'"They were out of control. You cannot manage a crowd of over two thousand people, there might have been serious injuries," added Véronique Vienet, stunned not only by the attitude of the vacationers, who thought they were helping yet made things worse, but also by a glancing blow to her head from the tail of the baby whale, whose chances for survival, now that it has been frightened back out to sea, are almost gone. "He's weak, and has lost a terrific amount of weight," the veterinarian observed soberly. "When I first saw him, he weighed between seven and eight tons, but now he's down to only three or four." The would-be rescuers, including three injured firemen who'd been manhandled by the crowd, were saddened by what had happened. "They were like hooligans at a soccer match. Everyone wanted to get in on it and bring back a trophy." The vacationers, in their attempt to help, have probably signed the young whale's death warrant.'"

The departure of Nicolas, Vanessa, and Alvin occupied us for the rest of the morning, since we had to exchange money for them because they had only dollars and wished to leave tips for the staff. This persuaded me that they were the only ones among our guests who had thought to do this and were thus the only ones to show kindness and good manners. Then we had to track down Anagan, who'd gone for a swim in the bay, and one of Vanessa's dresses, which had accidentally been placed in Astrid's closet, and watch our three travelers say good-bye to the entire household.

After which, Marie and I finally rendezvoused in my room, where we decided to cheat a little on our departing flight schedule so that we two could have lunch together at the Hôtel du Cap before taking the plane. So we told our parents we had to leave the house slightly earlier than planned, and after saying good-bye to them, Marie and I took a tour of the house. Everything was back to normal in the kitchen, where our own chef had returned and the menu was once more to our taste. Like the rest of L'Agapanthe, which seemed so unchanging. I thought about the end of a love affair, about how we make love with someone without realizing that it's for the last time, because nothing tells us solemnly that this moment will never come again, a moment we often try in vain to recall later on, when the affair is over.

Frédéric came to find me before I left.

"You know, your idea about chasing after suitors?" I said to him. "Idiotic!"

"I don't happen to agree," he replied. "Have you ever heard the story of the goat? A fellow goes to see his rabbi to complain. 'I live in a one-room apartment with my wife and our two children, we've no room to turn around, it's awful!' So the rabbi says to him, 'Get a goat, and come back to see me in a month.' The guy returns a month later and says, 'Well, I'm living in sheer hell! Why the devil did you tell me to get a goat?' And the rabbi replies, 'Nu, because once you've gotten rid of the goat, you'll be able to enjoy what you have.'"

I stared blankly at Frédéric.

"You mean to tell me *that's* why you suggested the plan to me? So that it would turn into a fiasco and give me time to get used to the idea that the house was going to be sold? I can't believe it."

# The road to Eden-Roc

*July 20, 1987*

*I am ten years old. A tedious road, unappealing, paved like
a city street. I have to watch my step, be careful not to fall
and twist my ankle or skin my knees or elbows, because I'm
clumsy and the road is full of bumps and potholes.*

*In any case, I don't know how to lift up my head and
dream away, just dream myself away from this punishing
walk. All I can do is gather up my courage, set out, and get it
over with.*

*But the heady scent wafting from the fig tree arching over
the asphalt on my right soon carries me into another world of
sweet languor, shady and cool. The moment is too brief and
the fragrance too fleeting for me to realize that this is where
I would like to stop and linger. Baffled by this new feeling, I*

have a hard time grasping the idea that simply breathing this soft and syrupy perfume would make me happy. It never occurs to me to dawdle, to stop and savor it. No one has suggested this to me or given me leave to do it. I only know what I'm supposed to do, and I have a long way to go.

So I walk on.

There is no shade anywhere except a narrow band, like a lane of shadow, cast by the low wall behind which lie our neighbors' modest, even humble homes.

A man is watching me with curiosity. A little nervous, I politely say hello because I don't want to seem like a stuck-up little girl. The neighbor doesn't smile or reply. But it doesn't matter.

I have to get going. Especially since I'm afraid of the dog barking behind the gate. I don't dare look over there, for fear of offending the man. I wouldn't want him to think I'm comparing his house with mine, or to feel judged, spied on, stared at, even though that's what he's doing with me.

I quicken my pace under the sun beating down on my skin lacquered with sweat. Trying to escape the bite of the sun, which stings like sea salt, I hug the little wall so close I'm almost scraping my side. When the pathway leads to a real road, the only available strip I can walk along becomes as thin as a ribbon. I put my feet one in front of the other like a tightrope walker, afraid of being swept away by the cars zooming past, but I can enjoy the refreshing sense of speed left in their wake. The cars are convertibles, as brightly colored as sourball candies.

Their hair streaming in the wind, the smiling passengers look happy, ready to take mysterious pleasure in what I do out of obligation: I must swim and play tennis every day to become an accomplished young woman. And I arrive at last.

The entrance gate, the front steps, the familiar doorman, and finally the gentle and often breezy slope leading down to the sea and the swimming pool. The winding path to the oppressively hot and dusty clay tennis courts is shady and more protected. The boring lessons drag along. I do as I'm asked. And I watch the other visitors to this palatial hotel, who seem so free, so cheerful. Why? I just don't understand their happiness. I understand only schedules and obligations.

The hour limps by. Soon I'll be done.

*Sunday, 1:00 p.m.*

The Hôtel du Cap seemed completely transformed to us, through the combined efforts of passing time and new management. They take credit cards now but no longer issue free beach passes to a privileged few. Thus Marie and I felt our welcome blow now cold, now hot, between a new protocol, made of rules and prohibitions suited to an impersonal and almost banal establishment, and the familiar charm of a priceless and singular place; between the pool attendant who inquired haughtily if we were guests at the hotel, and Michel, the Eden-Roc doorman who asked for news of the family while kissing us on the cheek.

"What's the event?" I asked him.

"The grand terrace has been reserved for a conference."

"Ah, I see! But we can still go there, can't we?"

"Yes, of course, go right ahead."

Marie and I toured the gastronomic restaurant, which no longer used the same china as before, and the main dining room, prettily repainted in white. Then we went down to the bar, where the lighting, mixing with that of the swimming pool, kept shifting from blue to green, and from rose to violet.

"It's really something, that design gadget! It gives the restaurant a fake nightclub atmosphere, don't you think?" asked Marie.

"Oh, my, that's quite a problem."

"But . . . what is the matter with you?"

And then I told her that there was a buyer for L'Agapanthe, and gave her the gory details of my doings with Alvin, and revealed my sadness at having spoken so little to her that weekend.

"In any case, those suitors? That idea was a farce," she said dismissively. "God only knows what got into us."

I remembered what Frédéric had said to me. But when I spoke to her, it was about what might have been the real heart of the matter.

"I think I wanted nothing to change, I wanted to

be able to keep the house, to stay together the way we were when we were little, but that's impossible. Anyway, to stay together, we have to evolve, to become more friends than sisters, and each have a life of our own. Because when we attempt to re-create our childhood, we remain—for life—the children of our parents. Haven't you ever wondered why we aren't married?"

"Well, because we haven't met our husbands yet!"

"No! It's because we weren't ready! We could have vetted every single guy on earth and it wouldn't have worked. First off, because you don't recruit a lover the way you do an office employee, and all that fancy planning never works, you simply have to fall in love. And second, it was an absurd idea to tie our love life to L'Agapanthe, which is a family home, and therefore *our parents' house*."

"True, and nothing worked in that mix, anyway. None of the suitors liked the house and we didn't like them *in* the house."

"Ah, except for Béno!"

"Oh, thanks a lot!"

"Seriously, how are you with that?"

"Don't worry, I'm fine. I've gotten over it, really."

"And that dog in Rio, are you still upset about that?"

"No, I'm over that, too."

"So it's just too bad about L'Agapanthe?"

Marie was about to agree when she looked off suddenly to my left, and I heard a voice I seemed to know, speaking English.

"Laure! You remember me?"

I turned, and there he was, nodding briefly in greeting to Marie.

"Rajiv! What are you doing here?"

"I'm running a conference!"

"Oh?" I said stupidly, unable to say anything more because I was so stunned to see in daylight this man who had such an effect on me.

"It is a discussion on economics as a moral science."

"And that is . . . ?"

"The idea that economics, unlike physics or chemistry, is not a hard science devoid of ideological bias, but is a discipline that requires ethical scrutiny and a deep understanding of the role political action plays within it."

"That's wonderful!" I exclaimed with a joy made real not only by my sincere interest but also by my longing to say something that would please those green eyes set like jewels in lashes as black and silken as velvet.

"You think so?" He was clearly surprised by my enthusiasm.

Embarrassed at having overdone it, I felt myself blush. Just as I was about to stammer something to fill the silence, I saw how moved he was by my emotional reaction.

"Would you like to come in?" he said with a grin, which brought laugh lines out by his eyes and put dimples in his cheeks.

"I . . ." I hesitated, glancing at Marie in a welter of conflicting feelings. How could I walk out on her in the middle of our important discussion? But how could I pass up this invitation from Rajiv, whose relaxed ease and gentle presence had practically left me in a daze?

"Actually, I was just about to tell Laure that I had to be on my way, I have a plane to catch," announced Marie with what only a sister would have recognized as a sly smile.

With a grateful glance at Marie, I turned back to Rajiv.

"Then yes, thank you, I'd like that very much."

The breeze picked up, and standing next to Rajiv, I smelled the delicate but intoxicating aroma of fresh, warm bread he had about him. In that moment, I wondered if it would be there in his wake that I would find my place.

# Thank-you letter

To Patrick Ettinguer
September 3, 1967

Dear Patrick,

While we were chatting on the phone the other day, a whole stream of images was flitting through my thoughts, reminding me how much memory has its own seasons. The languid beckoning of summer takes me back each year to L'Agapanthe through one cue or another—blooming plumbago or a lush green lawn—and even as I was speaking, I was following their lead: there was Uncle Jean with his smile and red hair; Aunt Flora emerging from an elevator as from a tabernacle and sweeping down the right-hand steps on her way to the beach. . . . Why do we always take the stairs on the right, never those on the left? There was the clicking of Montrelay's *clogs and the soft thudding of Pradenne Jacques's espadrilles. Meyer's ineffable dive into the sea, like an envelope plunged swiftly into a minister's portfolio. The fidgety tinkling of ice cubes in Leo's tomato juice. Edmond's unforgettable striped sweater, which made me lose all my Ping-Pong matches because I could never keep track of the ball against those stripes. There was Roland, always bowing and scraping, and Guillaume, whose inexorable march out to announce our mealtimes always came to a sudden halt on precisely the same flagstone in the loggia. Ada's voice on the stairs. And Jean de Bergh, who never failed, before joining any conversation, to cross his left leg over his right and then polish his glasses, so that I wondered no less unfailingly whether he intended to listen with his eyes and see with his ears. I remember Sacha de Courcy's bedroom eyes, his voice, his hands on the guitar; the large intimidating dinners and the small enchanting ones; the tall Castros and the tiny Blériots. And against this human backdrop, there was the library where I discovered Flaubert, the pink loggia, the indolent water lilies in the basin of the small fountain, the lawn damp with dew, the sea urchins under the diving board, the shoals of mullet, and the water's transparent depths, murmuring as in a dream. Those small terraces where no one ever lingered (there again, why?), inhabited by flowers that seemed careful not to breathe forth their perfume in full bloom, as if honoring* a kind of compromise between delight and decorum, which our parents' generation observed in their own homes and in all things. Our generation seems to live like a car eternally caught between the accelerator and the brakes, with a mobile perpetuum of noise, like a musical canon, looping from airplanes to lawn mowers. Which reminds me of Jean the gardener's mower and rake, their sound track tolerated for its regular hours, like a mechanical angelus in the monastic order of lawns . . .

*Five*

# APPENDICES

# The Characters

### THE FAMILY

Laure ETTINGUER, the narrator.

Marie ETTINGUER, the sister.

Flokie ETTINGUER, the mother.

Edmond ETTINGUER, the father.

### THE PILLARS

Gay WALLINGFORD, a cultured woman of the world.

Frédéric HOTTIN, a playwright and the "uncle" Laure would
    have loved to have.

### THE LITTLE BAND

Odon VIEL, an astrophysicist, the Nobel laureate of the
    group.

Polyséna DÉMAZURE, an Italian who is hard to understand
in any language, married to Henri.

Henri DÉMAZURE, an international lawyer.

Laszlo SCHWARTZ, a famous artist, Flokie Ettinguer's
"crush."

### THE ODDBALLS

Charles RAMSBOTHAM, an eccentric English lord,
passionately interested in gorillas.

Georgina de MARIEN, a Peruvian heiress, a nomad *de luxe*,
and the recognized companion of Edmond Ettinguer.

### THE END-OF-JULY REGULARS

Jean-Claude GIRAULT, a model of good manners and the
perfect guest.

Astrid GIRAULT, Jean-Claude's wife, prone to gaffes but
very nice.

### THE NEWCOMERS, WEEKEND OF JULY 14

Jean-Michel DESTRET, the first suitor, a French self-made
man and a nerd.

Laetitia BRAISSANT, a political public relations agent and a
leftist freeloader.

Bernard BRAISSANT, a political journalist and a freeloader
like his wife.

### THE NEWCOMERS, WEEKEND OF JULY 21

Béno GRUNWALD, the second suitor, a hedge-fund owner,
jet-setter, and playboy who lives in London.

Mathias CAVOYE, a second-rate art dealer.

Lou LÉVA, an unscrupulous starlet.

### THE NEWCOMERS, WEEKEND OF JULY 28

Alvin FISHBEIN, the third suitor, an American billionaire
obsessed with organic food and yoga.

Nicolas COURTRY, a French Internet billionaire, Laure's ex-
boyfriend, who divides his time between New York and
California.

Vanessa COURTRY, a bombshell of beauty and sex appeal
who is married to Nicolas.

Barry SULLIVAN, called ANAGAN, Alvin Fishbein's personal
guru, a teacher of Jivamukti yoga.

### THE STAFF

Roberto, the head butler.

Marcel, the under-butler.

Gérard, Roberto's temporary replacement as head butler.

Pauline, the senior Ettinguers' chambermaid.

Colette, a chambermaid.

Roland, the chauffeur.

And the chef, the caretaker, the gardener, and various
kitchen underlings.

## THE CAFETERIA CLUB

CHERYLA, a world-famous singer.

Héloise SALLOIS, the wife of François SALLOIS, a banker
and French heavyweight in mergers and acquisitions.

Alain GANDOUIN, a French intellectual and adviser to
politicians and business leaders.

And Maurice Saatchi, Lord Hinlip, Karl Lagerfeld, Martha
Stewart, Diane von Furstenberg, Barry Diller, Christian
Louboutin, Louis Benech, Larry Gagosian, Sandretto Re
Rebaudengo, Ty Warner . . .

# Staff Menu Notebook

**LUNCH:** Crab and avocado cocktail, tagliatelle with rabbit and mustard sauce, salad/cheeses, apple tart

**DINNER:** Leftovers, quiche, salad/cheeses/fruit

**LUNCH:** Tomatoes and mozzarella, roast chicken breasts, sauce diable, grated potato pancakes, salad/cheeses, lemon tart

**DINNER:** Leftovers, pasta bolognese

**LUNCH:** Tomato salad, cauliflower gratin, cutlets, salad/cheeses, vanilla pudding

**DINNER:** Quiche, roast lamb, ratatouille, salad/cheeses/fruit

**LUNCH:** Composed salad, roast chicken, fried potatoes, fruit

**DINNER:** Leftovers, potato omelet, salad/cheeses/fruit

**LUNCH:** Tomato salad, sauté of pork, salmon pâté, ratatouille

**DINNER:** Leftovers

**LUNCH:** Carrot salad, deviled eggs, sauté of pork, cauliflower gratin

**DINNER:** Leftovers, ratatouille omelet

# Kitchen Cabinet Inventory

### CUPBOARD A

1 mandoline

1 automatic piston funnel with stand

6 frying pans + 4 new + 4 old

8 crêpe pans

3 blini pans

2 extra large cooking pots

1 copper casserole

2 food mills

### CUPBOARD B

27 large springform pans

19 small springforms

grill racks

7 savarin molds

3 brioche pans

5 charlotte molds

3 mango pitters

1 loaf pan

6 tart plates

7 madeleine pans

2 large ice-cream scoops

4 small melon-ball scoops

2 terrine molds

4 sifters

1 series small tartlet molds

## CUPBOARD C

2 conical strainers

3 colanders

4 small strainers

21 whisks

16 ladles

9 skimmers

1 spider skimmer

1 scoop

1 sauce ladle

## CUPBOARD D (CASSEROLES)

7 double boilers

17 casseroles

4 sauté pans

14 lids

2 sauce warmers

# Recipe inventory

## PASTRIES AND DOUGHS

Pâte brisée

Pâte sucrée

Sweet shortbread

Puff pastry

Inverse puff pastry

Brioche

Sweet roll

Danish pastry

Savarin

Croissant

Crêpe

Fry cake

Cream puff

Sponge cake

Kneaded puff pastry

## ICINGS AND GLAZES

Chocolate

Bitter chocolate

Ganache

Chocolate cacao content Nos. 1, 2, 3

Opéra cake fillings (cream, white, currant, raspberry, lime,
coffee, mixed fruit)

## PETITS FOURS SECS

Cigarettes russes, cats' tongues, almond tuiles, orange
tuiles, raisin cookies, shortbread, macarons, light-glazed
petits fours (rolled cookies, sponges, miroirs)

# Recipes

**PASTA SALAD WITH CHICKEN**

**AND PINE NUTS (SERVES 8)**

*Ingredients*

2 lbs. penne rigate

6 chicken breasts

5 very ripe medium-size tomatoes

12 leaves basil

1/4 cup pine nuts

5 T mayonnaise

3 T Worcestershire sauce

Cook pasta in salted boiling water with a drizzle of olive oil. Drain, cool, and chill in refrigerator. Salt and pepper chicken breasts, drizzle with olive oil, cook in 325° oven for 7 to 8 minutes. Chill. Peel, seed, and julienne tomatoes. Tear basil into small pieces by hand. Toast pine nuts in fry pan. When all ingredients are cool, toss with dressing (mayonnaise and Worcestershire sauce). Layer pasta, basil, tomatoes, pine nuts. Slice chilled white meat into thin strips, arrange in rosette on pasta.

## COEUR À LA CRÈME (SERVES 8-10)

*Ingredients*

1 quart whipping cream

1-1/2 cups confectioners' sugar

3 cups plain yogurt

10 T sour cream

1 vanilla bean

Whip cream and sugar until stiff, chill in refrigerator. Whip yogurt and sour cream in large bowl until smooth. Open vanilla bean and scrape out seeds. With a rubber spatula, carefully fold together whipped cream, yogurt/cream cheese mixture, and vanilla seeds. Line a pierced, heart-shaped mold with cheesecloth, and pour the cream mixture into the mold. Fold the ends of the cheesecloth over the top and refrigerate at least eight hours.